10th
Anniversary

JAMES PATTERSON is one of the best-known and biggest-selling writers of all time. He is the author of some of the most popular series of the past decade – the Alex Cross, Women's Murder Club and Detective Michael Bennett novels – and he has written many other number one bestsellers including romance novels and stand-alone thrillers. He lives in Florida with his wife and son.

James is passionate about encouraging children to read. Inspired by his own son who was a reluctant reader, he also writes a range of books specifically for young readers. James has formed a partnership with the National Literacy Trust, an independent, UK-based charity that changes lives through literacy. In 2010, he was voted Author of the Year at the Children's Choice Book Awards in New York.

Also by James Patterson

A list of more titles by James Patterson is printed
at the back of this book

For Isabelle Patterson
and Madeline Paetro

Acknowledgments

Our thanks and gratitude to New York attorney Philip R. Hoffman, Captain Richard J. Conklin of the Stamford, Connecticut, Police Department, and Dr. Humphrey Germaniuk, Medical Examiner of Trumbull County, Ohio, for generously sharing their time and wealth of experience.

Our thanks, too, to our excellent researchers, Ingrid Taylar, Ellie Shurtleff, Melissa Pevy, and Lynn Colomello. And to Mary Jordan, who, as always, manned the control tower.

10th Anniversary

JAMES PATTERSON
AND MAXINE PAETRO

arrow books

Published by Arrow Books in 2012

3 5 7 9 10 8 6 4 2

First published in Great Britain in 2011 by Century

Arrow Books
Random House, 20 Vauxhall Bridge Road,
London SW1V 2SA

www.randomhouse.co.uk

Addresses for companies within The Random House Group Limited can be found
at: www.randomhouse.co.uk/offices.htm

The Random House Group Limited Reg. No. 954009

A CIP catalogue record for this book
is available from the British Library

ISBN 9780099525370
ISBN 9780099570745 (export edition)

Typeset by SX Composing DTP, Rayleigh, Essex, SS6 7XF

The Random House Group Limited supports The Forest Stewardship
Council (FSC®), the leading international forest certification organisation.
Our books carrying the FSC label are printed on FSC® certified paper.
FSC is the only forest certification scheme endorsed by the leading
environmental organisations, including Greenpeace. Our
paper procurement policy can be found at
www.randomhouse.co.uk/environment

MIX
Paper from
responsible sources
FSC® C016897

Printed and bound in Great Britain by Clays Ltd, St Ives PLC

WOMEN'S MURDER CLUB

Prologue

WITH BELLS ON

One

THIS WAS THE DAY I was getting married.

Our suite at the Ritz in Half Moon Bay was in chaos. My best friends and I had stripped down to our underwear, and our street clothes had been flung over the furniture. Sorbet-colored dresses hung from the moldings and door frames.

The scene looked like a Degas painting of ballerinas before the curtain went up, or maybe a romanticized bordello in the Wild West. Jokes were cracked. Giddiness reigned — and then the door opened and my sister Catherine stepped in, wearing her brave face: a tight smile, pain visible at the corners of her eyes.

"What's wrong, Cat?" I asked.

"He's not here."

I blinked, tried to ignore the sharp pang of disappointment. I said sarcastically, "Well, there's a shock."

Cat was talking about our father, Marty Boxer, who left home when we were kids and failed to show when my mom was dying. I'd seen him only twice in the past ten years and hadn't missed him, but after he'd told Cat he'd come to my wedding, I'd had an expectation.

"He *said* he would be here. He *promised*," Cat said.

I'm six years older than my sister and a century more jaded. I should have known better. I hugged her.

"Forget it," I said. "He can't hurt us. He's nobody to us."

Claire, my best bosom buddy, sat up in bed, swung her legs over, and put her bare feet on the floor. She's a large black woman and funny — acidly so. If she weren't a pathologist, she could do stand-up comedy.

"*I'll* give you away, Lindsay," she said. "But I want you back."

Cindy and I cracked up, and Yuki piped up, "I know who can stand in for Marty, that jerk."

She stepped into her pink satin dress, pulled it up over her tiny little bones, and zipped it herself. She said, "Be right back."

Getting things done was Yuki's specialty. Don't get in her way when she's in gear. Even if she's in the *wrong* gear.

"Yuki, wait," I called as she rushed out the door. I turned to Claire, saw that she was holding up what used to be called a foundation garment. It was boned and forbidding-looking.

"I don't mind wearing a dress that makes me look like a cupcake, but how in hell am I supposed to get into this?"

"I love my dress," said Cindy, fingering the peach-colored silk organza. She was probably the first bridesmaid in the world to express that sentiment, but Cindy was terminally lovesick. She turned her pretty face toward me and said dreamily, "You should get ready."

Two yards of creamy satin slid out of the garment bag. I wriggled into the strapless Vera Wang confection, then stood with my sister in front of the long freestanding mirror: a pair of tall brown-eyed blondes, looking so much like our dad.

"Grace Kelly never looked so good," said Cat, her eyes welling up.

"Dip your head, gorgeous," said Cindy.

She fastened her pearls around my neck.

I did a little pirouette, and Claire caught my hand and twirled me under her arm. She said, "Do you believe it, Linds? I'm going to dance at your wedding."

She didn't say "finally," but she was right to think it, having lived through my roller-coaster, long-distance romance with Joe, punctuated by his moving to San Francisco to be with me, my house burning down, a couple of near-death experiences, and a huge diamond engagement ring that I'd kept in a drawer for most of a year.

"Thanks for keeping the faith," I said.

"I wouldn't call it faith, darling," Claire cracked. "I never expected to *see* a miracle, let alone be *part* of one."

I gave her a playful jab on the arm. She ducked and feinted. The door opened and Yuki came in with my bouquet: a lavish bunch of peonies and roses tied with baby blue streamers.

"This hankie belonged to my grandmother," Cindy said, tucking a bit of lace into my cleavage, checking off the details. "Old, new, borrowed, blue. You're good."

"I cued up the music, Linds," said Yuki. "We're *on*."

My God.

Joe and I were really getting married.

Two

JACOBI MET ME IN THE hotel lobby, stuck out his elbow, and laughed out loud. Yuki had been right. Jacobi was the perfect stand-in Dad. I took his arm and he kissed my cheek.

First time ever.

"You look beautiful, Boxer. You know, more than usual."

Another first.

Jacobi and I had spent so much time in a squad car together, we could almost read each other's minds. But I didn't have to be clairvoyant to read the love in his eyes.

I grinned at him and said, "Thanks, Jacobi. Thanks a lot."

I squeezed his arm and we walked across an

acre of marble, through tall French doors, and into my future.

Jacobi had a limp and a wheeze, the remnants of a shooting a couple of years back in the Tenderloin. I'd thought we were both going to check out that night. But that was then.

Now the warm, salty air embraced me. The great lawns flowed around the shining white gazebo and down to the bluff. The Pacific crashed against the cliff side, and the setting sun tinted the clouds a glowing whiskey pink that you could never capture on film. I'd never seen a more beautiful place.

"Take it easy, now," Jacobi said. "No sprinting down the aisle. Just keep step with the music."

"If you insist," I said, laughing.

Two blocks of chairs had been set up facing the gazebo, and the aisle had been cordoned off with yellow crime scene tape. POLICE LINE. DO NOT CROSS.

The tape had to have been Conklin's idea. I was sure of it when he caught my eye and gave me a broad grin and a thumbs-up. Cat's young daughters skipped down the grassy aisle tossing rose petals as the wedding march began. My best friends stepped out in time, and I followed behind them.

Smiling faces turned to me. Charlie Clapper on the aisle, guys from the squad, and new and old friends were on the left. Five of Joe's look-alike brothers and their families were on my right. Joe's parents turned to beam at me from the front row.

Jacobi brought me up the gazebo steps to the altar and released my arm, and I looked up at my wonderful, handsome husband-to-be. Joe's eyes connected with mine, and I knew without any doubt that the roller-coaster ride had been worth it. I knew this man so well. Our tested love was rich and deep and solid.

Longtime family friend the Reverend Lynn Boyer put our hands together, Joe's hand over mine, then whispered theatrically so that everyone could hear, "Enjoy this moment, Joseph. This is the last time you'll have the upper hand with Lindsay."

Delighted laughter rang out and then hushed. With the sound of seagulls calling, Joe and I exchanged promises to love and cherish through good days and bad, through sickness and health, for as long as we both lived.

Do you take this man to be your wedded husband?

I do. I really do.

There were nervous titters as I fumbled with Joe's wedding band and it spun out of my hand. Joe and I both stooped, grabbed the ring at the same time, and held it between our fingers.

"Steady, Blondie," Joe said. "It only gets better from here."

I laughed, and when we resumed our positions, I got that gold band onto Joe's finger. The Reverend Boyer told Joe he could kiss the bride, and my husband held my face between his hands.

We kissed, and then again. And again. And again.

There was wild applause and a surge of music.

This was real. I was Mrs. Joseph Molinari. Joe took my hand and, grinning like little kids, we walked back up the aisle through a shower of rose petals.

WOMEN'S MURDER CLUB

Book One

LITTLE BOY LOST

Chapter 1

A TEENAGE GIRL wearing a neon green plastic poncho, naked underneath, stumbled along a dark road. She was scared out of her mind and in pain, the cramps coming like repeated blows to her gut and getting worse. Blood had started coming out of her a while ago, and now it was running fast and hot down her legs.

What had she done?

People always told her she was a smart kid, but—and this was a fact—she'd made a horrible mistake, and if she didn't get help soon, she was going to die.

But where was she?

She had the sense that she was walking in circles but getting nowhere. During the day, the area around Lake Merced was full of traffic—joggers, cyclists, a steady stream of cars on the road around the lake. But at night it was completely deserted. The darkness was bad enough, but now fog filled the basin. She couldn't see farther than a few yards in front of her.

And she was really scared.

People had gone missing around here. There had been *murders*. Plenty of them.

Her feet dragged. She really couldn't lift them, and then she felt herself fading out, just leaving her body. She reached out to brace her fall, and her hand found the trunk of a tree. She gripped it with both hands and held on hard to the rough bark until she felt rooted in the black, moonless night.

Oh my God. Where am I now?

Two cars had already passed her without stopping, and now she thought of abandoning her plan to flag down a car and return to the house. They were gone. She could sleep. Maybe the blood would stop flowing if she could lie down—but she was so lost. She didn't know which way to turn.

The girl stumbled forward, looking for light, any light.

Blood was running faster out of her body, dripping down her legs, and she felt so faint that her legs hardly held her up.

As she pushed herself forward, she stubbed her toe on something hard and unforgiving, a root or a stone, and she pitched forward. She put out her hands, bracing for the fall.

Her chin and knees and palms took the brunt of it, but she was all right. Panting from the pain, the girl got to her feet.

She could make out the trees along the roadside, the eucalyptus and the pines looming overhead. Grasses scratched at her arms and legs as she staggered through them.

She imagined a car stopping, or a house coming into view. She imagined how she would tell the story. Would she have a chance to do that? Please. She couldn't die now. She was only fifteen years old.

A dog barked in the distance and the girl changed course and headed toward that sound. A dog meant a house, a phone, a car, a hospital.

She was thinking of her room, of being safe there. She saw her bed and her desk and the pictures on the wall and her phone—oh, man, if only she still had her phone — and that's when her foot turned over, her ankle twisting, and she went down again, falling really hard, skinning half of her body.

This was too much. Too much.

She stayed down this time. Everything hurt so much. She made a pillow of her arms and just rested her head. Maybe if she took a little nap. Yeah, maybe some sleep was what she needed and then, in the morning . . . when the sun came up . . .

It took a long moment to understand that the dull light growing brighter in the fog was a pair of headlights coming toward her.

She put up her hand and there was a squeal of brakes.

A woman's voice said, "Oh my God. Are you hurt?"

"Help me," she said. "I need help."

"Stay with me," said the woman's voice. "Don't go to sleep, young lady. I'm calling nine one one. Look at me. Keep your eyes open."

"I've lost my baby," the girl said.

And then she didn't feel any more pain.

Chapter 2

RAIN WAS BATTERING the hood and sheeting down the windshield as I pulled my ancient Explorer into the lot next to the Medical Examiner's Office on Harriet Street, right behind the Hall of Justice. I had some anxiety about returning to work after taking time off to get married.

In a few minutes, I was going to have some catching up to do, and then there was a new fact I would have to deal with.

I would be reporting to a new lieutenant.

I was prepared for that—as much as I could be.

I pulled up the collar of my well-used blue blazer and made a wild, wet dash for the back entrance of the Hall, the gray granite building that housed the Justice Department, criminal court, two jails, and the Southern Station of the SFPD.

I badged Kevin at the back door, then took the stairs at a jog. When I got to the third floor, I opened the stairwell door to the Homicide Division and pushed through the double-hinged gate to the squad room.

It was a zoo.

I said, "Hey, there," to Brenda, who stood up and gave me a hug and a paper towel.

"I wish you so much happiness," she said.

I thanked Brenda, promised wedding pictures, and then mopped my face and hair. I took a visual inventory of who was on the job at 7:45 a.m.

The bullpen was packed.

The night shift was straightening up, sinking refuse into trash baskets, and a half-dozen day-shift cops were waiting for their desks. Last time I was here, Jacobi still occupied what we laughingly call the corner office: a ten-foot-square glass cubicle overlooking the James Lick Freeway.

Since then, Jacobi had been bumped upstairs to chief of police, and the new guy, Jackson Brady, had scored the lieutenant's job.

I had a little history with Brady. He had transferred to San Francisco from Miami PD only a month before, and in his first weeks as a floater, he had shown heroism in the field. I worked with him on the explosive multiple homicide case that put him on the short list for Jacobi's old job.

I'd been offered the job, too, thanks very much, but I'd turned it down. I'd already held down the corner office for a few years, until I got sick of the administrative overload: the budgets, payrolls, meetings with everyone, and layers of bureaucratic bull.

Brady could have the job with my blessing.

I just hoped he'd let me do mine.

I saw Brady through the walls of his cube. His white-blond hair was pulled back in a ponytail, and he wore a shoulder holster over a starched blue cotton shirt that stretched across his massive chest.

He looked up and signaled for me to come to his office. When I got there, he hung up the phone. Reaching across the desk that was once mine, he shook my hand and congratulated me.

"Are you using Boxer or Molinari?" he asked me.

"Boxer."

"Well, have a seat, Sergeant Boxer," he said, waving me toward the chair across from his desk. "I got a call from Major Case Division about ten minutes ago. They're short on manpower and asked for help. I want you and Conklin to check it out."

"The case is a homicide?" I asked.

"Could be. Or maybe not. Right now it's an open case. Your open case."

What kind of bull was this?

Step out of line for a couple of weeks, and the only open case was a spillover from another unit? Or was Brady testing me—alpha-dog management style?

"Conklin has the case file," Brady said. "Keep me in the loop. And welcome back, Boxer."

Welcome back, indeed.

I showed myself out, feeling like all eyes in the squad were on me as I crossed the room to find my partner.

Chapter 3

DR. ARI RIFKIN was intense and busy, judging from the incessant buzz of her pager. Still, she seemed eager to brief me and my partner, Richard Conklin, aka Inspector Hottie. Conklin scribbled in his notebook as Dr. Rifkin talked.

"Her name is Avis Richardson, age fifteen. She was hemorrhaging when she was brought into the ER last night," the doctor said, wiping her wire-rimmed specs with her coattail.

"From the looks of her, she delivered a baby within the past thirty-six hours. She got herself into grave trouble by running and falling down — too much activity too soon after giving birth."

"How'd she get here?" Conklin asked.

23

"A couple—uh, here's their names—John and Sarah McCann, found Avis lying in the street. Thought she'd been hit by a car. They told the police that they don't know her at all."

"Was Avis conscious when she came in?" I asked Dr. Rifkin.

"She was in shock. Going in and out of lucidity—mostly out. We sedated her, transfused her, gave her a D and C. Right now, she's in guarded but stable condition."

"When can we talk with her?" Conklin asked.

"Give me a moment," said the doctor.

She parted the curtains around the stall of the ICU where her patient was lying. I saw through the opening that the girl was young and white, with lank auburn hair. An IV line was in her arm and a vital-signs machine blinked her stats onto a monitor.

Dr. Rifkin exchanged a few words with her patient and then came out and said, "She says that she lost her baby. But given her state of mind, I don't know if she means that the baby died or that she misplaced it."

"Did she have a handbag with her?" I asked. "Did she have any kind of ID?"

"She was only wearing a thin plastic poncho. Dime-store variety."

"We'll need the poncho," I said. "And we need her statement."

"Give it a shot, Sergeant," said Dr. Rifkin.

Avis Richardson looked impossibly young to be a mother. She also looked as though she'd been dragged behind a truck. I noted the bruises and scrapes on her arms, her cheek, her palms, her chin.

I pulled up a chair and touched her arm.

"Hi, Avis," I said. "My name is Lindsay Boxer. I'm with the police department. Can you hear me?"

"Uh-huh," she said.

She half-opened her green eyes, then closed them again. I pleaded with her under my breath to stay awake. I had to find out what had happened to her. And by giving us this case, Brady had charged Conklin and me with finding her baby.

Avis opened her eyes again, and I asked a dozen basic questions: Where do you live? What's your phone number? Who is the baby's father? Who are your parents? But I might as well have been talking to a department-store dummy. Avis

Richardson kept nodding off without answering. So, after a half hour of that, I got up and gave my chair to Conklin.

To say that my partner has "a way with women" is to play up his charm and all-American good looks and cheapen his real gift for getting people to trust him.

I said, "Rich, you're on deck. Go for it."

He nodded, sat down, and said to Avis in his deep, calm voice, "My name is Rich Conklin. I work with Sergeant Boxer. We need to find your baby, Avis. Every minute that passes puts your little one in more danger. Please talk to me. We really need your help."

The girl's eyes seemed unfocused. Her gaze shifted from Conklin to me, to the door, to the IV lead in her arm. Then she said to Conklin, "A couple of months ago . . . I called the number. Help for pregnant girls? A man . . . he spoke with an accent. French accent. But . . . it wasn't authentic. I met them . . . outside my school . . ."

"Them?"

"Two men. Their car was a blue four-door? . . . And when I woke up, I was in a bed. I saw the baby," she said, tears gathering in her eyes, spilling over. "It was a little boy."

And now my heart was breaking apart.

What the hell was this crime? Baby trafficking? It was outrageous. It was a *sin*. Make that a lot of sins. I tallied up two counts of felony kidnapping before we even knew the fate of the baby.

Conklin said, "I want to hear the whole story from the beginning. Tell me what you remember, okay, Avis?"

I couldn't be sure, but it could have been that Avis Richardson was talking to herself. She said, "I saw my baby.... Then, I was on the street. Alone. In the dark."

Chapter 4

I STAYED at Avis Richardson's bedside for the next eight hours, hoping she'd wake up for real and tell me what had happened to her and her newborn. Time passed. Her sleep only deepened. And every minute that went by made me more certain that this girl's baby would not be found alive.

I still didn't know anything about what had happened to this teenager. Had she given birth alone and left the baby in a gas station bathroom? Had her child been snatched?

We couldn't even get the FBI involved until we knew if a crime had been committed.

While I sat at Avis's bedside, Conklin went back to the Hall and threw himself into the hands-on work of the case. He reached into the missing persons databases and ran searches for Avis Richardson or any missing Caucasian teenage girls matching her description.

He interviewed the couple who had brought Avis to the hospital and established the approximate area where they had found her: Lake Merced, near Brotherhood Way.

Working with the K-9 unit, Conklin went out into the field. Cops and hounds looked for the blood trail that Avis Richardson had surely left behind. If the house where she'd given birth could be located, there'd be evidence there, and maybe the truth.

As the hounds worked the scent, the crime lab processed the plastic poncho Avis had been wearing. It would hold prints, for sure, but a few dozen people at the hospital had handled that poncho. It didn't make any sense that she was wearing a rain poncho but no clothes.

Another mystery.

I kept vigil with a sleeping Avis. And the longer I sat, the more depressed I became. Where were the worried friends and parents? Why wasn't someone looking for this young girl?

Her eyelids fluttered.

"Avis?" I said.

"Huh," she answered. Then she closed her eyes again.

I took a break at around four in the afternoon, pushed dollar bills into a vending machine, and ate something with peanut butter and oats in it. Washed it down with a cup of bitter coffee.

I contacted a dozen hospitals to see if a motherless baby had been brought in and got in touch with Child Protective Services as well. I came up with nothing more than a mounting heap of frustration.

I borrowed Dr. Rifkin's laptop and went out to VICAP, the FBI's Violent Crime Apprehension Program database, to see what they had on the abduction of pregnant women.

I found a few crimes against pregnant women—domestic violence mainly, but no cases that resembled this one.

After my fruitless Internet crawl, I went back to the ICU and slept in the big vinyl-covered reclining chair beside Avis's bed. I woke up when she was wheeled out of the ICU and down the hall to a private room.

I called Brady, told him that we were still nowhere, my voice sounding defensive to my own ears.

"Anything on the baby?"

"Brady, this girl hasn't said boo."

When I hung up with Brady, my phone buzzed with an incoming call from Conklin.

"Talk to me," I said.

"The hounds found her trail."

I was instantly hopeful. I gripped my little phone, almost strangling it to death.

"She bled for about a mile," Conklin told me. "She put down a circular path at the southernmost part of Lake Merced."

"That sounds like she was looking for help. Desperately looking."

"The hounds are still on it, Lindsay, but the searchable area is expanding. They're working a grid on the golf course now. The gun club area is next. This could take years."

"I haven't found anything in missing persons," I said.

"Me, neither. I'm in the car, calling people with the name Richardson in San Francisco. There are over four hundred listings."

"I'll help with that. You start at A. Richardson. I'll start at Z. Richardson, and we'll work toward the middle," I said. "I'll meet you at the letter M."

When I hung up with Richie, Avis opened her pretty, green eyes. She focused them on me.

"Hey," I said. "How are you feeling?"

I had a white-knuckle grip on the rails of her bed.

"Where am I?" the girl asked me. "What happened to me?"

I bit back the words "Ah, shit" and told Avis Richardson what little I knew.

"We're trying to find your baby," I said.

Chapter 5

I PUT MY KEY in the lock of the front door to our apartment, and at that precise moment, I remembered that I hadn't called Joe to say I wouldn't be home for dinner. Actually, I hadn't spoken to him in about twelve hours.

Way to go, Lindsay. Brilliant.

My border collie, Martha, heard me at the front door, barked, and, with toenails clattering across the wooden floor, hurled herself at my chest.

I cooed to her, ruffled her ears, and then found Joe in the living room. He was sitting in an armchair, reading light on, with eight different newspapers lying on the floor around the chair in sections.

He looked at me with reproach in his eyes.

"Your mailbox is full."

"My mailbox?"

"Your phone."

"Is it? I'm sorry, Joe. I had to turn my phone off. I was in the hospital ICU all day. A new case I'm working."

"We were supposed to take my folks out for dinner tonight."

"Oh my God. I'm sorry," I said as my stomach dropped toward my toes. Joe had told me that we were going to take them out for some quality time and first-class steak at Harris'. I'd filed that information in a folder at the back of my mind and never looked back.

"They're on the flight back to New York."

"Honey, I'll call them tomorrow and apologize. I feel like crap. They're so great to me."

"They're treating us to a honeymoon. A little luxury shack in Hawaii. When we've got time."

"Ah, shit. Is that what they said? That makes me feel even more rotten. There's a baby missing..."

"Have you eaten?" he asked.

"Just vending machine stuff. A long time ago."

Joe got out of the chair and strolled to the

kitchen. I followed him like a puppy that had had an accident on the rug. Taking a chicken breast out of a bowl of marinade, he put a pan on the stove and fired it up.

"I can do that," I said.

"Tell me about your case."

I poured myself a giant glass of merlot and left the bottle on the counter. Then I dragged up a stool and watched Joe cook. It was one of my favorite things to do.

I told him that a teenage girl had been found in the street like roadkill, bleeding out from a recent pregnancy and delivery. That she'd almost died from loss of blood. That she was still barely lucid, so I had spent the past twelve hours running through missing persons files in every state in the union, waiting for her to talk.

"All we know is that her name is Avis Richardson," I said to Joe. "Conklin and I have called about two hundred Richardsons in the Bay Area. So far no luck. Wouldn't you think her parents—or someone—would have reported her missing?"

"You think she was abducted? Maybe she's not local."

"Good point," I said. "But still, no hits in VICAP." I worked on my butter-sautéed chicken. Slurped some wine. I was kind of hoping that between the sustenance and Joe's FBI-trained mind, some insight would come to me.

There was a newborn out there somewhere. He might be dying or dead, or in transit to another country. Dr. Rifkin said the gap in Avis Richardson's memory had to do with whatever medication she had taken and that she didn't know what kind it was or how long ago she had taken it. There was a chance Avis might *never* remember more than what she'd already told us. Particularly if she'd been knocked out during the trauma.

I was hoping that her body had a memory of giving birth and that she was emotionally aware of her terrible loss. That maybe that physical memory would trigger an actual one and she'd remember something critical if we gave her enough time.

"Joe, despite all that has happened to her recently, why can't she tell us how to reach her parents? Is she unable? Or unwilling?"

Joe said, "Maybe she was living on the street."

"She was found just about naked. Wearing a two-dollar rain poncho. You could be right."

Joe took away my empty plate, loaded the dishwasher according to a system of his own devising, and gave me a bowl of praline ice cream and a spoon. I got up from my stool and wrapped my arms around his neck.

"I don't deserve you," I said. "But I sure do love you to death."

He kissed me and said, "Did you try Facebook?"

"Facebook?"

"See if Avis has a page. And then here's an idea. Come to bed."

Chapter 6

"I'LL JOIN YOU IN A BIT," I said to Joe's back as he walked down the hall to our bedroom.

I took my laptop to the sofa and reclined with my head against the armrest, Martha lying across my feet.

I opened a Facebook account and did a search for Avis Richardson. After some fancy finger navigation, I found her home page, which wasn't privacy protected. I read the messages on her wall, mostly innocuous shout-outs and references to parties, all of which meant nothing to me. But I did learn that Avis attended Brighton Academy, a pricey boarding school near the Presidio.

I called Conklin at around midnight to tell him that we had to track down the head of

Brighton, but I got his voice mail. I left a message saying, "Call me anytime. I'm up." I made coffee and then accessed Brighton's website.

The site was designed to attract kids and their parents to the school and, if you could believe the hype and the photos, Brighton Academy was a little bit of heaven. The kids—all of them good-looking and well groomed—were shown studying, onstage in the auditorium, or on the soccer field. Avis was in a couple of those photos. I saw a happy kid who was nothing like the young woman lying in a hospital bed.

I recognized other kids, ones I'd seen on Avis's Facebook page.

I made a list of their names.

And then I heard a baby crying.

When I opened my eyes, I was still on the sofa, my laptop closed, with Martha on the floor beside me. She was whining in her dreams.

The digital clock on the DVR showed a couple of minutes before seven in the morning. I had a terrible realization. This was only my second night in our apartment as a married woman, and it was the first time, ever, that I'd slept in the same house as Joe but not in the same bed.

I poured out some kibble for Martha, then peeked into the bedroom where Joe was sleeping. I called his name and touched his face, but he rolled over and went deeper into sleep. I showered and dressed quietly and then walked Martha up and down Lake Street, thinking about Joe and our marriage vows and about what it meant to be part of this team of two.

I would have to be more considerate.

I had to remember that I wasn't single anymore.

A moment later, my mind boomeranged back to Avis Richardson and her missing baby.

That child. That child. Where was that baby?

Was he lying in the cold grass? Or had he been stuffed in a suitcase and into the cargo hold of a ship?

I called Conklin's cell at 7:30, and this time I got him.

"Avis Richardson goes to Brighton Academy. That's one of those boarding schools where parents who live out of state park their kids."

"It might explain why no one is looking for her," Conklin said. "I was just talking with K-9. The hounds are going in circles. If Avis was

40

transported from point A to point B by car, that would have broken the circular trail."

"Crap," I said. "So, she could have delivered the baby anywhere and then been dumped by the lake. No way to know where point A was."

"That's what I'm thinking," he said.

"I'll meet you at the hospital in fifteen minutes," I said. "Avis Richardson's memory is all we've got."

When we got to Avis Richardson's hospital room, it was empty, and so was her bed.

"What's this now? Did she *die?*" I asked my partner, my voice colored by unadulterated exasperation.

The nurse came in behind me on crepe-soled shoes. She was a tiny thing with very muscular arms and wild gray hair. I recognized her from the night before.

"It's not my fault, Sergeant. I checked on Ms. Richardson, then went down the hall for a quarter of a minute," said the nurse. "This girl of yours scampered when my back was turned. Appears she took some clothing from Mrs. Klein in the room next door. And then she must've just walked the hell out of here."

41

Chapter 7

AT 8:30 THAT MORNING, Yuki Castellano was sitting at the oak table in a small conference room in the DA's Office on the eighth floor of the Hall.

Predictably, she was anxious.

Right now, she was running a low-grade anxiety that would heat up as it got closer to the actual start of the trial.

Today was a big day. And a lot was at stake.

She'd put in a year of work on this case, and it was all going to happen in less than half an hour. Court would convene. Dr. Candace Martin would go on trial for murder in the first degree, and Yuki was the prosecuting attorney.

Yuki knew every angle of this case, every

witness, every crumb of physical and circumstantial evidence.

The defendant was guilty, and Yuki needed to convict her, for the sake of her reputation in the office and for her belief in herself.

Yuki was satisfied with the jury selection. The case folders stored on her laptop were in perfect order. She had exhibits in an accordion file, and a short stack of index cards to prompt her in case she got stuck while giving her opening statement.

She'd been practicing her opener for several days, rehearsing with her boss and several of her ADA colleagues. She'd rehearsed again with her deputy and second chair, Nick Gaines.

She had her opening statement down cold, and the case would simply flow from there.

Just then, Nick came into the conference room, bringing coffee for two, a smile on his face, his shaggy hair hanging over his collar.

"You look hot," he said to her.

Yuki waved away the compliment. She was in what she called her "full-court dress": a white button-down silk-blend shirt, her late mother's pearls, a navy-blue pin-striped suit, and short stacked heels. One magenta streak blazed in her shoulder-length black hair.

"I want to look *cool*," she said. "Unflappable. Prepared. And I want to scare the snot out of the defense."

Gaines laughed. And then Yuki did, too.

"What do you say, Nicky? Let's get there early," she said.

The two ADAs walked through the maze of cubicles out to the hallway. They got on the elevator and rode down to the third floor, where doors to the courtrooms lined both sides of the main corridor.

Yuki was inside her head, psyching herself up as she made this walk. She reminded herself that she was dedicated. She was smart. She was buttoned up to her chin and she knew what she was going to say.

And now for the hardest thing.

She had to kick doubt's ass right out of her mind.

Chapter 8

GAINES HELD THE DOOR for Yuki, then followed her into the wood-paneled courtroom. The defense table was empty. There were only half a dozen people in the gallery.

They settled in at the prosecutors' table behind the bar. Yuki straightened her jacket and her hair and then squared her notebook computer with the edge of the table.

"If I get stuck, just smile at me," Yuki said to her second chair.

Gaines grinned, gave her a thumbs-up, and said, "You've heard of *Cool Hand Luke?* When you see this, it means Cool Hand Yuki."

"Thanks, Nicky."

Yuki was always prepared, but she'd lost a

number of cases she had been favored to win. And that losing streak had taken a bite out of her confidence. She'd won her last case, but her opponent had given her a parting shot that still stung.

"What's that, Yuki?" the jerk had said. "Your first win in how long?"

Now she was going up against Philip Hoffman, and she'd lost to him before. Hoffman was no jerk. In fact, he was a gentleman. He wasn't theatrical. He wasn't snide. He was a serious dude, partner in a law firm of the highest order, and he specialized in criminal defense of the wealthy.

Hoffman's client, Dr. Candace Martin, was a well-known heart surgeon who'd killed her philandering louse of a husband.

Candace Martin was pleading not guilty. She said she didn't kill Dennis Martin, but that was a monumental lie. There was enough evidence to convict her a few times over. And yes, the People even had the smoking gun.

Yuki's nervousness faded.

She knew her stuff. And she had the evidence to prove it.

Chapter 9

CINDY THOMAS was one of two dozen people in the editorial meeting in the big conference room at the *San Francisco Chronicle*. The meeting had started an hour ago and it looked as though it could go on for another hour.

Used to be that these meetings were collegial and fun, with people making cracks and busting chops, but ever since the economic downturn and the free-and-easy access to the Internet as a news source, editorial meetings had a scary subtext.

Who would keep their job?

Who would be doing the job of two people?

And could the paper stay in business for another year?

There was a new gunslinger in town: Lisa Greening, who had come in as managing editor under the publisher. Lisa had eight years of management experience, two years at the *New York Times*, three at the *Chicago Tribune,* and three at the *L.A. Times.*

Her claim to fame had been an investigative report for the latter on the PC Killer, a smooth con man with a foot fetish who'd terrorized the Pacific Coast, luring women, killing them, and keeping their feet in his freezer as trophies.

Greening had won a Pulitzer for that story and had parlayed it into her new post at the *Chronicle*.

Since Cindy was the *Chronicle*'s crime desk reporter, she felt particularly vulnerable. Lisa Greening knew the crime beat as well as Cindy did—probably better—and if she failed to live up to a very high standard, Cindy knew she could become a budget cut. Greening would pick up her territory, and Cindy would become a freelancer working for scraps.

Half the editors in the room had given status reports, and Abadaya Premawardena, the travel editor, was up.

Prem was talking about cruise ship packages and discounts on Fiji and Samoa when Cindy got up and went to the back of the room and refilled her mug at the coffee urn.

Her last big story, which was about Hello Kitty, a jewel thief who preyed on the rich and famous, had been a huge and splashy success. The thief had either skipped town or retired, probably due to the work Cindy had done. But that was old news now, and the next big story, the kind that sold newspapers, had yet to appear.

Cindy sat back down as Prem finished his report, and Lisa Greening turned her sharp gray eyes on Cindy.

"Cynthia, what's coming up for us this week?"

"My ATM mugger story is wrapping up," Cindy said. "The kid was arraigned and is being held without bond."

"That was in your column yesterday, Cynthia. What's up for today?"

"I'm working on a couple of ideas," she said.

"Speak up if you need assistance."

"I'm good," said Cindy. "Not a problem."

She flashed a smile at Greening, a smile that was both charming and confident, and the editor moved on to the next in line. Cindy couldn't have reported anything about the next hour.

Only that it was finally over.

Chapter 10

CINDY LEFT the editorial meeting in a deep funk. She walked down the hall to her office and before even sitting down called Hai Nguyen, her cop contact in Robbery.

"Anything new on ATM Boy?" she asked.

Nguyen said, "Sorry, Cindy, but we've got no comment at this time."

Cindy believed that Nguyen would help her if he could, but that woulda-coulda sentiment was of no help to her. While the cops and robber worked out their deal, Cindy still had eight column inches to fill by four o'clock today.

How was she going to do that?

She had just hung her coat on the hanger behind her office door when her desk phone rang.

The caller ID read "Metro Hospital ER."

She grabbed the receiver and said, "Crime desk. Thomas."

"Cindy, it's me, Joyce."

Joyce Miller was an ER nurse, smart, compassionate, and companionable. She and Cindy had once lived in the same apartment building and had bonded over single-girl nights, drinking cheap Bordeaux and watching movies on Sundance.

"Joyce. What's wrong?"

"My cousin Laura, she's acting weird. Like she's just visited an alternate universe. You met her at my birthday. She works for a law firm. She *loved* you. Listen, I talked her into coming into the ER by saying I'd get her some sleep meds, but she won't let a doctor touch her and she won't call the police."

"What do you mean, she's 'acting weird'?"

"She must've been drugged. And I think something happened to her while she was out. For *eight hours*. Woke up in the shrubbery near her front door. That's what I mean by acting weird. I love this girl, Cindy. Will you come here while I've got her? I think together we can get her to talk."

"Right now?" Cindy asked. She looked at her Swatch. Only six hours until her drop-dead deadline at four o'clock. Eight empty column inches that she'd told Lisa Greening she could fill. It was a crevasse of empty space.

"She's like a sister to me, Cindy," Joyce said, her voice breaking with emotion.

Cindy sighed.

She forwarded her calls to the front desk and left the building. She took BART to 24th, walked four blocks to Metropolitan Hospital at Valencia and 26th, and met Joyce just outside the ambulance bay. The friends hugged, and then Joyce led Cindy into the crush and swarm of the ER.

Chapter 11

LAURA RIZZO sat at the edge of a hospital bed in the ER. She was about Cindy's age, around thirty-five, raven-haired with an athletic build, and she was wearing jeans and a dark blue Boston U sweatshirt. Her movements were jerky and her eyes were open so wide, you could see a margin of white completely surrounding her irises. She looked like she'd been plugged into an electric outlet.

"Laura," Joyce said. "You remember Cindy Thomas?"

"Yeah.... Hi. Why—why are you here?"

Joyce said, "Cindy is smart about things like this. I want you to tell her what happened to you."

"Look. It's nice of you to come, I guess, but

54

what is this, Joyce? I didn't tell you so that you'd bring in reinforcements. I'm *fine*. I just need something for *sleep*."

"Listen, Laura. Get real, would you, please? You called me because you're freaked out, and you should be freaked out. Something happened to you. Something *bad*."

Laura glared at Joyce, then turned and said to Cindy, "I have to say, my mind's a blank. I was coming home from work last night. I remember thinking about getting pizza for dinner and a bottle of wine. I woke up lying in the hydrangeas outside my apartment building at around 2 a.m. No pizza. No wine. And I don't know how I got there."

"Good lord," Joyce said, shaking her head. "So you just got up and went inside?"

"What else could I do? My bag was right there. Everything was in it, so I hadn't been robbed. I went upstairs and took a shower. I noticed then that I felt sore—"

"Sore where? Like you'd been in a fight?" Cindy asked.

"Here," Laura said, pointing to the crotch of her jeans.

"You were assaulted?"

"Yeah. Like that. And as I'm standing there in the shower, I have like this vague memory of a man's voice. Something about winning a lot of money, but I sure don't feel like I won anything."

"Did you go somewhere after work? A bar or a party?"

"I'm not a party girl, Cindy. I'm like a nun. I was going home. Somehow, I—I don't know," Laura said. "Joyce, even if I let a doctor examine me, I don't want to tell the cops. I *know* cops. My uncle was a cop. If I tell them that I don't know anything about what happened to me, they're going to think I'm a wacko."

Chapter 12

PHIL HOFFMAN PACED in front of the reception desk at the seventh-floor jail in the Hall of Justice. He was waiting for his client Dr. Candace Martin, who was changing out of her prison uniform in preparation for her first day of trial.

Candace was holding up well.

She was determined. She was focused. And while she was uncomfortable in her present circumstances, she had borne up well under the confinement—the close contact with the other inmates, the rules—because that was what it took to get to this day.

Now it was up to him.

If Phil won an acquittal, Candace would go back to her job as head of cardiac surgery at

Mercy Hospital. The stain on her name would be eradicated. She would be able to pick up the parenting of her two children, who were, even now, waiting for them outside the courtroom.

Phil had talked to both of the kids, and in his judgment they could handle the pressure. But he did expect a challenge from opposing counsel.

Phil had gone up against Yuki Castellano before, and he quite liked her. She was feisty and she was smart, but Hoffman knew her greatest weakness, too. Yuki bulled ahead, wielding her passion while skipping over potholes and ignoring warning signs that the bridge ahead was out.

Without being cocky about it, he liked his odds of winning better than hers.

Phil stopped pacing. There was a clanking of barred doors, then the echo of footsteps, and Candace came through the door in a tailored suit and handcuffs.

"Hey, Phil," Candace said.

Phil came toward her, touched her shoulder, and said, "How are you doing? Okay?"

"Way better than okay, Phil. I've been waiting for this day for a lifetime. A year, anyway."

The guard removed her handcuffs and said,

"Good luck, Dr. Martin."

Candace rubbed her wrists. "Thanks, Dede. See you later."

Phil held the elevator door for Candace and smiled at her as they descended to the third floor.

He'd also been waiting for this day for more than a year. And he was pretty sure that today was going to be a very good day.

Chapter 13

ALL TWO HUNDRED people in courtroom 3B seemed to be talking at once. Yuki was texting her boss to tell him there'd been a mysterious delay when, at just after ten, the bailiff called out, "All rise for His Honor, Judge Byron LaVan," and the judge entered the oak-paneled courtroom.

LaVan was fifty-two, a square-jawed man with wild dark hair and black-rimmed glasses. He was known to be a short-tempered judge with an impressive background in criminal law.

He took the bench, the seal of the state of California behind him, the American flag to his right, the state flag to his left. Laptop open in front of him, he was ready to start.

When the gallery was reseated, the judge

brusquely apologized for his lateness, saying there had been a family emergency. Then he asked the bailiff to bring in the jury.

The twelve jurors and two alternates filed into the jury box, fumbled with their handbags and notebooks, and settled into their maroon swivel chairs. To Yuki's right, Phil Hoffman whispered to his client, Dr. Candace Martin.

Sitting in the first row, directly behind Dr. Martin, were her two beautiful young children, Caitlin and Duncan, looking like angels. Angels who didn't know what the hell was happening.

So, that was how Hoffman was going to play it, Yuki thought. He was going to go for sympathy from the jury.

Suddenly Yuki was struck with a sickening realization. Bringing the kids to court wasn't just a bid for sympathy from the jury. Hoffman was forcing her to dial down her rhetoric so that she wouldn't upset the kids.

Controlling son of a bitch.

She couldn't let him get away with that.

Yuki listened to the judge instruct the jury, but a part of her mind was on her former, lucrative job in a big-deal law firm, which she'd quit so that she could do something meaningful—for herself and for the people of San Francisco.

Not that she was a selfless do-gooder. After two years of defending the rich, Yuki had become highly motivated to put away killers like Candace Martin who thought they could hire a thousand-dollar-an-hour defense attorney and beat the rap.

The judge finished his talk to the jury and turned to face the courtroom. Yuki got to her feet and said, "Your Honor, may I approach the bench?"

Judge LaVan looked at her like she had farted in court. Too bad, she thought. She stood firm until the judge signaled to Yuki and Hoffman to step forward.

Hoffman's sequoia-like height dwarfed Yuki's five foot two. She felt young and small by comparison, the top of her head about level with Hoffman's armpit.

Yuki said, "Your Honor, I object to the defendant's young children being present in the courtroom. The State is accusing their mother of killing their father. When I say what I have to say, the kids are going to get upset, which is going to make the jury sympathize with the defendant."

LaVan said, "Mr. Hoffman? Have you got a position on this?"

"The kids are well behaved and they know the truth, Your Honor. Their mother is innocent. They're here to show their support."

LaVan cleaned his glasses with a tissue, repositioned them on the bridge of his nose, and said, "Ms. Castellano, do your job. Ignore the kids. I'll instruct the jury to do the same. Let's get on with it, shall we? Is the prosecution ready?"

"Yes, Your Honor, we are."

"Then tell us what you've got."

Chapter 14

YUKI'S HEART WAS PUMPING pure hot adrenaline as she crossed the well of the courtroom and took the lectern. She reminded herself to relax her shoulders and smile as she swept the jury box with her eyes. Then she launched into her opening argument.

"The defendant is charged with premeditated murder — that is, murder in the first degree," Yuki said, her voice ringing out over the courtroom.

"In the next few days, the State will prove beyond a reasonable doubt that the defendant, Candace Martin, shot and killed her husband, Dennis Martin. We will introduce physical evidence and testimony that will show that Dr. Martin's hands are not just dirty, they're as black as sin."

There was a gratifying intake of breath in the courtroom, and Yuki waited out the whispers moving like a wind across the gallery. Then she began to lay out the prosecution's case as neatly as a hand of solitaire.

"Dennis Martin was shot to death in the foyer of his home on the night of September fourteenth of last year. This is not in dispute.

"The four people who were in the house at the time of the murder were Candace Martin, her two children, and the family cook. All were questioned by the police, and evidence was taken. The twenty-two-caliber handgun that was used to kill Dennis Martin was collected at the scene of the crime and so was the gunshot residue on Candace Martin's hands.

"There is only one way to get GSR on your hands," Yuki told the jury. "You get it by firing a *gun*."

Yuki told the jury that Candace Martin had the means and the opportunity to kill her husband.

"We're not required to show motive, but we will tell you why Candace Martin planned and executed this murder.

"Dennis Martin was a habitual womanizer, and at the time of his death, he was having another affair. But Mr. Martin didn't try to cover up his activities.

"During their thirteen years of marriage, Mr. Martin taunted his wife with his infidelity and finally, on September fourteenth, she'd had enough.

"In our society, marital infidelity is punishable by divorce, but Candace Martin figured her husband deserved the death penalty. With her husband dead, she'd get the kids, the three-point-five-million-dollar home, and everything in their combined bank accounts. She'd also get the meal that is best served cold — revenge."

Yuki sneaked a glance at the Martin children. The little boy's mouth was hanging open. The little girl was scowling. The judge had said "Ignore them" and Yuki tried to do that as she preemptively set fire to the defense's position.

"Mr. Hoffman will tell you that his client didn't do it," Yuki told the jurors. "He will say that the defendant was in her home office when she heard shots in the foyer. He will say that she found her husband bleeding on the floor, that she checked his pulse, that she realized that her husband was dead. And then—what do you know? She heard an intruder leaving by the front door.

"Mr. Hoffman will tell you that Candace Martin called out and that the intruder was startled and dropped his gun. And he will tell you that his client picked up the gun and followed the intruder outside and fired at him.

"That's the defense's explanation for the gunshot residue on Candace Martin's hands.

"There's only one problem," Yuki said to the fourteen men and women in the jury box. "This story is entirely *bogus*.

"There was no intruder.

"There was no forced entry into the house, and nothing was stolen.

"But Candace Martin had told several people that she wanted her husband dead, and the *very evening* of the fatal incident she was seen handling a gun.

"Our job in the DA's office is to speak for the victim," Yuki said, "and we will do that. But if Mr. Martin could speak for himself, he'd tell you who killed him," said Yuki, pointing at the pretty, blond heart surgeon who was chewing on the ends of her hair.

"He'd tell you that his dear wife shot him dead."

Chapter 15

SUSIE'S CARIBBEAN CAFÉ is a mood changer in the best possible way. The walls are yellow, the calypso music is live, the food is hot, and the beer is cold. Susie's is also the unofficial clubhouse of our gang of four, branded the Women's Murder Club by our friend, girl reporter Cindy Thomas.

I desperately needed an hour at Susie's. Conklin and I had spent the day looking for a newborn baby. We'd walked with cadaver dogs, checked in with divers at the edge of Lake Merced, and made an all-day, fruitless canvass of houses in the area, with Avis Richardson's photo in hand, asking, "Have you seen this girl?"

Then, ten minutes ago, a stunning call had

come in to Jacobi. Avis Richardson had turned up behind the locked doors of a schoolmate's parents' apartment on Russian Hill. These "do-gooders" were keeping Avis away from the cops until her parents could arrive from New Zealand. So Avis had been located, but we still had no leads on her baby, who was either missing or dead.

Probably both.

Claire and I drove to Susie's together in my car and parked in a miraculously empty spot on Jackson Street near the corner of Montgomery. We came through the door into the lilting beat of steel drums and laughter, and waved to casual friends. We passed the bar and took the narrow and aromatic aisle past the kitchen to the cozy back room where Yuki was already holding down our booth.

Lorraine called out, "Hey, y'all," and brought over a frosty pitcher of beer, along with Yuki's watermelon margarita. Yuki cannot hold her liquor, but that doesn't stop her from drinking it.

I slid into the banquette next to Yuki, while Claire took the other side of the booth. Yuki lifted her glass of pink liquid mind-bender and took a slug.

"Sip it!" we shouted to her in unison.

Yuki snorted tequila up her nose and sputtered, "I have earned the right to get drunk. I made a brilliant opener and then the judge gets a call. His sick mother is fading fast. He adjourns court for the day. By tomorrow, Phil Hoffman will have read the transcript and will pick my bones clean in his opener."

At that, Cindy, dependably the last to arrive, scooted into the booth next to Claire and bumped her hip, saying, "Give me a couple of inches here, girlfriend."

Claire said, "Are you all going to listen to what happened to me today? Or do I have to fight for the talking stick? Because I will do it."

"You go first," Yuki said, holding up her empty glass to the light. Claire didn't wait for anyone to object.

"I get called to go to this house in the Sacramento Delta," she said. "A friend of mine called in a favor. So I drive to this swampland—can only get there by these veiny little roads and levees—and I find this hunting cabin.

"This old dude who lives there paid all his bills two weeks in advance and hasn't been seen since.

71

Now people are starting to ask, 'What happened to Mr. Wingnut?'"

Cindy was thumbing the keys on her Crackberry while Claire told her story.

"There's this long lump under the bedcovers," Claire said, plucking the PDA out of Cindy's hand, putting it in her pocket, treating Cindy like she was a little girl.

"Hey!" said Cindy.

I had to laugh—and I did.

Claire went on, ignoring Cindy pawing at her pocket and retrieving her phone. "I pull back the blankets and the dead man has been mummified by the heat and he's holding a freakin' AK forty-seven in his hands."

Cindy stopped what she was doing and stared at Claire.

"He was dead? Holding an AK forty-seven?"

"He killed himself with that gun," Claire said. "Sent my pulse rocketing into the low one-eighties. You can believe that."

Cindy looked stricken.

"I'm okay, now, sugar," said Claire. "It was just a scare."

Cindy swiveled her head toward me, her

blond curls bouncing, her clear blue eyes locking on mine.

"That text I just got was from Metro Emergency," she said. "Another girl thinks she was raped."

"Another girl? *Thinks* she was raped?"

"Linds, I feel it in my gut. A very wonky story is brewing. Do me a favor, will you? Give me a lift to the hospital."

Chapter 16

I GUNNED MY CAR along Columbus Avenue to Montgomery Street and past the Transamerica Pyramid, my siren whooping to clear a lane in the dinner-hour rush.

Beside me Cindy clung to her armrest and told me about Laura Rizzo, a woman who might have been drugged and assaulted the same night Avis Richardson was found wandering under a moonless sky fifteen miles north of the city.

I had to check out Cindy's "wonky story."

Two girls had been assaulted now, maybe three—and none of them had memories of the assaults? Could there be a connection to Avis Richardson? Or was I just wishing for a lead— any lead?

I brought Cindy up to speed on the Richardson case as I reached the intersection of Montgomery and Market streets. I came close to clipping a big-assed Lexus and ran onto the trolley tracks along Market. I jerked the wheel again and put the traffic jam behind me. Cindy was pale, but I just kept driving.

"A teenage girl was brought into Metro ER by passersby a couple of nights ago," I told Cindy. "That's off the record."

"Okay."

"Okay? Seriously."

"Yes, Lindsay. O. Kay. It's off the record."

I nodded, took a hard right, and turned onto Mission on two wheels, flying past Yerba Buena Gardens on my left. You almost had to get promises from Cindy in writing. She's honest, but what can I say? She's a reporter. And we weren't ready to churn the waters with a kidnapped baby story.

I still didn't know what we had. Was Avis Richardson a victim of multiple savage crimes? Or had she killed her own child? I kept my foot on the gas as if that would actually bring the Richardson baby home.

"This teenager had recently given birth," I went on, taking the car through the heart of the Hispanic area of town. We passed check-cashing holes-in-the-wall and cheap souvenir vendors selling T-shirts out of the old 1920s theaters under their cracked and faded marquees.

I turned right onto 26th, still talking. "But the thing is, Cindy, no baby was found. The girl didn't remember the delivery, and now that the shock is wearing off and she might be able to talk to us, she won't do it."

"Why the hell not?"

"I swear I don't know."

Cindy made me promise to tell her *whatever* I could, *whenever* I could, *on* the record. I nodded yes as I turned left on Valencia and parked my old heap in front of the hospital.

Chapter 17

CINDY AND I entered the crowded lobby of Metropolitan Hospital and found Cindy's friend, Joyce Miller, waiting for us at the main desk. She was a dark-haired woman, maybe thirty-five, wearing a nurse's uniform.

She pumped my hand with both of hers.

"Thanks for coming, Lindsay. Thanks so much."

We followed Joyce down a number of branching linoleum-tiled corridors, around corners, and then through the ER, an obstacle course of gurneys and wheelchairs, before we came to a partitioned stall where we met Anne Bennett, a possible rape victim.

Ms. Bennett was a travel agent in her early

forties. She looked as fatigued as if she'd been running on a treadmill for the past eight hours.

Her voice quavered as she said that she remembered taking a cab to her office this morning but she woke up behind a Dumpster in an alley a block from her house.

"I don't remember a damned thing," Ms. Bennett told me. "My blouse had been buttoned wrong. My pantyhose were gone, but I was still wearing my black pumps with the gold buckles. My handbag was on my chest and my phone and my wallet were still in it. Forty-four bucks. Just what I'd had."

"And you remember nothing of the ten hours between leaving for work and waking up?"

"It was as if someone had turned off my lights," Anne Bennett said, looking up at me with bloodshot eyes.

"The doctor said it appeared I'd suffered sexual trauma. The last time I had sex with my boyfriend was four days ago. And there was nothing traumatic about it. We've been together so long, it's no-drama sex, and that's just the way I like it."

Anne Bennett was telling the story straight

and clearly, but panic flashed in her eyes. It was like she was searching her memory — and finding nothing there.

Chapter 18

HOFFMAN STOOD AS COURT was called to order and the jury filed in. He retook his seat, thinking about juror number three, Valerie Truman, the single mother who worked at a library and earned a thousandth of what Candace Martin made in a year. And he thought of number seven, William Breitling, a retired golf pro with a ton of charisma. Breitling wasn't the foreman, but Hoffman believed he could influence the jury.

When Judge LaVan asked Hoffman if he was ready to present his case, he said that he was and walked from his seat beside Candace Martin directly to the jury box.

He rested his hand on the railing, greeted the jurors, and began.

"Yesterday, the prosecution gave their opening statement. I think Ms. Castellano did a pretty good job, but she left out a couple of important points. For starters, Dr. Martin is innocent."

William Breitling smiled with a full set of veneers, and Hoffman felt the ice melt in the jury box.

"Here's what happened on the evening of September fourteenth," Hoffman said. "Dr. Martin had just come home from the hospital. She had successfully repaired a man's heart that day and she was satisfied that her patient was going to recover completely.

"She said hello to each of her children, then went down the hall to her home office to call the patient's wife.

"Dr. Martin had removed her glasses so she could rub her eyes and was about to make the call when she heard what sounded like shots coming from the foyer.

"The shots startled her and she knocked her glasses to the floor. This is one of those important points I mentioned."

Hoffman walked the length of the jury box, touching the rail now and then for emphasis.

The jurors followed him with their eyes as he described how his client had found her husband lying on the floor, saw the blood, and, after checking, discovered that Dennis Martin had no vital signs.

"When she looked up, she saw someone, an intruder, who was in the shadows of the foyer. Dr. Martin couldn't make out the intruder's face and she was terrified. She shouted in surprise, and the intruder dropped his gun and ran. My client picked the gun up and ran after him, through the front door and out onto the front steps.

"Dr. Martin had never fired a gun before, but she let off a couple of shots into the air. She hit nothing. That is how she got gunshot residue on her hands.

"Immediately after firing those shots, Dr. Martin went back into her house and called the police. That is the act of an innocent person," Hoffman said.

"The prosecution says that Dennis Martin was a philandering rat but that being a rat isn't a crime punishable by death. Well, that's true. And Dr. Martin knew it. She also knew that her marriage was going through a bad spell.

She, too, was having an affair.

"She wasn't jealous. She figured the marriage would right itself in due course or it would end. She was prepared for either outcome.

"Candace Martin is a modern and successful woman. She isn't a Pollyanna and she isn't the Orange Blossom princess, but she is a highly respected cardiac surgeon and a marvelous mother, and she also loved her husband."

Hoffman turned toward his client.

"I want you to look at her now," he said to the jurors, "and see her for what she is: the victim of an overworked police department that took the easy solution—blame the spouse. And she's being tried by an overzealous prosecutor who, for her own reasons, needs to score a big win."

Chapter 19

YUKI FELT PHIL HOFFMAN'S smash return right between her eyes. Holy crap. Hoffman's shot at her was outrageous and maybe even defamatory. She had a flash fantasy of making an objection: *"Your Honor, opposing counsel is freaking desperate and should be thrown out of the court."*

Nick Gaines, Yuki's second chair and wingman, pushed a notepad toward her. He was a gifted cartoonist and in a few strokes had captured a lanky Phil Hoffman grabbing at his throat and a stick-figure Yuki with a slingshot and a title: "Underdog."

Yuki pushed the pad back to Gaines. She got his point. The jury would like her more as a result of Hoffman's low blow. She would overcome the slam. As for now she reminded herself, "Never let 'em see you sweat."

She stood and said, "Your Honor, will you please remind the jury that opening statements are not evidence?"

"Consider it done, Ms. Castellano," LaVan said with a sigh.

Yuki's first witness was the uniformed patrolman who answered the radio call to the Martins' house. Officer Patrick Lawrence testified that he was only blocks away and had arrived with his partner within a minute of the call. He said that he had interviewed Dr. Martin and kept her company as the EMS arrived and until Inspector Chi of Homicide and Lieutenant Clapper of the Crime Scene Unit took possession of the scene.

Yuki established that Dr. Martin seemed in control of her emotions and that because of Officer Lawrence's quick arrival, Candace Martin hadn't had a chance to wash her hands or clean up the crime scene.

After Officer Lawrence left the stand, Yuki called private investigator Joseph Podesta, and he was sworn in. Podesta was a neat and pleasant-looking man in his fifties who had been hired by Dennis Martin to snoop on his wife.

Yuki questioned Podesta on his credentials, and he told the jury that he had been an investigator for the district attorney in Sacramento for twelve years and a private investigator, first in Chicago and currently in San Francisco, for a combined twenty years.

"Why did Dennis Martin hire you, Mr. Podesta?" Yuki asked.

"Mr. Martin knew that his wife was having an affair and he wanted pictures of them, uh, in flagrante delicto."

"Did you get pictures of the defendant with her lover?"

"Yes, I did."

"Did you learn anything else during the time she was the subject of your investigation?" Yuki asked.

"Yes."

"Please tell us what you learned."

"On one of the nights I was tailing her, Candace Martin met with a man I believe to be a contract killer."

A rumble came up from the gallery, and Hoffman shot to his feet with an objection.

"Your Honor, this is pure hearsay. How can this witness know that the man he says he saw is a contract killer? If he was so sure, why didn't he call the police? Instead, the State is using this extremely dubious testimony to impugn the reputation of a heart surgeon. How does this make any sense?"

The judge quieted the room with two hard bangs of his gavel and said, "I'd like to hear this, Mr. Hoffman."

When she could speak again, Yuki asked, "You have proof of this meeting, Mr. Podesta?"

"I followed Dr. Martin from her house in St. Francis Wood to Hunters Point. I followed her to Davidson Avenue. That's a dead end. A late-model Toyota SUV was parked at the end of the street, where it butts up against the I-280 overpass. This is a bad neighborhood, but I was able to watch without being seen."

"Go on, Mr. Podesta."

"The meeting was clearly clandestine," Podesta said. "I took photographs of Dr. Martin getting into this SUV. When I downloaded them onto my computer later, I thought I'd seen the man's face before."

"And what happened next?"

"Two weeks later Dennis Martin was murdered."

"What did you do, Mr. Podesta?"

"I compared my picture of the man in the SUV to pictures on the FBI's Most Wanted list. In my opinion, the man I saw talking to Dr. Martin was Gregor Guzman."

"And why is Mr. Guzman on the FBI list?"

"Your Honor. Is this witness an FBI agent? What the—?"

"Sit down, Mr. Hoffman. The witness may answer to the best of his knowledge."

"Gregor Guzman is wanted on suspicion of murder in California as well as a few other states and other countries. He's never been arrested. I contacted the FBI three times, but no one ever got back to me."

Yuki introduced the photograph of Candace Martin sitting in a dark sports utility vehicle with a balding man with a shock of hair at the front of his scalp. It was a grainy photo, taken with a long lens at night, but it appeared as Podesta described it.

"Thank you," Yuki said. "That's all I have for you, Mr. Podesta."

Chapter 20

"YOUR HONOR, SIDEBAR?" Hoffman said stiffly.

The judge waved the two attorneys in toward the bench and said, "Go ahead, Mr. Hoffman."

"Your Honor, this witness is a private investigator. He's not even a cop. His testimony is pure guesswork. Where is this so-called hit man? Why isn't *he* on the witness list? How do we know *why* my client was seeing this man, or even if this person is who the witness says he is?"

"Ms. Castellano?"

"Mr. Podesta didn't say he was an expert witness. He followed the defendant, who got into a car with a man who resembles Gregor Guzman. Mr. Podesta took pictures of a clandestine meeting between them. He compared the picture of the man in the SUV with photos of Gregor Guzman issued by the FBI. He made a match—*in his opinion*. That's his testimony."

"Mr. Hoffman, I've heard you. Now, please cross-examine the witness," LaVan said.

Phil Hoffman addressed Joseph Podesta from his seat beside his client, trying to show the jury how little regard he had for the witness.

"Mr. Podesta, I don't know which piece of fiction to begin with. Okay, I've got it," he said before Yuki could object.

"First, have you ever worked for the FBI?"

"No."

"Do you have any specialized training in the identification of contract killers?"

"I have a very good eye."

"That wasn't my question, Mr. Podesta. Do you have any specialized training in the identification of contract killers? Did you get this man's fingerprints? Did you get his DNA? Do you have a tape recording of this assumed conversation?"

"Objection," Yuki said. "Which question does counsel want the witness to answer?"

"I'll withdraw all of them," Hoffman said,

"but I object to this exhibit. The quality of this photograph stinks and it proves nothing. In fact, I object to this entire testimony and move that it be stricken from the record."

"Overruled," said the judge. "If you're finished questioning this witness, Mr. Hoffman, he may step down."

Chapter 21

"THE PEOPLE CALL Ellen Lafferty," Yuki said.

The doors opened at the back, and a pretty, auburn-haired woman in her early twenties wearing a tight blue suit and a blouse with a bow at the neck came into the courtroom and walked down the aisle. She passed through the gate to the witness stand, where she was sworn in.

"Are you employed by Candace and the late Dennis Martin?" Yuki asked her witness.

"I am."

"In what capacity?"

"I am the children's nanny. I work days and live out."

"How long have you worked in the Martin house?" Yuki asked.

"Just about three years."

Yuki nodded encouragingly. "In your opinion, what was the state of the Martin marriage?" she asked.

"In a word," Lafferty said, "explosive."

"Could you give us a couple more words?"

"They hated each other," said the nanny. "Dennis wanted to divorce Candace, and she was furious about it. She once told me she thought getting a divorce would be messy. It would hurt her children as well as her standing in the medical community."

"I see," Yuki said. The witness was describing a marriage held together by practical considerations rather than love, and Yuki knew the jury would understand that.

"Were you in the Martin house on the day that Dennis Martin was killed?"

"Yes. I was," Lafferty said. She had kept her eyes on Yuki until this moment, but now she swung her gaze toward the defendant and fixed it there.

"Did something remarkable happen that evening?"

"Absolutely."

"Please go on."

Lafferty turned back to Yuki.

"I was getting ready to leave for the day. It was six o'clock and I was going to meet a girlfriend at Dow's Imperial Chinese at six-fifteen. We hadn't seen each other in a while and I was really looking forward to seeing her."

"Go on," Yuki said.

Lafferty said, "I was putting on my lipstick when Dr. Martin came home. She had a funny look on her face. Distracted, or maybe angry. I went into her office to ask her if everything was okay, and when I got there, she was putting a handgun in her desk drawer."

"You're sure it was a gun?" Yuki asked.

"Oh, absolutely."

"Did Dr. Martin ever tell you she wished her husband were dead?"

"Many times. Too many to count."

"Too many to count," Yuki said pointedly to the jury.

"And did Mr. Martin tell you about his feelings for his wife?"

"He said she was cold. He used to say that he didn't trust her."

94

"Thank you, Ms. Lafferty. That's all I have for this witness."

Hoffman stood, his chair scraping noisily against the oak floor. He put his hands in his pockets and approached the witness, who stiffened her shoulders and looked up at him.

"Ellen. May I call you Ellen?"

"No. I'd rather you didn't."

"I'm sorry. Ms. Lafferty. Did you think Dr. Martin was going to kill her husband?"

"I don't know. Maybe."

"So, if you thought she was going to commit murder and you saw Dr. Martin with a weapon, why didn't you call the police?"

Yuki watched Lafferty's righteous indignation melt into an expression of grief.

She said, almost begging Hoffman and the jury to understand, "I wasn't thinking about her that night. I was in a hurry. In hindsight, I should have called the police or warned Mr. Martin. I blame myself. If I'd done something, Mr. Martin would still be alive and the children would still have their father."

The little boy's wail cut through the air like a siren: "*Ellllllll-ennnnnnnn.*"

The witness leaned forward in her chair and called out across the well of the courtroom, "Duncan. Baby. I'm right here, sweetie."

That's when Judge LaVan went nuts.

Chapter 22

YUKI TOOK THE ELEVATOR up to the DA's offices, her mind still busy with the sound of the child's scream and Judge LaVan's reaction.

Christ. It was as if Duncan Martin had yelled, *"Stop beating me!"* There was a good chance Hoffman's sympathy ploy had worked.

Yuki left her briefcase in her windowless office, made her way to the corner office facing Bryant Street, and knocked on the open door.

Leonard Parisi, deputy district attorney and her direct superior, asked her to come in and sit down.

Parisi had been nicknamed Red Dog for his thick red hair and his unshakable determination. He was a large, pear-shaped man of fifty with coarse skin and clogged arteries, but the expression on his face was just beautiful.

He was smiling. At her.

"I peeked in this morning. Saw your examination of that private eye. Fantastic job, Yuki," he said. "I'm impressed."

"Thanks, Len. LaVan just called us into chambers," Yuki said, taking the chair in front of his desk.

"Oh? What was that about?"

"Hoffman had the defendant's kids in the courtroom, half to gain sympathy from the jury, half to rattle me. I objected, but LaVan overruled me.

"So I've got the Martins' nanny on the stand, and she says if she'd called the police on Candace, Dennis would still be alive. And, Len, the little boy just *screams* for his nanny. Nanny calls out to him from the stand, 'There, there, I'm here, baby.'"

"Huh, huh, huh," Parisi grunted sympathetically.

"Court's adjourned for the day. The judge says to me and Hoffman, 'You two. See you in back.' He tells Hoffman, any more out of the kids, he's barring them from the courthouse."

"Good. LaVan doesn't kid around."

"Len, tell me what you make of this. Hoffman came up to me afterward," Yuki told her boss. "He said, 'You know, Ellen Lafferty's testimony was a pack of lies.' I said, 'Well, I sure didn't see that on cross.' Hoffman wanted to talk to me about it, but I didn't have time. I knew it was just going to be more of his B.S."

"Sure. He's trying to mess with your head, Yuki. Shake your confidence. Disrupt your momentum, that SOB. Listen, switching gears, I've been wanting to tell you. Craig Jasper is leaving. Moving to San Diego at the end of the month."

Craig Jasper was a bright light in the department and had been Parisi's protégé. Yuki told Red Dog she was sorry, but he waved the comment away.

"I see opportunities for you, Yuki. You just need a couple of wins under your belt."

Yuki's face brightened and she nodded. She would love to get an upgrade in status and pay grade. It was really time. The Martin case had been important a minute ago, and it just got more important.

"I've got a good feeling about this case," she said, standing to leave.

"Me, too," said Red Dog. And he smiled again.

Yuki fixed her makeup in the bathroom at the end of the hallway. She was psyched at the idea of the job and more responsibility, but it also meant more pressure. And she already had no shortage of that.

She had a date later with a guy who was almost too gorgeous for her. She hoped she could calm down and not talk too much, not scare the guy off.

They had a lot in common. The guy was a cop.

Chapter 23

I WAS LEAVING for the day when Phil Hoffman galloped up to me in the all-day lot across from the Hall. I like Hoffman, even though his job is getting off killers and perverts and other living human garbage. He was one of the few criminal defense attorneys I'd met who could actually pull off this kind of dirty work without acting smug about it.

On the other hand, Yuki was locked in mortal combat with Hoffman and she was my friend.

"Hey, Phil," I said as he pulled up next to the spot where I'd parked my Explorer. I took off my jacket and tossed it into the backseat.

"Lindsay, I need your help."

"Can we talk tomorrow?" I asked him. "I've

been slogging through hell all day," I said, thinking of the dozens of consecutive hours I'd been working on finding the Richardson baby.

"This will only take a minute."

"Okay, then. Shoot."

"You're aware of Candace Martin?"

"Sure. My colleague Paul Chi worked the Martin case. And Yuki, of course."

"Yes. That's right," Hoffman said, putting his briefcase down on the asphalt. He ran a hand through his hair. "Something new has come up regarding the testimony of one of the witnesses. I asked Yuki to hear me out, but I'm the enemy. She's not inclined to believe anything I say."

"Phil, why don't you just say your piece in court?"

"If I could get Yuki's ear out of court, it would be better for all concerned. This new information I have is going to reverse the trial. Let me be clear. The case will be dismissed and you'll be booking someone else for Dennis Martin's murder."

My mind spun. I heard what he said, but I didn't get why Hoffman was talking to me. "How can I help you?"

"I want you to talk to my client."

"Me?"

"Yes. After that, maybe you can get Yuki to hear me out."

"So if I get this right, this is the long way around in getting Yuki to talk to you."

Everything about Hoffman's request was inappropriate. I was the wrong cop and he was going around everyone in the Hall of Justice. But Paul Chi reported to me. I had to worry if the SFPD and the District Attorney's Office had the wrong person in the dock.

Hoffman's request made me uncomfortable. But off the record? Unofficially?

Phil Hoffman had definitely gotten my attention.

Chapter 24

INSPECTOR PAUL CHI is a certified genius and a lifelong student of criminal behavior. It was hard to believe that he had arrested the wrong person for the murder of Dennis Martin.

So what was Hoffman up to?

I left Joe a message saying I'd be late, then retraced my steps into the stream of Justice Department workers leaving the lobby of 850 Bryant.

Chi and McNeill were with Brady in the corner office when I rapped on the glass. Brady waved me in and Cappy McNeill stood, sucked in his stomach so I could get past him, and then gave me his chair. McNeill has five years on me both in age and time in grade. He's not ambitious, but he's steady. He's all about instinct and experience and bringing down the bad guys.

As for Brady, I'd seen him go through a firestorm and confront a killer who had nothing to lose. Brady had guts to spare, but he was new to San Francisco. He didn't know Phil Hoffman, and he hadn't been in charge of Homicide when Candace Martin was investigated for murder.

I reset my ponytail and then laid out my conversation with Hoffman in the parking lot. "Bottom line, Hoffman says the wrong person is being charged with murder. He says we should withdraw the charges, reopen the case, and bring in the person who really killed Dennis Martin."

"Really? And who does Hoffman say did it?" Chi asked me.

"Hoffman said his client will tell me."

"Ah, shit, Lindsay," McNeill grumbled. "Candace Martin damn well is the doer. Hoffman is cornered, so he's working any angle he can dream up. And I gotta give him credit. This angle is pretty damned creative."

"This case opened and shut itself," said Chi. "And then it tied itself with a big red bow." He started ticking off the physical evidence on his fingers: gun, prints, GSR.

"You're saying that no innocent person has ever been convicted?" I asked Chi.

"What's in this for you, Sergeant, because I just don't get where you're going," Brady said. He texted a message, closed the phone, and put his eyes on me. "How many hours have you worked in the past twenty-four?"

"I don't keep track."

"I do. You've gone about eighteen hours straight. The Martin case was closed—what, a year ago? It's in the hands of the justice system. So go home, Boxer. Get some sleep. Tomorrow let's see some progress on Richardson."

I felt the little hairs on the back of my neck stand at attention. First time I'd ever felt this kind of opposition from Chi and McNeill. As for the new lieutenant? I didn't know if his mind was just closed—or if he was right.

I threw up my hands, said okay, and left the squad room again. I called Hoffman from the stairwell and told him I'd meet him on the seventh floor in five minutes.

He thanked me and said, "You won't be sorry."

I was already sorry. Phil Hoffman's story had gotten to me, and now I was bucking the boss with absolutely nothing to gain.

Chapter 25

THERE ARE TWO JAILS at the Hall, each with separate elevators that go only from the lobby to the jail. Prisoners awaiting trial are held in the jail on the seventh floor, and that's where I met Phil Hoffman.

Hoffman's expression showed that he was relieved to see me, but my stomach heaved with anxiety. I didn't belong here, doing *this*. Not my job.

"Thanks for coming, Lindsay," Hoffman said. Doors buzzed open as we walked along grimy, overlit corridors toward a meeting room used for prisoners and their lawyers.

"I'm doing this on my own time, Phil. Nothing official about it."

"I understand and I appreciate it."

A moment later, Candace Martin was escorted by a guard into the room. She was wearing jailhouse orange, and somehow it looked good on her. She wore no makeup and had her blond hair tucked behind her ears, and she looked younger than her forty years. Hoffman introduced us and we all sat down.

"Candace, tell Sergeant Boxer what you told me."

"First, thanks for coming, Sergeant Boxer," she said. "I know you're doing a big favor for Phil."

"I only have a few minutes."

Candace Martin nodded and said, "Ellen flat out lied. I never had a gun in my office. The gun came into my house with the killer," she said. "So why did Ellen lie? It makes no sense, unless she's trying to get me convicted."

"Why would she want to do that?" I asked.

"My husband was handsome and a self-described sex addict. He would screw a tree if it breathed. He liked to tell me that Ellen was 'a treasure,' and he'd put a little spin on it to see what I would do. But I never gave him the satisfaction of a reaction."

Now Candace Martin clenched her fists on the tabletop. "You know what I cared about, Sergeant? The kids. Caitlin and Duncan love Ellen. I wanted to trust her, so I did."

I said, "I don't see where this is going, Dr. Martin. Whatever was going on between Ellen Lafferty and your husband, why would she commit perjury? Why would she accuse you of murder?"

"Here's what I think, Sergeant. I didn't understand why an intruder would shoot Dennis. But today, when Ellen turned the air purple with her lies, it clicked.

"What if Dennis was screwing her? What if he was making promises to her about divorcing me, and it wasn't happening fast enough? What if she gave him an ultimatum and he didn't go for it? What if *she* was the so-called intruder who shot my husband?"

I said, "That's a lot of what ifs and no evidence at all." I stood up, already projecting myself out of the Hall, heading home to my husband, leaving this whole questionable action behind me.

"I know, I know," Candace said, putting her head in her hands. "I know it's just speculation, but if you knew what a manipulative prick Dennis was, you'd see how he could use her to enrage me—and use me to enrage her."

"Sorry, Dr. Martin. It's an interesting theory," I said, "but that's all it is."

I was acting tough, but Candace Martin was getting to me. I'd once been on trial, accused of wrongful death, and had been abandoned by everyone but my attorneys. What Candace Martin said made sense. I sympathized with her and I even liked her.

Still. This was not my job.

"Please, Sergeant. Do something," Candace Martin said, as I signaled to the guard to open the door. "I didn't kill my husband. That girl is taking care of my kids while I'm in a cage and on trial for my life."

Chapter 26

THE NEXT MORNING, Conklin and I were in the Richardsons' posh wood-and-amber-toned luxury suite at the Mark Hopkins, simply one of the most elegant, beautiful hotels in San Francisco, with a view of the world from the top of Nob Hill.

Conklin questioned Avis Richardson as her devastated, borderline-hysterical parents hovered in the background.

Conklin was not only kind to Avis, he was sincere, and his first-class interview should have yielded more from her than "I don't remember anything."

More than three days after she was admitted to the hospital, she still looked bombed-out and withdrawn. Her body language told me that she wasn't really listening to Conklin, that her mind was on the far side of the moon.

Paul Richardson paused in his pacing around the Oriental carpet to say, "Avis, try, for God's sake. Give Inspector Conklin something to work with. This is life and death. Do you understand me? Do you?"

Room service rang the doorbell.

Sonja Richardson brought her daughter a mug of hot chocolate, then pulled me aside to say, "Avis is not herself. Normally, she's quick. She's funny. I tell you, she's having a nervous breakdown. Oh my God, I can't believe we listened to her. She begged us to let her stay here when Paul was transferred. She had friends, and the staff at Brighton... We felt she was safe at that school."

I went back to the sitting room and sat a few feet from Avis. Her eyes were vacant. She'd been physically hurt. Her baby was gone. And I was guessing that she blamed herself.

Still, why didn't Avis ask about her son? She should have had a lot of questions: What were we doing to find him? Was there any chance he was alive? But she didn't ask a thing.

Did she know that he was dead?

Had she buried him herself?

Was the baby's father involved in this horror story?

Conklin took a new tack. He said, "Avis, were you threatened? Is that it? Did someone tell you that if you spoke to the police they'd hurt the baby?"

I could almost see the lightbulb go on over her head. Avis turned her eyes up and to the right and said, "Yeah. The Frenchman said he'd kill my baby if I talked to the police."

My bull-crap alarm went off, a three-alarm clamor.

Avis had just lied.

I stood up from the chubby armchair, cast my five-foot-ten shadow across the girl on the couch, and said, "I have to talk to Avis alone."

There was silence for a full three seconds and then Conklin said, "Mr. and Mrs. Richardson, let's go into the other room. I need to get some contact information and so forth."

The girl looked up at me as the room cleared, and I saw fear in her eyes. She was afraid of me. Maybe she figured that Conklin was the good cop and I was the other one.

She got that right.

I said, "It's time, Avis. I want to find your baby and I'm staying in your face, here or at the police station, until you tell me the *truth*. Do you understand?"

"I'm the victim," she whined. "I was kidnapped. You can't hold me responsible."

"I can damn well hold you responsible. I can hold you as a material witness for forty-eight hours. During that time, I won't be bringing you hot cocoa. I will make you as miserable as possible, and when I get tired, I'll send in a fresh team of bullies."

"No."

"Yes. Right now, cops are getting a warrant for your phone records," I said, picking up the armchair and setting it down hard, closer to the couch. "We're going to know the names of everyone you've spoken to in the past year. We *will* find something."

No comment.

Her silence was infuriating.

"Dammit, little girl. Your baby is missing. Maybe he's *dead*. You're his *mother*. You're all he *has*. And you're all *I* have. The bullshit stops now. Do you read me?"

Avis Richardson shot a furtive look at the door. "They'll kill me," she said.

I crossed the floor, locked the door to the adjoining room, threw the bolt, and sat back down. My heart was pumping like it was about to explode.

Tears gathered in Avis Richardson's eyes. Then she started to talk.

Chapter 27

"I DIDN'T WANT my parents to know that I was...pregnant," Avis Richardson said.

She sat scrunched against the back of the couch, her knees tucked up to her chin, her black-painted toenails peeking out from under a blanket. "I saw an ad on Prattslist a couple of months back," she said.

Prattslist. It was a message board for virtual tag sales and personal ads, and it also functioned as the yellow pages for prostitutes and sex offenders and predators of all types and stripes prowling for victims.

"Tell me about the ad," I said.

"It said something like 'Pregnant? We'll help you from birth to...uh, placement with your baby's new parents.'" She gave me a glancing look. "So I called the number."

I shook my head, sick that this girl who could have had the best medical care in the world had hidden her pregnancy from people who cared about her. Then she'd turned her life over to an anonymous phone number on Pervs "R" Us. I said, "Go on."

Avis said that her call had been answered by the man with a French accent who told her to call again when she was in labor. He'd said there would be papers to sign.

"He said that he was a doctor and that the delivery would be as safe as if I were in a hospital. He told me that the adopting parents would be completely vetted. And he said I'd be reimbursed ten thousand dollars for prenatal expenses."

Holy crap. Avis Richardson had sold her baby.

I was furious, frustrated, and still hopeful that the child was alive, but I kept emotion out of my voice.

I said, "You believed all this, Avis? You weren't suspicious at all?"

"I was grateful."

I didn't know whether to spit or go blind.

Avis Richardson had known what had happened to her baby from the start. She had lied to the SFPD, and we'd pressed half of our resources into a phony dragnet that had wasted time and manpower and could never have turned up her baby.

Well, at least the time for lying was over.

If Avis didn't want to sleep in general holding tonight, she was going to tell me the truth about everything she knew.

Chapter 28

AVIS RICHARDSON PICKED at her nail polish as she told me that two months after her first call to "the Frenchman" she'd found on Prattslist, she started having contractions. She called the number again and arranged to be picked up a couple of blocks from the school.

"You've got the number?"

"No one answers it anymore."

And then she returned to her story.

"I was nervous that someone might see me standing on the street like that," she said. "When the car pulled up, I saw that it was a regular four-door type. Dark color. Clean. I ducked into the backseat really quick."

Rental car, I thought.

Avis said there were two men in the front seat of the car, but their faces were in shadow and after she was inside, all she saw were the backs of their heads. She was told to lie down on the floor in back and cover herself with a blanket.

"How long was the drive?" I asked. "Did you hear anything that could help us figure out where you were taken?"

"I don't know how long I was in the car. An hour? They turned on the radio," Avis told me. "Lite music station. Pretty soon after that, I felt a needle stab my hip, right through the blanket. Next thing I knew, I was being hustled out of the car and helped up a walk toward a house. Sergeant Boxer, I was in agony."

"What can you remember about the house? Color? Style? Was it on a residential block?"

"I don't know. I was hanging on to the men's arms, looking at my feet.... I think I heard the door slam behind me, but I was knocked out again, and when I woke up, I was in a bed having contractions every couple of minutes," she said.

I sighed. Put my anger down. This was such a bleeping awful story. Maybe the only way the kid could deal with what had happened to her was to distance herself as she had done.

"Next time I woke up, there was a light shining in my face. It was clipped to a door. One of those aluminum bowl-shaped lights?"

I nodded and noted the non-clue detail.

"I couldn't see anyone because of the light in my eyes, and I was numb," she said. "They gave me some water out of a red bottle with a sippy straw.

"I heard the baby cry. I asked to see it," she went on, her voice and expression as flat as a photograph. "I was told, no, it wouldn't do me any good. That he was a healthy baby boy. And then I woke up on the street," she told me.

"It was dark," Avis said. "I didn't know where I was. Then I saw a street sign that said Lake Merced. My clothes were bloody and disgusting. I found a rain poncho blown into some bushes, so I took off my clothes and put it on."

The green plastic poncho, the only hard evidence we had, hadn't even been handled by the men who'd taken her. So much for the thirty-six hours of lab time spent processing traces off it.

"They could have killed me," she said.

I nodded. "It's hard to say you were lucky, but you were."

The girl's sharpest memories were utterly useless. Fake French accent. Dark sedan. Aluminum lamp. Red bottle with a sippy straw. Green plastic poncho that had never had contact with the perps. Everything led to nothing.

I understood why Avis had blocked more traumatic memories.

But her continued lack of interest in the baby stunned me. It didn't matter that she didn't care. *I* cared.

I would find that baby boy or die trying.

"Do you know where your baby is?"

"No."

"Have you been honest with me?"

"Yes. I swear," Avis said.

My bullshit meter went on the blink. I couldn't tell if she was lying or not. But there was another entire line of inquiry we hadn't yet pursued.

"Who is the baby's father?" I asked.

Chapter 29

BRIGHTON ACADEMY is in the Presidio Heights area, tucked away, nearly hidden behind trees and a neighborhood of sleepy, Victorian-lined streets. It was a surprise to turn a corner and see four handsome stone buildings set in a square around a compact campus of clipped lawns punctuated with carved boxwood cones and hedges.

High-school kids played field hockey and tennis, and others were grouped on benches or lying under trees in the quad.

The whole place smelled green. Greenback green.

Like Hogwarts for the really, truly rich.

Conklin and I checked in at the Administration Office, where we met with Dean Hanover, a big man wearing a pink shirt and polka-dot bow tie under his blue blazer.

We told him about our investigation into the possible kidnapping of Avis Richardson and the disappearance of her child. Hanover was sweating on a cool day, and I knew why. The dean had a big problem.

"This goes beyond nightmare," Hanover said to me. "That poor kid. And, of course, her parents are going to sue us to the walls."

I got the dean's in loco parentis permission to interview Avis's boyfriend, E. Lawrence Foster, as well as my short list of Avis's six best friends.

"Tell me about these kids," I said.

"Foster is an average kid, friendly. Parents own a magazine in New York. He's got a lot of friends, but I confess I don't know much about his relationship with Avis."

Hanover gave us one-paragraph bios on the other kids: all children of wealthy parents who lived in other states or other countries. Avis's roommate, Kristin Beale, was no exception. Her parents were in the military, stationed overseas.

We left the sweaty dean, headed out through the stone-arch entrance to the Administration

Office, and took one of the shrub-lined paths toward the main hall.

"You want to be the good cop for a change?" Rich asked me.

"I would if I could," I told him.

Chapter 30

WE FOUND LARRY FOSTER in the high-tech chemistry lab in the southernmost wing of the school. He was as the dean had described him: a friendly, good-looking tenth-grader from the East Coast. He was neatly dressed in the school uniform—blazer, necktie, gray pants, and state-of-the-art cross-trainers.

We invited Larry into an empty classroom and seated ourselves at desks. I sent up a prayer that this teenage boy would know something that would lead us to his son.

"You think *I'm* the father? I'm *not*," Larry Foster said. His sleepy gray eyes opened wide. His lower lip quivered. "Avis and I are friends. That's all."

"Friends, huh," said Conklin. "Avis said you were closer than that. Why would she lie?"

"I don't *know* why she would lie. We never hooked up, not ever," the kid said. "I never had those kinds of feelings about Avis, I swear."

"You knew she was pregnant?" I said.

"Yeah, like since last week, and I didn't tell anyone. Avis said she was having the baby for an infertile couple. I told her she was full of it, and she said, 'Yeah, full of baby.' And then I thought, Hey, she hasn't called me back the past couple of days. Is she okay?"

"We have reason to believe that Avis got pregnant the regular way," Conklin said. "If that is true, who's your first guess for the father of her baby?"

"No idea. I didn't even know she was with anyone," the kid said.

Next up was Brandon Tucker, a kid with a future as a professional soccer player. He was taller than me and he had a disarmingly wicked smile. I'd seen a lot of pictures of this kid on Avis's Facebook page.

Was he baby Richardson's father?

After the preliminary introductions, I asked

Tucker what he knew about Avis—her pregnancy, her baby, and her whereabouts over the past three days.

"Ma'am, I don't know anything about a baby," said Tucker. "I only heard that she was pregnant, like, a week ago. And I was, like, totally shocked. Avis is a very quiet girl. And heavy. I just thought she was bulking up."

"So, what was she to you?" I asked. "She has you on her Facebook friends list."

"Like that means anything. She asked to friend me. I said okay. She used to help me with my French," he laughed. "She tutored me for exams once in a while. I paid her by the hour. For *tutoring*," he said.

"You ever hook up with Avis?" Conklin asked.

The kid looked offended.

"Me? Hell, no. Not my type, dude. Not even if I was drunk—she just wasn't my type."

"Who was her type?" I asked.

"Larry Foster, right?"

We used the same classroom to talk to three other teens, and by this time, they all knew why we were there. Not one of those kids admitted to knowing that Avis was pregnant until a week ago, and no one knew the identity of the father of her child.

We were told repeatedly that she was a quiet girl, intelligent, not popular, not an outcast, either. She got good grades and kept to herself.

Even the girls we interviewed, when implored to help us find the baby, said they didn't have an idea in the world.

"You believe this?" Conklin said to me when the last kid had left the room. "A school like this. Avis was nine months pregnant, and no one knew nothin'."

"Reminds me of something I once heard," I said to my partner. "How do you know if a teenager is lying?"

"How?" Conklin asked.

"Their lips are moving."

Chapter 31

AVIS AND KRISTIN BEALE had been bunking in the same room for more than a year. Logically, of all the people who knew Avis, her roommate, given their daily contact, should have had the most intimate knowledge. I figured she might very well know what Avis had been thinking, doing, and planning for herself and her baby.

Kristin Beale was our best hope — and maybe our last.

Conklin knocked on the paneled door in a corridor lined with them. A voice called out, "Come innnnn."

We did — and the smell of marijuana came out to greet us.

The dorm room was just big enough for two

beds, two closets, and two desks. It looked out over the Presidio, and I could see a sliver of the bay over the tops of trees.

In front of the view was Kristin Beale.

She was lying on her back in the window seat, her long legs bent, her bare feet pressed against the wall. She was pretty, with a wild mop of dark brown hair, and had on footless leggings and a man's dress shirt. White wires were plugged into her ears.

The girl startled when she saw us, straightened her legs and sat up, and pulled out her earbuds. She was thin — too thin.

She said, "Who are you?"

As I did the introductions and told her why we had come, I looked the girl over. Even from fifteen feet away, I could see that Kristin Beale's pupils were dilated.

I also took in the state of the room.

Kristin's side had a post-tornado, morning-after look. The floor around her unmade bed was strewn with clothes, books, and candy wrappers.

The other side, Avis's side, was as tidy as a banker's desk. A pillow on the bed was embroidered with the letter *A*, and there was a picture of the Richardson family on her dresser.

Avis's closet was open. I quickly went through her clothes and saw that she had them in two sizes. Size eight and extra large.

Her computer was turned off on her desk, untouchable without a warrant.

"Is Avis okay?" Kristin asked, in a tone that told me she didn't care at all.

"She's with her parents," I said. "She's doing okay, but she's been through an ordeal. Kristin, has Avis called you or written to you? We're trying to find her baby."

"Baby? I don't know anything about a baby."

"Avis was nine months pregnant," I said. "You saw her every day. Unless you're blind, you must have known she was pregnant."

"Well, I didn't," the girl said. "She was a pretty good eater and she didn't work out."

Turning to Conklin, I said, "You know, Inspector, I'm getting sick of these kids lying their faces off."

"I don't think they understand that we are homicide cops," he said. "Maybe they think that because they go to a rich kids' school, they're outside of the law."

The girl was staring at us now, eyes going back and forth between us and darting to a spot on the floor. I followed her eyes to a pile of laundry and saw the corner of a plastic bag under a sock.

I said to Conklin, "You're right. They're spoiled. They're living in a separate universe. A universe where this," I said, toeing the sock aside, "a few ounces of marijuana, isn't illegal. But, of course it's possession of an illegal substance, and in this case, given how much you have here, Kristin, I'm thinking it could even be possession with intent to sell."

"That's not mine. I never saw it before."

I had to laugh. Two feet from her bed and she'd never seen it before.

"I say it's your grass and that your urine is going to show that you've been smoking it."

I reached under my coat for my cuffs, and the girl backed up.

"Kristin Beale, you're under arrest for possession of narcotics."

"No . . . what, are you — kidding? I'll get kicked out of here. Okay, okay, okay. Like, what do you want to know?"

"Where is the baby?"

"I don't know."

"Who is the father of Avis's baby?" I said.

"She never told me. I am telling you the *truth*."

"Someone got her pregnant," said Conklin.

"She's gone out with boys, but no one regularly."

"More lies," I said. "I think you'll tell us the truth at the station. Of course, we'll have to call your parents."

"I think she was going out with a married man," the kid yelled at me. "Look. She didn't tell me. One time, I asked her if she was pregnant. She said, 'I don't want to talk about it.' I asked if her secret boyfriend was married, and she gave me a look. Like *this*. And she told me to never tell anyone. And that is everything I know. Everything. She never talked about the baby again. Maybe she told Larry Foster. Those guys are tight."

Chapter 32

I PUT MY CARD on Kristin's desk and told her to call me if she had any thoughts she'd like to share that might save a baby's life. I flushed the weed down the toilet in the bathroom down the hall, and then, muttering under my breath about teenagers, my partner and I left the dorm.

During the six hours we had spent interviewing Avis's friends at Brighton, her parents had called me a dozen times. I had nothing for them, so I'd let the calls go through to voice mail. But as we were driving away from the campus empty-handed, Brady called.

I picked up the call on the third ring.

The lieutenant sounded agitated.

"The press has the story," he said. "It's going to

hit the fan on the networks in a couple of hours, but it's already broken on cable news and the Web."

Cindy was my next caller.

"Lindsay. How could you not call me? You promised the story to me. You *swore*."

"I've got nothing, Cindy. Nothing at all. Zero. Zip. Legwork with no payoff."

Conklin's phone rang, too. It was Paul Richardson saying that the media were gathering outside their hotel, clamoring for a statement.

"Don't tell them anything," Conklin told Avis's father. "Stay in your room and get the hotel to block your incoming calls. Use only your cell phone."

"The press is going to do cartwheels with this story," I said to Conklin as we got back into the car.

"Maybe a lead will come out of it," he said.

"I like your optimism."

I'd seen similar stories spin out of control and confuse evidence, spawn hoaxters, and contaminate jury pools. "Baby missing" could become kidnapping, child trafficking, even witchcraft or alien abduction. And that would be before the supermarket tabloids got hold of the story.

"We need to catch a break," Conklin said as we got back on the road.

I sighed loudly.

I wished I felt upbeat about this one. But I was feeling that it was too late to strap in. We'd already hit the wall.

Chapter 33

THE PRESS-MOBILES were already parked in front of the Hall, satellite trucks and setups with talking heads using the gray, granite edifice as a backdrop.

Conklin pulled into the lot off Harriet Street and I got a buzz in my hip pocket. Yuki was texting me to say she wanted to see me, tell me about her date last night. She'd put a picket fence of exclamation marks at the end of her message.

I fired back a message in return, saying that I had to see her, too. Important!!!!!

At just after six, I edged into the standing-room-only crowd at MacBain's Beers o' the World Saloon, a cop-lawyer-bail-bondsman hangout two blocks from the Hall. There were peanut shells on the floor, exotic beer on tap, and a pool table in back. Yuki was at the bar.

I opened my jacket and, revealing my badge hooked to my belt, flashed it at the guy sitting to Yuki's right.

"I didn't do it, Sergeant," he said, holding up his hands. We both laughed. "Congratulations on, you know, getting married," he said.

"Thanks for the seat, Reynolds."

I said, "Hey, girlfriend," to Yuki, kissed her cheek, planted myself on the bar stool. Then I ordered a Corona and plunged ahead. "I met with Candace Martin last night."

"You did *what?* I don't think I heard you right."

Yuki was only sitting a foot away from me, but she jacked up the volume to a yell. She'd never been angry with me before, and frankly I felt ashamed.

I flashed back to that trial of mine a couple of years ago, when I'd been accused of wrongful death in the shooting of a teenage girl who had fired on me and Jacobi without provocation.

It was absolutely self-defense, but I was put on trial anyway. The city of San Francisco couldn't help me. I could have lost my job, my life savings, my reputation, but that didn't happen.

Yuki Castellano had been on my defense team. She had fought for me and we had won. I owed her a lot.

I said to Yuki now, "Phil Hoffman asked me to see her. He said we've got the wrong person for Dennis Martin's killing."

"Are you ka-razy?" Yuki said.

And then she let loose with her trademark breathless verbal fusillade. "You listened to a *defense* lawyer? You went behind my *back* and interviewed the defendant in my *case?* How could you *do* that, Lindsay? What made you even think you had the *right?*"

"Chi and McNeill report to me," I said, feeling my cheeks flaming. "If they made a bad arrest, I had to know."

I could have called Yuki. I *should* have called Yuki. But she would have been aboard the same train as Brady, Chi, and McNeill. She would have said, "Don't do it."

"I just *talked* to her, dammit," I said. "All I did was *talk* to her."

Yuki signaled the bartender, a wiry young woman with big breasts named Nicole.

"Hit me again," Yuki said, pushing her beer

mug forward, dumping a bowl of peanuts over the bartender's side of the bar.

"That's three," Nikki said.

"Yeah?" Yuki shot back. "So what?"

"Just sayin'."

"Well, *don't*."

Yuki swung around to face me. "So, while you were just *talking* to Candace Martin, what did she say?"

"She said that Ellen Lafferty was likely having an affair with her husband and she has a theory. Candace thinks either Ellen got dumped or she knew she was being played by a player. Candace thinks Ellen shot Dennis."

"*Wow*," said Yuki. "Candace is saying, 'The other dude did it.' What a shock."

Christ, Yuki was mad.

I said, "It answers the big unanswered question, Yuki. Who was the unknown intruder? If Ellen Lafferty didn't leave the house for her evening off, she was already on the scene."

"Lindsay, this whole setup is a Phil Hoffman distraction. Maybe Santa came down the chimney and did it. Maybe Dennis Martin pressed the gun into his wife's hand and pulled the trigger on himself. You should have kept your nose out of this. You've made me look bad and for what?"

"Paul Chi. It was his case."

"*Good point.* Why didn't Hoffman go to *Chi?* He went to you because we're friends and he's trying to undermine my case," Yuki said, slamming her beer mug down on the bar.

"You're being jerked around, so enjoy that. I'm going to get that woman convicted. Because it wasn't the other dude, Lindsay. *Candace Martin did it.*

Chapter 34

ENTERING THE COURTROOM the next morning, Nick Gaines said to Yuki, "What's this? Some adorable little kids are missing from the front row."

Yuki put her briefcase on the table and stole a look at the row of seats behind the defense table. She saw strangers there. They looked young and intense. Probably law students. The Martin kids were gone. She guessed they'd served their purpose—before Duncan went off-road and got the judge mad.

Court was called into session. Judge LaVan called on Yuki, asking her to put on her next witness. She was ready.

"The People call Felix Ashton."

A fortyish man with black hair and mustache, wearing an expensive-looking gray jacket and dark pants, was sworn in.

Yuki asked him to state his name, then his profession. "Real-estate broker. High-end residential properties," Ashton said.

Yuki paced in the well and said, "How well do you know Candace Martin?"

"We've been seeing each other for about a year."

"By 'seeing each other,' you mean romantically?"

"Yes."

"And how did you meet her?"

"Dennis Martin asked me to appraise the house that he and Candace owned together. She contacted me after I did the appraisal and asked me to give her the information."

"I see," Yuki said. She glanced at her notes, looked back up at the witness.

"And what was the value of the house?"

"In that neighborhood and in that excellent condition, no less than three-point-five million. Some would go as high as five."

"Did you have occasion to meet Dennis Martin more than once?"

"Yes."

"Under what circumstances?"

"Every couple of weeks, he'd show up in the restaurant where Candace and I were having dinner and take a table near us. He sat next to us at the movie theater a couple of times. He followed Candace to antagonize her. He used those occasions to have sarcastic buddy-buddy talks with me."

"So he was stalking her. Did that make Candace angry?"

"Objection," Hoffman said. "Leading the witness."

"I'll allow it. Answer the question, Mr. Ashton."

Ashton said, "Dennis Martin needled Candace all the time. He bragged to her and to me that he was seeing a lot of different women. He told me that he'd divorce Candace in a flash, if she gave him what he wanted—the house and alimony and the kids. He said he wanted it all. And so he was trying to torment her until she gave in."

"And did Candace ever tell you that she was going to agree to his terms?"

"No."

"Do you love Dr. Martin?" Yuki asked.

"Yes, I do."

"And has she told you that she loves you?"

"Yes."

"But she wouldn't give her husband a divorce."

"He was a mean guy. If he hadn't insisted on custody of the kids, she would have cut him loose. But she didn't want to give him joint custody."

"Nice of her."

Hoffman got to his feet and objected.

Yuki said, "I withdraw the comment. I have only one more question, Mr. Ashton. You say the two of you were in love. Yet Dennis Martin was in your way. Did Candace Martin ever tell you that she'd like to kill her husband?"

"Well . . . not that she would actually do it."

"Yes or no, Mr. Ashton? You're under oath. And we have your deposition."

"Ah. Yes, she said that, but—"

"The answer is yes. That's all, Mr. Ashton. Thank you."

"Cross, Mr. Hoffman?" LaVan asked.

Phil Hoffman stood, buttoned his jacket, straightened his Hermès tie, and walked smartly to the witness box.

"Mr. Ashton, based on your conversations

with Candace, did you think she was actually going to kill her husband?"

"Objection, Your Honor. Calls for speculation," Yuki said.

"Overruled," Judge LaVan said. "The witness may answer."

"No. Candace isn't violent."

"Let me ask this," Hoffman said. "You've known the defendant for a year. In that time, did she ever show you a gun or say that she had one?"

"No, she did not."

"Thank you. I have no further questions."

"The witness may step down," said the judge.

Chapter 35

YUKI SAT ON HER INCREASING RAGE at Hoffman and focused on her witness, Cyndi Parrish, the Martins' live-in cook.

Parrish had been a jet-engine mechanic in the Navy and was now in her fifties, a soft and billowy woman with blurry tattoos on her forearms.

"And how long have you lived in the Martin household?" Yuki asked the cook.

"It will be eleven years next month. I came to the Martins after Caitlin was born."

"And would you say, as a member of the household, that you have an informed opinion about the Martin marriage?"

"Yes, I would say so."

"How did they get along?"

"They didn't get along at all."

"Ms. Parrish, do you have a close relationship with Dr. Martin?"

The large woman looked uncomfortable. She glanced down at her hands and muttered, "Yes. She confides in me."

Yuki lobbed the next question, a softball, but it was right across the plate.

"Was Dennis Martin seeing someone? That is, was he in a sexual relationship with someone other than his wife?"

"I can't say."

"*Can't,* Ms. Parrish?"

"He never talked to me about anything other than food," said the cook, earning a nice burst of laughter from the gallery.

Yuki smiled, let the laughter fade away, and then asked, "Did Dr. Martin speak to you about her husband's affairs?"

"She did in the early days. Lately, not so much."

"Ms. Parrish, let me be more precise. Did Candace Martin tell you how she felt about her husband the week before he was shot to death?"

"Yes. He tormented her, constantly. Night

before the shooting, she said she hated him. She said she'd kill him if she could. I suppose that's what you want me to say."

"Just tell the truth, Ms. Parrish."

"It wasn't a pretty marriage. Neither one of them had any use for the other one."

"Did Candace Martin ever say that she'd like to kill her husband?"

"Yes."

"I have no further questions," said Yuki, heading back to her table.

"Can I say something else?"

"That's all, Ms. Parrish. We're done."

Phil Hoffman stood and approached Yuki's witness to do his cross-examination.

He said, "What did you want to say, Ms. Parrish?"

"I wanted to say that Dr. Martin is a good person. And she loves her kids."

"Indeed. Ms. Parrish, did you ever see a gun in the house?"

"No, I never did."

"Thank you. That's all I have."

Yuki pressed her palms down on the table, stood up, and said, "Redirect, Your Honor."

151

The judge said, "Go ahead, Ms. Castellano."

"Ms. Parrish, does Dr. Martin love her kids enough to kill for them?"

"Objection," Hoffman said. "Leading the witness. Calling for speculation."

"Sustained."

"Withdrawn," said Yuki. "I'm done, Your Honor."

"Anyone would," the cook said.

"Thank you, Ms. Parrish. You may stand down," said the judge.

"Anyone would kill for their kids," the cook muttered loudly, as she got up from her seat. "It's a law of nature."

Hoffman stood to object, but the judge said, "I've got it, Mr. Hoffman. Ms. Parrish, you've testified under oath. It's over. The jury will disregard the witness's offhand remarks."

"I won't be silenced," said the cook, as she lumbered across the well. "*Anyone* would kill for their kids."

Chapter 36

CINDY STARED at her computer monitor, far too aware of the timer in the left-hand corner ticking off the seconds toward her four-o'clock deadline.

Oh, man, she was so stuck.

After nailing yesterday's deadline, she still didn't know how to write this story. The heart-rending and truly terrifying interviews with the rape victims were quite vivid in her mind, but she couldn't name the witnesses, couldn't quote the nurses, and there was no "source close to the police," because the cops weren't actually working the case.

Cindy had boiled the facts down to their bare bones.

The attacks had happened to women who lived

and worked in three different places in the city. The women were not of a single type. They were of different ages, occupations, and ethnicities. They looked nothing alike. And the worst fact of all: Cindy could scare women readers half to death with this story, but she had no idea how they could protect themselves from the rapist.

Cindy reread her notes from her interview this morning with the latest victim, Inez Fleming. Like Laura Rizzo and Anne Bennett, Inez Fleming had woken up near her home after a blackout of many hours. During that time, she'd been raped, sloppily redressed in her own clothes, and dumped.

Fleming had been examined at nine that morning by a doctor in the emergency room at St. Francis. The head nurse had called Joyce Miller to say that she had a rape victim like the ones who had come into Metro earlier in the week.

Joyce had called Cindy. And Cindy had gone to see Fleming.

The first thing Cindy noticed about Inez Fleming was that she was no weakling. Weighing in at about two hundred pounds, Inez worked as a substitute teacher in a public school in the

Mission. She seemed streetwise, and unlike the first two victims, Inez was married.

Inez told Cindy that she remembered hearing something when she was in some kind of dream state. She'd said, "It was about some kind of 'big day.' What's that?"

Cindy wanted to know, too.

It was similar to the fragmented memories the other women had reported. Like Laura and Anne, Inez couldn't even state that it was a memory. It could have been a fantasy or even something she overheard while she was lying in the alley.

Inez Fleming's husband had arrived right then and told Inez not to talk to the press, and now, six hours later, Cindy was foundering in quicksand and running out of time.

Chapter 37

CINDY FLEXED HER FINGERS and tried out a headline: "Rapist Dopes and Dumps Victims." She was typing her lede—*Three women reported being raped and drugged when they awoke from a blackout*—when her phone rang. She glanced at the caller ID.

It was Richie.

Should she take the call or let it go to voice mail? The time was 3:23. There was no time to talk to him. Not now. This was her only story and she had to work it.

On the third ring, she grabbed the phone.

"Can I call you back, Rich? I'm on deadline."

"Just take a second," he said, a playful tone in

his voice. "There's someone important I want you to meet."

Cindy laughed, spun her chair around so that she wouldn't see the clock. "Really? Who is this important person?"

"I'm not saying. Not right now."

"What if it's off the record?" Cindy asked.

"I like your style, Cin, but you still have to wait."

"Bummer. Where are you now?"

"I'm on the street outside the Mark Hopkins, waiting for Lindsay. She's with the Richardsons. Should be down in a second."

Cindy pictured Richie leaning against the unmarked car, wearing blue like he always did, his soft light brown hair falling across his forehead.

"Any news on the baby?" she asked.

"Nope. We have miles and miles of not one fricking thing," he said. "Lindsay is taking this one personally."

"Don't we all?" Cindy said.

"Damn right," Rich said. "When you get home, put on something dressy. I'll pick you up — Cin, I gotta go. I'll see you later."

"Wait. What time?"

"Seven, okay?"

"Perfect."

Cindy wrote her story fast and with confidence, the way she did when there was no time to spare. She looked at the clock in the corner of her computer screen and saw that she could even manage a quick polish. The clock showed 3:59 when she pushed *send*. She shook out her hands and leaned back in her chair. Her story would be on the streets in the morning.

The cops would read it, and maybe the rapist would, too.

What would happen next?

Chapter 38

CINDY KICKED OFF HER SHOES in the small foyer, and removing her clothes as she walked into the bedroom, she dropped them on the bed as she walked to the shower. "Dressy," Rich had said. She couldn't even guess what he was planning. Where were they going and who was this important person she was going to meet?

The shower was hot and invigorating. Cindy kept her eyes closed and stood there, letting the water beat down on her head. She didn't move at all, but her mind was in motion.

She was thinking about Richie—about how when she'd first met Lindsay's new partner, he'd not only rocked her world, he'd knocked a few neighboring planets off course, as well. Yes, he was gorgeous, but thank God she'd been able to keep her lovesick wits together long enough to realize that Rich Conklin's cover-guy looks were only the gift wrapping. He was a good person. He was intelligent. He was easy to talk to. He was protective. He was the one for her, most definitely. And he was mad about her, too.

Admittedly, there had been a time when she worried that Rich had a major crush on Lindsay. You could see the electricity when they were together. But when she'd asked, they'd both said, "No, no, no. We're just partners."

Now that she and Richie were living together, she worried about one thing only—that he would come home safely every night.

Cindy got out of the shower, dried her hair, and stepped into a small, black Nicole Miller dress with a deep neckline that Rich hadn't seen her wear before. As she returned the hanger to the closet they shared, she thought about where she'd lived before she and Richie had found a place together.

Her old apartment building was on the border of two neighborhoods—one on the rise, the other on the edge of hell. She'd gone for the gentrification sales pitch because she really loved the open, sunny rooms in the Blakely Arms. And then accidental deaths in the building had turned out to be murders.

She and Rich had become friends while she was both living in the building and writing the story about the killings. Rich and Lindsay were investigating the crimes. Later, when she and Rich had started dating, he'd told her that he wished she worked any desk but crime.

Sometimes she wished it, too.

But more often she was grateful for her job at the *Chronicle*. Writing about, and sometimes even confronting, people so dangerous they scared her curls straight had given her confidence and made her a better journalist.

Cindy fastened her necklace of small glinting crystals and put a rhinestone clip in her hair. Then she turned on the news. An interview was in progress. A reporter from KWTV was talking to a woman whose face had been pixilated to protect her identity, but Cindy recognized her.

It was the rape victim she'd met that morning.

Inez Fleming.

"All I remember is leaving work last night,"

Fleming was saying. "A sanitation worker woke me up in the early morning in an alley near my house. I still had all my stuff. Purse, et cetera. Maybe whoever drugged me and raped me looked in my wallet and knew where I lived. Or maybe he's someone I know. I can only say to women, don't trust anybody."

Cindy fumbled with the remote, rewound the DVR, and watched the interview again.

She'd been scooped.

The story was out, but the mystery remained. Who did it? What happened? Why were the victims targeted? Was it personal or random? And how many women would this guy rape before he was caught?

This she knew: she would stick with this story until the end.

The phone rang beside the bed and she scooped the receiver off the cradle.

"Richie?"

"Come downstairs, honey. Expect the unexpected. Yep, that's what I said. Be ready for *anything*."

Chapter 39

YUKI'S DATE WAS SITTING next to her in a booth at Renegade, an elegant waterfront restaurant in SoMa with a full view of the Bay Bridge. A floor-to-ceiling waterfall sheeted down a copper wall behind him. His thigh was touching hers, his sun-bleached hair, combed back and cut straight, was falling loose around his collar, and he was telling her about the last case he'd worked in Miami.

Yuki was mesmerized by the sound of his voice.

"Guy runs out of a bank with dynamite strapped to his chest, duffel bag over his shoulder. He gets into his car, guns the engine and—plows into the car right in front of him."

"On, no. Come onnn," Yuki said.

"Yeah, he did," Jackson Brady said. "Rams his Chevy into the trunk of this Honda. Then he backs up and peels out, and the guy in the Honda calls the cops. Honda got a good look at Mr. Dynamite and he's got a partial plate on the Chevy."

"Whoa. Way to go."

"Meanwhile, the teller has pulled the alarm, and now a caravan of cops takes off after the Chevy and finds it abandoned in a canal off the side of the road. The so-called dynamite is in the front seat, made out of painted dowels and wire. But anyway, the guy stole four grand, and they have his plate number, his address, and so on. His name is Timberland Carson and there's an outstanding warrant on him, armed robbery of a convenience store."

Brady stopped and took a swig of his beer.

"Don't stop now," Yuki said. She sipped her drink. Just sipped it. It was delicious, but she did not want to get drunk on her second date in one week with Jackson Brady.

"So now I catch the case because the convenience store robbery was mine," Jackson continued. "We go to Carson's apartment, pound on the door," Jackson said, punching the air to demonstrate. "'Miami PD. Open up, Mr. Carson.'

"Carson opens the door. 'Oh, you found my car already? I was just going to report it stolen.'"

Brady laughed and Yuki laughed along with him. Brady had great timing and he could mimic voices. What a howl.

Brady said, "Meanwhile, I can see the car keys with the little Chevy fob on it hanging from the hook next to the door. I say, 'Anyone else here, Mr. Carson?'

"'No,' he says, and so now we're in the house. He's got to let us in because he's the victim. Someone boosted his car, right? So my partner puts Carson up against the wall, says, 'You're under arrest for that convenience store.' While he cuffs Carson, I'm looking around for the bank bag full of cash. There's nothing in plain sight, but I can see that the lock on the bedroom door is busted," Brady told her.

"I push it open with my shoulder, and Carson's roommate—who isn't supposed to be there— flies off the bed into the crack between the mattress and the wall."

"Hel-lo."

"Yeah. Hello, roommate—and on the bed is a suitcase full of weapons—guns and knives, like a booth at a flea market."

"You've got your gun out?" Yuki asked.

"Yeah, and I'm aiming at the bed, yelling, 'Come outta there, hands in the air.' You know. 'Don't do anything stupid.' And the guy pops up with a semiautomatic, says, 'I can kill you. Maybe both of you. Or you can let me leave.'

"I'm yelling, 'Put down your weapon, put down your weapon.' But the idiot fires, bullets go through the doorway, and in the second before I return fire, he's put a shot into Carson's ear."

"Holy crap. So you shot the roommate?" Yuki asked.

Brady said, "Yeah. Damn right. I had to do it."

"So, two guys dead."

"Ah, look at me telling you war stories."

"I like hearing your war stories," Yuki said.

"Uh-oh," Brady said. "Because they say what you like about a person when you meet them is what drives you crazy about them later on."

Yuki laughed. "I'm not worried," she said. Then she added, "You wanted me to know you killed someone. Why?"

Brady nodded, his hands clasped together on the table. "By the time IAB was done with me, I wanted to leave Miami. I wanted you to know that. I'm here to stay."

The waiter came over and said, "Your table is ready."

Yuki followed the waiter upstairs to the mezzanine, with its view of the lights on the bridge, the promenade below, and *Cupid's Span,* a huge piece of public art, an arrow piercing the ground.

She was aware of Brady walking behind her and liked the feeling of having him at her back.

But, she was also worried. Not because Brady had killed a man, but because she was going to have to tell Lindsay that she was going out with her boss.

Chapter 40

CINDY LOOKED THROUGH the window facing Kirkham Street and saw a smart-looking black Town Car coming up the block. It pulled up to the modest three-story apartment building where she lived with Richie.

There were no celebrities or wealthy people living in this building, so she made a mental note that this might turn out to be an interesting development. The driver got out of the car and headed up the front steps.

The buzzer rang in her foyer.

Cindy thought, Wrong number, and walked to the intercom.

"Hello?"

"Ms. Thomas. Your car is here."

"*My* car?"

"Are you Cindy Thomas?"

"I'll be right down," she said.

Cindy threw on her best coat, a black cashmere blend with antique buttons. She locked up, ran down the three flights and the front steps to the sidewalk. Richie was standing next to the car, a big bunch of pink sweetheart roses in his hand.

He was wearing a suit.

It was a blue one, Rich's only color, and he also wore a starched white shirt and a striped silver-and-blue tie. It took Cindy a second to fully get that yes, this was Richard Conklin wearing a suit, and he had a look of triumph in his eyes.

It wasn't her birthday. It wasn't his either. Who on earth was this someone he'd said he wanted her to meet?

"God, you're gorgeous," Rich said when Cindy was close enough to see the shaving nick on his jaw.

"You stole my line," she said.

She flung herself into his arms and they kissed a few times before Rich broke away, laughing, and said, "May I show you to our private room?"

"Where are we going?" she asked once they

were settled into the back of the car, her legs across his lap. "Who's the mystery person? Tell me right now."

"I'm not saying."

Cindy gave him a soft sock to the arm as the car traveled from Golden Gate Park to Oak Street, along the panhandle, a wide tree-covered median, and then from Van Ness past City Hall to California. "Every now and then I like to try to keep something from you," Rich said.

Cindy laughed and said, "Well, you got me, Inspector. I am clueless." And she was still clueless when the car pulled up in front of Grace Cathedral and stopped.

Grace Cathedral was a stupendous Gothic structure with a long history going back to before the earthquake and fire of 1906 and through its reconstruction to the present day.

The cathedral was such a short distance from where she and Richie lived that she'd passed by it many times, always gripped by the awesome sight of the exaggerated arches and spires and the Ghiberti Doors of Paradise, Old Testament–inspired replicas of the gilded originals in Florence.

You saw this cathedral and you had to think of God.

Cindy didn't even know for sure where she came out on the God question, but a cathedral was meaningful, even for the nonreligious. Not only was it a place of worship, but it embodied the history of the times and the course of generations, the birth through death of entire families.

Cindy was speechless and trembling as she and Rich walked up the steps, through the open doors, and across the inscribed limestone labyrinth that was thirty-five feet across.

As she entered the nave, Cindy's eyes were drawn upward to the stained-glass windows and then along the murals that led from the back of the church to the altar.

Cindy was dazzled.

She didn't know what it was, but *something* momentous was about to happen.

Chapter 41

RICH'S HEART POUNDED as he walked with Cindy down the center aisle of Grace Cathedral, awestruck as he always was by the monumental vaulted ceiling and the gold crucifix behind the altar.

Cindy was squeezing the circulation out of his hand, staring up at him, searching his face, speechless for the first time since he'd met her.

She started to ask, "What's go —?" but her foot turned and her high heels started to go out from under her. Rich had his hand under her elbow and at the small of her back. He caught her before she went down and smiled at her. He felt a laugh fighting to get free.

"Can't take you anywhere," he said.

"Clearly not," she said.

The altar seemed a mile away down the aisle flanked with hundreds of rows of mostly empty pews. Rich felt his heart knocking against his ribs. His mouth was dry. And he never felt more certain of anything in his life.

Images of Cindy blew through his mind: the first time he'd seen her with Lindsay, all big eyes and questions, the way her slightly overlapping front teeth made her smile so cute, an endless source of delight. And the way she looked now, her endearing face framed by all those blond curls.

His Cindy. The woman he knew so very well.

He flashed on the time she'd been a virtual third cop on their team, when he and Lindsay were working the string of homicides in the apartment building where Cindy lived at the time.

He'd learned a lot about her then.

How steadfast she was when facing danger. How hard she pushed herself forward when she was afraid. He admired her so much for those qualities.

But they made him worry about her, too.

And then they were at the altar.

The deacon smiled, very nearly winked, and then disappeared into the shadows—and they were alone.

"Who are we meeting here?" Cindy asked softly.

"I'm hoping he's your future husband, Cin. What would you think of getting married right here?"

"Is that a proposal, Richie?"

Richie dropped to one knee. He said, "Cindy. If I know anything, it is that you are the love of my life. I want to spend the rest of my years getting to know you and love you even more than I do now. Will you marry me?"

He pulled the little velvet box from his jacket pocket and opened the lid. His mother's solitaire diamond engagement ring lay inside. She had given it to him, saying, "Someday you'll give this to a very special woman."

Cindy stared at the ring, then back at him.

"I guess so," she said.

Then she laughed, stuck out her ring finger, which was shaking so hard that, with his hand shaking, too, it was truly a triumph that Rich got the ring in place.

"Our first hurdle," he said.

"How did you get to be so funny?" she said, pulling him to his feet, going into his strong arms, and speaking right next to his ear.

"Listen. This is the real deal and it's on the record. I love you to death. I am honored to be your one true wife."

Conklin said to his bride to be, "You had that all ready to go, didn't you?"

"Maybe I did," Cindy said. "Because that's how I really feel about you, Richie."

"Thanks for saying yes," he said, hugging her right off the floor. They kissed and the jewelry box clattered to the marble floor. Parishioners sitting in the front rows applauded, a sound that echoed like doves' wings beating overhead.

Chapter 42

JOE WAS ON A BUSINESS TRIP, inspecting the port in L.A., and he hadn't been sure when he'd be home.

I ran with Martha down Lake Street from the Temple Emanu-El to Sea Cliff and back, my eyes locking on dark-colored sedans. I thought about Avis Richardson's baby all the way. I couldn't help myself, and after three miles of checking cars and beating the pavement with my Adidas, I was done.

Our apartment was dark when I walked in breathless and soaked with sweat.

I switched on some lights, showered, poured myself a glass of chardonnay, and then got busy in the kitchen. I decanted some doggy beef stew for Martha, filled up her water bowl, and turned on the TV. Chris Matthews was doing the Politics Fix segment of his show while I heated up the jambalaya that Joe had cooked a few days before. And then the phone rang.

The phone always rang.

A month back, I'd made the decision not to answer the phone—neither our landline nor my cell. In so doing, I had missed a phone call that could have changed my life.

Jacobi had called—four times, in fact—to offer me the lieutenant's job he was leaving by moving up to captain. By the time I finally spoke with him, the job had been tentatively offered to Brady. I thought it was a sign that Brady should take the job.

That was okay with me. I liked the hands-on job of being a homicide cop. It was exhausting, and you could never put it down, not even for a night, but like for my father before me, working the street was my calling.

Jackson Brady, on the other hand, was ambitious. He had a history as a good cop, and I knew he was the future of the SFPD.

I'd done the right thing in stepping aside, but

I was a little more careful these days to answer ringing phones.

The cordless on the kitchen counter was beginning its third ring. I peered at the caller ID. It was Cindy, so I snatched the receiver off its base.

"*I'm getting married,*" Cindy yelled into my ear.

"What? What did you say?"

"We're getting *married*. Richie and me. He just *proposed*."

"Oh my God. That's *fantastic,*" I said, feeling some conflict between whoo-hooo and a fear of Cindy getting too much off-the-record information every night from my partner.

Plus, I had liked being number one on Richie's speed dial.

That selfish thought faded as Cindy jabbered away into the phone about Richie's bended-knee proposal at the Grace Cathedral, the diamond ring, and the happiness that was giving her heart flight.

"It's wonderful, Cin. Let me congratulate Rich."

"He's on with his dad. I'll tell him to call you. Oh, I'm getting incoming," she said. "My mom is calling me back."

"Go ahead, Cindy. I'm so happy for you both."

I switched the channel to a ball game and watched the home team slaughter the visitors as I ate my dinner. Then the telephone rang again.

It was Yuki. What *now*?

"Linds, am I catching you at a bad time?"

Yuki had been stiff with me since I'd told her about my interview with Candace Martin two days ago. I was hoping that maybe this call would be a break in the cloud cover.

"It's fine," I said. "This is a good time."

"I was going to tell you something the other day, but we got sidetracked. I don't know how you're going to take this, Linds."

"Yuki, there's nothing you can't tell me," I said.

"Okay. Uh. It's about Brady."

"What about him?"

"He asked me out. I went out to dinner with him. Twice. It went well. So, uh . . . we're dating."

I stopped breathing and just held the receiver hard to my ear, waiting for the next shoe to drop.

"Linds?"

"*Jackson* Brady? You're kidding me. Say you're joking."

179

"I really like him, Linds. I just wanted you to hear it from me."

I'd thought there was nothing Yuki couldn't tell me, but I'd been wrong. This news had shaken me. And I didn't know how to tell my good friend why I felt stricken to my bones.

"Lindsay, will you please say something?"

"There's no good way to say this. I checked Brady out when he joined the squad," I said. "He's *married*, Yuki. Did Brady tell you that he's married?"

WOMEN'S MURDER CLUB

Book Two

LIES, LIES, AND MORE LIES

Chapter 43

THAT SUNDAY was all mine.

I had ordered eggs and hash browns at Louis', a greasy spoon on Point Lobos Avenue. It was a great barn of a place, built in 1937 on a cliff overlooking the ocean. True, Louis' drew tourists, but it was still a local hangout, especially in the early morning.

The day was still too young for tourists, so Louis' was full of regulars, mostly runners and walkers from the coastal trail at Lands End, now relaxing and reading papers at the counter. Nobody was bothering anyone.

I sighed with contentment.

From my seat in a booth, I had a view of the Sutro Baths at Lands End and I could also see my parking spot in front of Louis' and Martha in the driver's seat of my Explorer. Before coming here, we'd made a stop at Crissy Field so that Martha could run on a sandy beach and swim in the surf of the bay.

"Careful, the plate's hot," the waitress said, setting down my breakfast. She refilled my chunky brown mug with fresh-brewed Colombian java.

"Thanks. It looks perfect," I said.

My cell phone rang, just as I picked up my fork. Why was I so goddamned popular? I looked at my phone, but didn't recognize the name on the caller ID. Who was W. Steihl?

Should I take the call? Or should I let it go to voice mail?

I flipped a quarter and smacked it on the back of my hand. I took a peek.

"Boxer," I said with a sigh into the phone.

"Sergeant Boxer, this is Wilhelmina Steihl. Willy. I met you the other day at Brighton?"

Now, I remembered her. Willy Steihl was one of Avis Richardson's school friends. She had shiny black hair to her shoulders and steel-rimmed glasses, and she wore bright red lipstick.

I also remembered how hesitant she was to talk to Rich and me a few days ago, but from the sound of her voice, she had something urgent to tell me now.

"I couldn't say anything when you were here," Willy Steihl said to me. "People would have figured out that I was the rat."

"Let's not worry about being a rat," I said. "Rats can be heroes, too. Do you know where we can find Avis's baby?"

"No, no, I don't know that. I'm a friend of Larry Foster? He said I should call you. Are you near a computer?"

"No, but my phone is pretty slick. What should I look up?"

"I want to show you some pictures. On Facebook. But I don't want to give you my password."

The kid was worrying about a password—something she could change in a couple of keystrokes—but I didn't want to go balls to the wall with her. Willy was a minor. She didn't have to talk to me at all.

"What if I meet you at your dorm?" I said. I signaled to the waitress to bring me my check.

"Not there. I don't want anyone to see me talking to you," Willy said.

I stifled a groan and told her I'd meet her at the entrance to 850 Bryant in an hour.

"I'll be there," Willy told me.

Was she going to help me find Avis's baby? Or was this going to be another lead to nowhere?

I put a ten and a fiver on top of the check and left Louis' still hungry.

Chapter 44

IT WAS JUST ABOUT TEN and an overcast sixty-four degrees when I rolled the window down a few inches for Martha and left my car in the lot across from the Hall.

Willy Steihl was not outside the large granite cube where I worked, so I waited on the corner, tapping my foot as traffic breezed by at a steady clip even for a Sunday.

Ten minutes later, a cab draw up curbside and I opened the door for young Willy Steihl. She said hi and, keeping a good six feet between us, followed me through the double glass doors into the red-marbled lobby of the Hall of Justice.

Willy took off her belt, put it in a tote, and went through the scanners at the entrance. I badged security and took the girl with black hair, black clothes, and a bite-me expression up to the squad room, where the swing shift was at work.

I asked Sergeant Bob Nardone if I could use my desk, and he said, "Sure, Boxer. And I should do what? Work on my air computer?"

"Get up, Nardone. Heat up your coffee. Take a break. We won't be long."

I commandeered the desk chair, and Willy Steihl stood beside me as I logged on to my account. Then I gave the girl my chair so she could enter her information on my computer.

She hunched over the keyboard as she typed in her password and ID, saying, "Give me a second, okay? I'm opening the folder I was telling you about."

I was drumming my fingers on my desk as Willy Steihl tapped on the keys. Finally she said, "Got it."

I turned the monitor toward me and stared at a picture of a soccer game. Kids were flying across the field, the ball was in play, and people were cheering at the sidelines. A typical high-school sports event.

"See," she said. "This was us against the

Warriors. I was taking pictures of Larry."

She enlarged the picture, focusing not on the field but on the people watching the game. I saw Avis Richardson with her profile to the camera, wearing Burberry-plaid pajama bottoms and a school sweatshirt that effectively hid her pregnancy.

She was standing very close to a tall, dark, and handsome man who, to my eyes, was definitely not a student.

Willy clicked the mouse and another picture came up, then another, and with each picture she enlarged the frame and closed in on Avis Richardson. In one of the pictures, I saw that Avis's hand was tucked into the hand of the good-looking man.

"Who is that?" I asked Willy.

"That's Mr. Ritter. He teaches sophomore English," she said.

"What are you implying, Willy? Don't make me guess."

The girl squirmed in the chair.

"Willy. Do not waste my time."

I wanted to give her a good shake, but she made up her mind without more help from me.

"We all knew that Avis and Mr. Ritter were close," she said. "She got excellent grades in English, so we thought she was his favorite student, or maybe they were *really* close. You know what I mean? Because Avis lied when she told you that she was dating Larry Foster.

"She wasn't dating him. I am."

Chapter 45

WILLY STEIHL had dropped a bomb.

She was leading me to believe that there was a relationship between a fifteen-year-old girl and her English teacher. What the hell was that? Statutory rape, that's what it was, a crime that could come with jail time for Mr. Ritter if he was convicted. And, if he'd been involved in the death of a baby? He'd be serving life in a federal prison.

I said to Willy, "Apart from these pictures, is there anything else you can tell me? Did Avis say anything to you about Mr. Ritter? Have you ever seen them alone together?"

Willy Steihl shrugged, then shook her head no. She looked as though she were trying to disappear through the back of the chair.

"Willy, this is very helpful and it's also very serious. Could Mr. Ritter be the father of Avis's baby?"

"I don't know. I just wanted you to see the pictures and draw your own conclusions, okay?"

Not okay.

"A baby is *missing*, Willy. Try to imagine what Avis must be feeling. What her parents are going through. That little boy is helpless. He may be alone. He may be dying. If you know anything that could help us find him, you have to tell me. It's your obligation. In fact, if you know something and don't tell me, that makes you an accessory to a crime."

"I shouldn't have come," said the girl in black, scrambling out of the chair, swinging her backpack over her shoulder. "I don't know anything. I have to get out of here."

I hadn't been subtle. I'd hammered the kid and threatened her, and now she was done. I wished for the thousandth time that I had even 10 percent of Conklin's tact. I offered Willy a lift back to school, but she said, "I'll get a taxi. Don't mention me to anyone, please."

"I have to use my judgment, Willy."

She looked at me like I was going to sink my fangs into her neck and then left the squad room without closing out her Facebook account.

Sergeant Nardone swooped in like a condor. I told him to keep his pants on, then took the opportunity to pry.

I tapped on the keyboard, did a search for photo tags for Ritter, and found more pictures of the English teacher on Willy's home pages and on those of her friends.

According to the Web chat and notes written on virtual walls, Ritter was frequently discussed by the girls in Willy's circle. Many of them commented on his good looks and his manner in class and speculated about what he'd be like in bed.

I clicked on the link to Avis Richardson's home page. I'd seen her page when Joe suggested it, but now I was looking with a specific purpose. I scrutinized photos of Avis mugging with Larry Foster, doing shots with girlfriends at parties, and cheering at sporting events— but there was not one picture of her with Jordan Ritter.

I cut and pasted what I might need later into an e-mail that I then sent to myself. After that,

I closed down the computer and gave Nardone back his chair.

"You're a gent, Nardone."

"Don't mention it, Boxer. By the way, I ate your Cheetos in the bottom drawer."

"I knew that," I said, pointing to the orange prints on a drawer pull. Nardone laughed. "You're good," he said.

I called Richie twice on my way out to my car. Both times I got his voice mail, and after the second time, I left a message. "I've got a lead, Rich. Good one. Call me."

Next, I called Jordan Ritter. I told Ritter I was working the abduction of Avis Richardson and hoped he could give me some insights into her personality.

Ritter said, "I don't know her all that well, but sure, I'll be happy to help."

Jordan Ritter lived only a few blocks from Brighton Academy. I drove Martha home, then headed east along California to Broderick.

It was still early on Sunday afternoon when I parked my car on the pretty residential block near the corner of Broderick and Pine. The building where Ritter lived was a three-story apartment house, Italianate, clay-colored, trimmed in white, with two columns of bay windows.

He lived on the ground floor.

I rang the bell in the alcove and said my name into the speaker. Ritter's footsteps got louder as he came to the door.

Chapter 46

JORDAN RITTER OPENED THE DOOR of his apartment, placed one palm on the doorjamb, and, taking his time, looked me over.

I was doing the same to him.

Ritter was in his early thirties, fit, unshaven, good hair, good teeth, and was wearing a T-shirt and Burberry pajama bottoms. I'd seen Avis Richardson wearing pajamas just like those.

A trend? A coincidence? Or had Avis been wearing her boyfriend's pj's?

"Well, look at you," he said.

The nervy bastard was hitting on me.

"Mr. Ritter? I'm Sergeant Boxer," I snapped. I also flashed my badge.

"Come in. Can I get you some coffee? I just made it."

I said, "Sure," and walked around him into the apartment.

The place had a prepackaged look, as if it had been rented furnished or bought all in one day in a department store. I followed Ritter through the living room, noticing the Sunday paper on the floor and a couple of coffee mugs on the low table in front of the couch.

Anyone with an online degree in Forensics for Dummies could've figured out that Ritter had had a sleepover guest. Or else he was cagey and had staged a red herring for my benefit.

In the kitchen Ritter said, "Cream and sugar, Sergeant?"

"Black will be fine."

"Like I said on the phone," Ritter said, "I hardly know Avis. She's in my class this year, but apart from her grades—which were excellent—I don't know much about her."

I followed Ritter back into the living room and took a chair opposite the one he sprawled in.

"I think we both know that's not true," I said.

Ritter laughed.

"You're saying I'm lying? Golly. That's bold."

"Mr. Ritter, let's just get to the point, okay? So I can get out of here and you can have your weekend back. How well did you know Avis Richardson? I have witnesses who say the two of you were very close."

"Aw, come on. A lot of girls like me. It's a cliché for schoolgirls to get crushes on their teachers. I didn't even notice Avis. That's the truth."

"I have photos that show otherwise."

"Photos. Of what? Oh, now I get it. Willy Steihl has been talking to you. Don't you know, Sergeant, how jealous these girls can get? Willy has been stalking me for most of the year."

"Is that so?"

"That's so. There are no incriminating photos of me and Avis because I hardly know her. Is there anything else?"

"Yes. In case the baby shows up, I'd like to prove that it isn't yours." I pulled a buccal swab kit from my pocket and said, "It's a cheek swab. Takes less than a second."

"I can't do something like that, Sergeant. I mean, if I'm a suspect, you should talk to my dad. He's listed in the phone book under attorneys-at-law."

"I'll note that you didn't want to cooperate. That's all for now."

"Well, thanks for stopping by, Sergeant."

I put my card on his coffee table between the two coffee mugs and left Ritter's apartment. My phone rang as soon as I strapped into my car. Rich.

"Hey," I said.

"Hey-hey," he sang into the phone.

"Congratulations, partner," I said. "Don't screw it up."

He thanked me, told me that he was the happiest guy in the world. When I could get a couple of words in, I told him about my morning.

"You're saying that you suspect Ritter of getting Avis pregnant?"

"I've got a picture on Facebook of Avis and Ritter holding hands. All that means is that he's a liar, which is something and nothing at the same time. I'll see you tomorrow," I said.

"You bet," he said.

It was now a week since Avis had gotten into

a black or dark blue sedan driven by a French-speaking man, taken a drive to somewhere or nowhere, and had her baby in a field by the lake or in a bed lit by an aluminum lamp.

It would be a miracle if her baby was still alive.

Chapter 47

"AVIS ISN'T HERE," Paul Richardson said when he let me into their suite. He invited me in and offered me a drink, which I turned down. It was only three in the afternoon, but he was swaying on his feet as he made his way around the coffee table to an armchair.

"Avis wanted to go out and see her friends," Sonja told me. "She was feeling better and said she wanted to 'hang out.'"

I wondered if she'd been hanging out with Jordan Ritter just before I arrived at his door.

"She'll be back here for dinner," her father said to me. "And she wants to go back to class tomorrow. I guess there's no reason to say no."

"Is there any news, Sergeant? Please give me

some hope," Sonja Richardson said. Avis's mother looked wrung out and had her arms wrapped tightly around her body as if to hold herself together.

"We have almost nothing to go on," I told her. "There was no ad on Prattslist that matched the one your daughter said she answered. I can't explain that, can you?"

"She's like any kid. She makes things up. I don't know if you should believe her or not."

"Has she ever mentioned her English teacher? Mr. Jordan Ritter."

"Dear?" Sonja Richardson asked her husband. "Has Avis mentioned Jordan Ritter?"

Paul Richardson was swirling his drink and didn't look up or answer.

"I don't think I've heard her talking about him recently, although I remember she was happy about being in his class," Sonja Richardson said. "He's a novelist, you know. And Avis thinks she'd like to write someday. Why are you asking about Mr. Ritter? Does he know something?"

"His name came up. I met him. He says he hardly knows Avis. Which is what she says about him, too."

Sonja Richardson touched the corner of an eye with a tissue. "I guess we just have to get used to the idea that the baby is gone. But it's hard, Sergeant. We never saw him. We don't even know for sure if he's alive or dead."

When I got home at dusk, Joe was on the doorstep. I saw his wonderful smile from a hundred feet away. I ran and threw my arms around his neck and jumped into his arms, locking my legs around his waist. Joe's hug was the warmest, safest place in my world.

"Let's make a baby," I said.

"If it involves sex, I'm in," Joe said.

It did. And he was.

Chapter 48

AFTER CINDY TOOK a couple of giddy laps around the office to show off her sparkly new engagement ring, she closed her office door and got to work. Line one was flashing, and she answered it as she logged on to her crime-tipsters blog.

She announced her name into the mouthpiece, and the man on the other end of the line announced his.

"This is Red Sanchez."

"Ray Sanchez?"

"Red. The color. I think I saw something that could help you with that story you wrote about the guy raping women."

"Okay, I'm listening. Whatcha got?"

Cindy adjusted her headphones and mic, opened a blank page in Word, and typed Red Sanchez in the top-left-hand corner with the phone number she took off the caller ID.

"That large woman who was on the TV?"

"I know who you mean," Cindy said.

Sanchez was talking about Inez Fleming.

"They didn't show her face, but I recognized her anyway."

"When did you see her?" Cindy asked.

"It was night before last. I was walking my dog on Baker Street, right near the corner of Clay. Sadie is old. If I don't walk her when she whines, it's a mess on the carpet and my wife goes crazy—"

"Mr. Sanchez."

"Call me Red."

"Red, when you saw the woman you think might have been the one who was interviewed on TV, what was she doing?"

"She was doing nothing. That woman was out. I mean O-U-T. I thought she was drunk. Maybe she *was* drunk. The driver was half holding her up, half dragging her toward an apartment building. Here. I got the address. It's not too far from my place."

Sanchez read off the numbers of a house address on Baker Street. It was a few numbers from Inez Fleming's home address, but then, Inez had woken up in an alley near her building. Cindy typed the house number on her file.

"Red, what do you mean 'driver'? Driver of what?"

"Sorry. I thought I said it was a taxi. Like one of those minivan types."

"What color was this minivan?" she asked. "Any marks or signs, or maybe you saw a phone number on the van's door?"

Sanchez said, "It was a regular yellow-cab-color minivan. I think I did see something, like an ad on the back of it. Like for a movie. The name eludes me. I'll think about it."

"What about the driver? Did you get a good look at him?"

"Nah. I was putting my newspaper down for Sadie. I saw this man, he had dark hair, I think. Yeah, I know, that's quite a clue. Anyway, this man was half dragging this lady along the sidewalk. I thought, 'Man, is she drunk,' and by the time my dog had done her business, both of them were gone."

Cindy thanked Sanchez and asked him to call again if he remembered anything else. Then she called Richie.

"Sweetheart? I think I've got a lead on the serial rapist."

Chapter 49

YUKI AND NICK Gaines were leaving her office on the way to court that Monday morning, a half hour early, as Yuki insisted they be.

Nick looked Yuki up and down and said, "Something's different about you this morning."

"What do you mean?"

"You're smiling," he said.

"You're saying I don't smile?"

"You don't smile on the way to court. Huh. I know what it is. You had *sex*, didn't you? I'm staring at post–boom boom glow, right?"

Yuki laughed. "No. Shut up. I had a doughnut. I'm on a sugar high and you're not the Mentalist. I hope Angela Walker shows up. What did you think? Did she sound solid to you?"

"She sounded eager. It would be crazy if she didn't show."

They were now walking the long green-floored corridor that was the feeder artery to the courtrooms. Panels of fluorescent buzzed overhead. Yuki tipped her chin up to signal Nicky as she passed the woman sitting on one of the backless benches along the wall, talking to a bailiff.

It was Angela Walker, their surprise witness.

Walker was forty, had spun-sugar, strawberry-blond hair piled on top of her head, and was wearing a V-necked French-blue sweater and a dark blazer and tailored pants. Yuki thought, If Angela Walker's testimony is half as good as she looks, this witness will do fine.

Yuki and Nick entered 3B, walked to the prosecution table, and nodded to Hoffman and his second chair, Kara Battinelli, one of those brainy grads a couple of years out of Boalt Law.

Battinelli gave Yuki a cat-that-got-the-cream look—which Yuki returned in kind.

Nick set up his laptop and Yuki's and got them both squared away before the proceedings began.

The bailiff, a bald and expressionless man in a green uniform, called court into session, and Judge LaVan entered the packed courtroom, wearing a scowl. The gallery rose and then sat, causing a rustle to bounce and boomerang off the oak paneling. When the room was quiet again, LaVan greeted the jury.

Then, he said, "Ms. Castellano. You're up."

Yuki stood and asked that Ms. Angela Walker be called.

All eyes swiveled toward the aisle as a woman who, even to Yuki's eyes, looked edible made her languid way to the witness stand and was sworn in.

Chapter 50

"MS. WALKER," YUKI said to her lovely looking witness, "do you know the defendant, Dr. Candace Martin?"

"I've never met her. But of course I know who she is."

"Did you know her husband, Dennis Martin?"

"Yes. I was seeing Dennis for a couple of years. Until about a month before his death."

Yuki tucked her hair behind her ears and said to Walker, "By 'seeing' Dennis Martin, do you mean you were having a sexual relationship with him?"

"Yes. I saw him two, three nights a week."

"And you knew he was married?"

"Yes. Yes. I knew. But he told me his marriage

was a sham. He was staying with his wife for the sake of the kids."

Yuki liked what the witness was saying and the way she was saying it. She was calm and sounded credible and honest.

"Ms. Walker, can you tell the court why your relationship with Mr. Martin ended?"

"He told me he was seeing someone else and that it was serious. He said he just couldn't contain the messiness of his social life anymore."

"Did you believe him?"

"Oh yes. He was a hound. A goat. A snake. A shark. A skunk. Pick your animal, and that was Dennis."

"And where were you when Dennis was killed?"

"Sydney, Australia. As far away from him as I could get."

"Ms. Walker. Did you call the Martin house while you were in Sydney?"

"I hate to admit it, but I called Candace. Might have set this whole debacle into motion."

"Really. Could you be more specific?"

"I was heartbroken. I wanted to get back at Dennis, so I called Candace and told her about my two-year affair with her husband. And I told her that he was still seeing someone."

"Did you know who Dennis was seeing?"

"Nope. Didn't have a clue."

"And how did Candace Martin react to your phone call?"

"She was really cold. She said, 'You're right. He's an animal. Someone ought to put him down. I might do it myself.'"

"Thank you. Your witness," Yuki said, walking away.

Chapter 51

PHIL HOFFMAN STOOD UP behind the defense table. He looked well rested and at the top of his game, a study in gray pinstripes and old school tie.

Yuki took note of the way the jurors looked at Phil. They liked him.

"Ms. Walker, you don't like Candace Martin, do you?" Hoffman asked.

"I don't dislike her. Like I said, I've never met her."

"Well, you clearly had no regard for her. You were sleeping with her husband for two years, knowing full well that he had a home, two young children, and a wife. Isn't that right?"

"Your Honor, counsel is leading the witness."

"Sustained. Don't do that, Mr. Hoffman."

"Sorry, Your Honor."

Hoffman jingled the coins in his pocket, turned back to the witness, and asked, "Do you have any regard for the defendant?"

"Not really." The woman squirmed in her seat. Patted her hair.

"In fact," said Hoffman, "you don't care if Candace lives or dies. Excuse me. Let me make that a question. Ms. Walker, do you care if Candace Martin lives or dies?"

"No, I guess not."

"Would it be fair to say about you that hell hath no fury like a woman scorned?"

"Your Honor!" Yuki said.

Hoffman smiled and said, "I have nothing further for this witness."

Chapter 52

YUKI WAS AT the bar in MacBain's when Cindy breezed in, looking like she'd sprouted wings. She was obviously that over-the-moon happy. Yuki hugged her friend and said, "I hope this high you're on is contagious."

"Me, too," said Cindy.

Yuki grinned and patted the stool next to her, and as Cindy flung herself onto the seat, Yuki said, "Tell me all about that bended-knee proposal in front of God and all his angels."

Cindy laughed and Yuki leaned in to hear all about it—and Cindy didn't spare any detail.

Yuki had always liked Rich. It was rare to find a guy who was both movie-star gorgeous and not in love with himself. Yuki knew Rich to be the opposite of a narcissist. He was a genuinely sweet guy of the old-fashioned, chivalrous kind. Perfect man for Cindy.

And now Yuki was dating a cop, too.

A married one.

"Hey, I've done all the talking," Cindy said. "I think that's a first. Tell me something I don't know."

Yuki blurted, "I'm going out with Jackson Brady."

"No. You are *not*," Cindy said. "Are you kidding me?"

Yuki took a look around to make sure Brady hadn't come inside the saloon while she wasn't looking.

"I swear. It's true."

"Holy cow," Cindy said, the shocked look on her face saying that she was way impressed. "Tell me everything. Don't leave out a word."

Yuki laughed, then filled her friend in on the whole story: the conferences with Brady regarding the Martin case, their first date at First Crush, a cool wine bar and restaurant, perfectly named. And she told Cindy about her date with Brady Friday night at Renegade.

"He told me things about himself that were pretty revealing."

"Did you sleep with him?" Cindy asked.

"Everyone is so interested in my sex life. Why?"

"Well, did you?"

"No. No, I didn't. But I wanted to."

"When are you seeing him again?"

"Well...if I remember correctly, Saturday night," Yuki said, with a coy smile.

"Hah! Well, I have a feeling you're going to have another chance to get his clothes off. Jeez. You'd better tell me all about it, girlfriend. I'm not kidding. This, I gotta hear."

The waiter carried their drinks to a small table by the window. He brought their lunches right after that, saying, "Please be careful. These plates are hot. Can I get you ladies another drink?"

Yuki passed on a second beer and removed the onions from her burger and cut it in half. "I find Brady tremendously attractive," she said.

"Who doesn't?" said Cindy, taking aim at her fries with a ketchup bottle, thwacking the bottom. "He's like Don Johnson in that old show *Miami Vice*. Tubbs. No, Crockett."

"One problem," Yuki said.

"Only one?"

"He's married. Lindsay says."

"Wait. He's *married*? And he didn't tell you?"

"No, but he will. Don't forget what I do for a living."

"Be careful, Yuki. You're hooked, you're cooked. That plate is hot."

"I'm on it," Yuki said. "I am." She finished most of her burger, checked her watch, and pictured setting off Judge LaVan if she was late. "Crap. I've got to go."

"I'll get the check," Cindy said.

"But I'm taking you out to lunch."

"Next time," Cindy said.

Yuki dabbed her lips with a napkin, kissed Cindy's cheek, and rubbed her engagement ring with her thumb as if making a wish on Aladdin's lamp. With Cindy's laughter in her ears, Yuki ran out of the bar.

Chapter 53

YUKI'S WITNESS LOOKED surprised but pleased to find himself the center of attention.

"Mr. White, you own a store called Oldies But Goodies on Pierce?" she asked him.

"Yes, that's right. On Pierce near Haight."

"And what do you sell in your store?"

"Lots of different things. Jukeboxes. Musical instruments. Vinyl LPs. Odds and ends."

"Do you sell guns?"

"Rarely, but yes."

"In April of last year, did you sell a twenty-two-caliber Smith and Wesson handgun to Mr. Dennis Martin?"

"Yes. He had a license to carry. I checked it and I checked his driver's license. It was him."

"Your Honor," Yuki said, "I'd like to admit this receipt, which documents the sale of a twenty-two Smith and Wesson handgun to Dennis Martin."

Yuki handed the sales slip up to the judge, who passed it to the clerk, who showed it to Phil Hoffman.

"Any objections, Mr. Hoffman?" LaVan asked.

"None."

"People's exhibit number thirty is admitted into evidence," LaVan said.

Yuki asked, "When did you contact the police, Mr. White?"

"Last week. When I saw the story about this trial in the paper. I recognized Mr. Martin's picture."

"Thank you, sir. Your witness," Yuki said to opposing counsel.

Hoffman stood, walked across the well, and greeted the witness.

"Mr. White, I think you know that the serial number of the gun you sold Mr. Martin is not on the sales receipt. Did you file a transfer of registration, as required?"

"I'm not a gun dealer. I'm in the antiques

business. I bought that gun as part of a box lot at an auction last year."

"So you didn't comply with the law?"

"Like I just said, I didn't even know there was a gun in the box I bought for thirty bucks. I'm not a gun dealer. I work alone in the store. Man comes in, sees the gun in the case. He also bought a fountain pen. And a book on electricity from the 1920s. These things are memorabilia. I wrote up a receipt. I didn't know I had to file anything. Look, I checked his gun license. I don't think a lot of people with my kind of business would even have done that."

Stephen White cast his eyes toward Yuki as if to say, "Did I just get into trouble here?"

Hoffman continued his cross-examination.

"So, to be clear, you didn't write down the serial number of the gun you sold to Mr. Martin on the receipt. Do you have the serial number anywhere?"

"Extremely doubtful."

"So there's no way to know if the gun you sold Dennis Martin is the gun that killed him, isn't that right?"

"I didn't say I did know."

"That's all, Mr. White. Thank you."

The judge folded his hands on his desk. "Redirect, Ms. Castellano?"

"Yes, Your Honor."

Yuki opened the folder in front of her, pulled a photograph from the file, and walked toward the witness. This was going just the way she'd hoped it would.

"Mr. White. This is a picture of the murder gun, a Smith and Wesson twenty-two. Is this the type of gun you sold to Mr. Martin?"

"Yes."

"How many of these guns did you sell in April last year?"

"I sold just the one."

"How many twenty-two Smith and Wesson guns did you sell in the entire year?"

"I sold just the one."

"To Mr. Dennis Martin?"

"Yes, exactly like I said. I wrote his name on that receipt."

"Thanks, Mr. White. I'm finished, Your Honor."

Yuki kept her expression neutral as she walked back to the prosecution table, but she was doing handsprings in her mind.

White was a very credible witness. He'd checked Dennis Martin's gun license and driver's license and he'd positively identified Dennis Martin from his photo. And he'd positively sold Dennis Martin a gun.

It wasn't proof—but it was damning testimony.

Yuki waited for Stephen White to step down from the box and then called her next witness.

Chapter 54

I STOOD IN THE BACK of the packed courtroom watching Yuki interrogate level-two investigator Sharon Carothers, the CSI who had tested Candace Martin's hands for GSR less than a half hour after Dennis Martin was gunned down.

I'd known Carothers for about four years and had worked a dozen cases with her, and I had never known her to make a mistake. She went strictly by the book but knew how to look around corners without breaking the rules.

"Ms. Carothers, are you the lead investigator on the Martin case?"

"Yes, I am."

"Did you test Dr. Martin's hands for gunshot

residue at approximately six-forty-five on the night of September fourteenth?" Yuki asked.

"I did. The test was positive for GSR."

A woman sitting near the wall broke into a fit of wet coughing that seemed like it would never quit. Yuki waited it out, every last sputter, then asked, "Ms. Carothers, did you ask the defendant if she fired the gun that was found on the scene?"

"Yes, I did. She said she had."

"And what was her explanation for firing the gun?"

"She had one explanation before I tested her hands and a more detailed explanation afterward."

"She had two explanations?" Yuki said, turning to shoot Candace Martin a look. Had that look been a gun, it would've gone *bang*.

I was torn, both rooting for Yuki and at the same time feeling compassion and fear for Candace Martin. A lot of people I knew and respected had bet their careers on their belief that Candace Martin had killed her husband. Could they all be wrong?

Why was my gut telling me that she was innocent?

Yuki said to her witness, "Please tell us about those two explanations."

Carothers turned unblinking eyes on the jury and said, "Before I did the test for GSR, Dr. Martin told me that an intruder shot her husband. After the test, she repeated that an intruder had shot her husband but added that when she called out to her husband, the intruder dropped the gun and took off. She said that she picked up the gun and ran after the intruder. That she had fired out toward the street to scare him off."

I left the courtroom quietly. I was still nowhere on the Richardson case and Brady had made it superclear to me that the Candace Martin case was closed.

What he didn't know was that I had gone through the Martin case file last night. I had read all of Paul Chi's notes and had found a lead I wanted to check out. I *needed* to check it out so that I could shut down Candace Martin's voice in my head saying, "I didn't kill him, Sergeant. Please help me. I'm on trial for my life."

227

Chapter 55

WHAT I HAD gleaned from Chi's notes was that Caitlin and Duncan Martin had a piano teacher who came to their home to give them lessons twice a week.

His name was Bernard St. John.

Chi had interviewed St. John during the Martin investigation, and according to his notes, St. John had no idea who the killer was. In fact, he'd made a point of saying that he did not believe that Candace Martin shot her husband.

Chi had never interviewed St. John again, but because the piano teacher felt so strongly that Candace Martin was innocent, I wanted to hear from him how and why he had formed that opinion.

St. John's rented apartment was in a Victorian house in the mostly residential 2400 block of Octavia Street. He was expecting me, and when I rang the bell on the ground floor, he buzzed me in.

I sized St. John up at his doorway.

He was in his early forties, five foot eight, with a slim build and spiky hair. I followed him into his apartment and saw that he clearly liked drama in his furnishings. The parlor was gold with red draperies, faux zebra-skin rugs were flung about, and a very nice Steinway grand sat near the bay window.

After offering me a chair, St. John sat down on a tassel-fringed hassock and told me he was glad that I had called.

"But I don't understand why the police want to talk to me now," he said. "No one wanted me as a witness."

"You weren't in the Martin house the night of the murder, were you?"

"No. I wasn't there. I saw no gun. Heard no threats," he said with a shrug.

"From what you said in our phone call, I take it that you were privy to certain behaviors in the household that you thought might be important."

229

"Well, I have some thoughts and observations, Sergeant. I certainly do. Starting with when Candace had breast cancer a couple of years ago."

St. John needed no encouragement to fill me in on the last two years of his employment with the Martins, a story laced with petty complaints and gossip. Still, the fact that he was a gossip didn't make him a bad witness.

On the contrary.

"Candace was bitchy to everyone when she was in chemo," he said. "Especially to Ellen."

"Ellen Lafferty. The children's nanny."

"That's right," St. John told me. "I don't know when it started, but it was well over a year ago when Ellen confided in me," St. John said. "She told me that she was having an affair with Dennis."

"Why didn't you tell this to the police?"

"I didn't think it was important. Is it?"

"I'm not sure. But tell me—why did you say to Inspector Chi that you didn't think Candace was capable of shooting her husband?"

"She's a doctor. 'First, do no harm.' Killing Dennis would have harmed everyone in the house. And look. It did."

I closed my notebook and thanked St. John for his time. As I left his apartment, I thought about Phil Hoffman telling me that what he knew about Ellen Lafferty could cause the charges against Candace Martin to be dismissed.

Candace had speculated that her husband had been sleeping with Ellen Lafferty, and now Bernard St. John had confirmed that part of her theory.

Had Lafferty gotten jealous, as Candace had suggested?

Was Ellen Lafferty the so-called intruder who killed Dennis Martin?

Chapter 56

I THOUGHT PAUL Chi might still be steamed at me for questioning the slam-dunk first-degree murder charge against Candace Martin. If he wasn't fuming now, he would be after I told him I was still turning over stones on his case, that I still wasn't prepared to let it go.

It was about 5 p.m. when I brought him a latte and sat down across from him at his very tidy desk in the squad room.

Chi looked at me, his expression absolutely blank, and said, "You still trying to pry open my closed case?"

I nodded. "You just have to let me get this out of my system," I said. "If you were me, you'd do the same."

"You're the boss."

"You remember Bernard St. John?" I asked him.

"The piano teacher. How could I forget that guy?"

"I just spoke with him."

"I'm not pissed off, Lindsay. I just want to understand you better. Fifty homicides a year come through here. We solve only half of them. And that's in a good year. So, here we got one that we actually close. Why has *this* case gotten to you?"

"I can't explain it."

"Can't explain an insult to me, McNeill, Brady, the SFPD as a whole, and the DA's entire office? You think this is going to score us any points with the DA?"

"I've got to do this, Paul. If Candace Martin is guilty, my poking around isn't going to change that."

"But you don't think she is guilty, do you?"

"I don't know."

Chi grinned. A rare occurrence. Like a blue moon in June.

"What's funny?" I asked him.

"I like this about you, Lindsay. You never give up. But you know, Brady doesn't have a sense of humor."

"I'll deal with him when I have to."

Chi shrugged and said, "So what did Bernard St. John tell you?"

"That Dennis Martin was sleeping with Ellen Lafferty. Lafferty confided in him."

"Whoa-ho. Well, there's your motive, Sergeant. You're making the case against Dr. Martin even stronger. Candace found out her husband was sleeping with the nanny, so she shot him. Motive as old as the history of mankind."

"Or — what if it was the other way around?"

"You think *Lafferty* was the shooter?"

"It's not so crazy, Paul. I want to talk to you about that contract killer. Gregor Guzman."

Chi just shook his head and sighed.

"Doggedness suits you, Lindsay. Okay, what do you want to know about Gregor Guzman?"

"Tell me everything you've got."

Chapter 57

AS CHI TAPPED on the computer keyboard, he told me, "Eleven hits are attributed to Guzman— that's eleven unsolved that match his MO."

I scooted the chair so close to Chi's desk, I could see my reflection in the monitor.

"It's a very elegant MO," Chi was saying. "First, he's stealthy. He's never seen and he leaves no evidence. Two, he always uses a twenty-two and his kill shots are head shots. His first shot does the job. His second shot is almost on top of the first. I'd say that second shot is just for insurance. He's a hell of a marksman."

"Dennis Martin took two shots to the *chest.*"

"That's correct."

Chi hit some keys on his computer and brought

up a series of photos of the elusive hit man. The first was a grainy black-and-white still shot that had been lifted from a video of a man leaving Circus Circus, the famous casino in Vegas.

The next photo was of a balding man in a car, taken by a tollbooth surveillance cam outside of Bogotá.

The third picture was of possibly the same man in a dark suit, standing beside an advertising kiosk, watching the crowd enter a public building. The picture was titled, "Lincoln Center, New York."

The last picture was the money shot.

It was taken at night with a long lens pointed at the passenger-side window of a dark SUV, time-dated September 1 of last year. Candace Martin was in profile in the passenger's seat. The way her hair fell obscured part of her face.

Next to her in the driver's seat was a balding man who had turned to face her. His features were difficult to make out because of the shadow inside the car's interior.

It was hard to say if the man pictured was Gregor Guzman or even if the woman in the passenger seat was Candace Martin.

"How sure are you that this man is Guzman?" I asked Chi.

"All pictures of Guzman are educated guesswork. We have no official photos to compare them to, but the face-recognition software found an eighty-three percent correlation between the four photos I just showed you."

"Paul, if your case hung on this picture in the SUV, Candace Martin would walk."

"The DA wanted to use it. It shows premeditation. I gotta admit something to you, Lindsay."

"I'm right here, Paul. And I'm listening."

"Apart from this piece-a-crap picture with Candace Martin, no one in law enforcement has reported seeing Gregor Guzman in the past three years. Who knows if he's even alive?"

Chapter 58

CINDY STOOD AT the windy corner of Turk and Jones just before six that evening. The Tenderloin was a rough neighborhood, arguably the worst in San Francisco.

As a light rain came down, the homeless pulled up their hoodies, hunched over their shopping carts, crouched under the eaves of the rent-by-the-hour Ethel Hotel and Aunt Vicky's, the down-and-dirty gay bar next to it.

Cindy buttoned her coat and pulled up her collar, staring at the cab company across the street that took up the northeast corner of the intersection. There were two plate-glass windows at the street level, each with a flickering neon sign, one reading QUICK EXPRESS TAXI, the other, CORPORATE

ACCOUNTS WELCOME. There was nothing welcoming about that storefront.

Rich had told her to meet him in a coffee shop a couple of doors down, but Cindy couldn't wait. She called Rich, and when she got his voice mail, she left him a message and then crossed Turk against the light.

As she approached Quick Express, Cindy noticed the cab company's vehicle entrance on Turk: a cave of an opening that sheltered a ramp down to the lower parking levels. Yellow cabs were lined up at the curb. Men stood in the drizzle, smoking on the sidewalk, taking swigs from paper bags.

Cindy walked up to the window and saw the dispatch office on the other side of the glass, much like a ticket office in a movie theater but bigger. She knocked on the glass.

The man in the office was regular height, in his forties, with dark hair and a pale moon face. He was wearing a rumpled plaid shirt and khakis. He looked agitated as he worked the phone lines while delivering blunt instructions into a radio mic.

Cindy had to speak loudly over the sound of incoming radio calls.

"I'm Cindy Thomas," she said into the grill. "Are you the owner here?"

"No, I'm the manager and dispatcher, Al Wysocki. What can I do for you?"

"I'm a reporter at the *Chronicle*," she said. She dug her press pass out of her handbag and held it against the window.

"What's this about?"

"One of your drivers might have saved someone who was having a heart attack. The person who called the paper only remembers that the driver was in a taxi minivan," Cindy lied.

"You got a name?"

"No."

"And what's the driver look like?"

"All this person remembers is that the minivan had a movie ad on it."

"Gee. A movie ad," Wysocki said. "Okay, look. We have six vans in the fleet. Three are in. Three are out. But you understand, none of the drivers has a call on any of these cabs. They drive what's here when their shifts start."

"May I take a look anyway? It shouldn't take long."

"Knock yourself out."

Wysocki told Cindy that the garage had three levels—the main floor, which she was on, and two subterranean levels. Two of the vans were on the first floor down, and the third was on the second floor down.

Cindy thanked the man and began her tour of the parked taxis in the dark, grimy, stinking-from-gas-fumes underground garage. Twenty minutes later, she'd located all three vans, none of which had a movie ad on its side.

She took the stairs back to the main floor and left her card with the dispatcher, taking his card in return.

"Okay if I call you again?"

"Feel free," said Wysocki, who grabbed his microphone and barked a street address to a cabbie.

Cindy left the garage through the front door on Turk and found Richie waiting for her on the street corner.

"You were suppposed to wait for me in the coffee shop," he said.

"I'm sorry, Rich. I was a bit early so I thought I'd follow up on something. Honey, this is just legwork. And this is just a cab company."

"A cab company, and you suspect a cabbie of being the last person to see a woman who was drugged and raped."

"Well, none of the cabs here is the one."

"I don't like the chances you take to get a story, Cindy," Rich said, opening the passenger-side door for her. "This is muggers' alley. I'm dropping you home. Then I've got to meet Lindsay."

Cindy looked up at her fiancé, stretched up onto her toes, and kissed him. She said, "You're very damned overprotective, Richie. And this is the weird part: I kind of like it."

Chapter 59

CONKLIN AND I met with the Richardsons once again in their pricey suite at the Mark Hopkins, with its billion-dollar nightscape of Nob Hill and Union Square. The view embraced the Transamerica Pyramid and skyscrapers of the Financial District, San Francisco Bay, and the western span of the Bay Bridge, reaching to Treasure Island.

I've lived in San Francisco my whole life, and I've rarely seen the city from a vantage point like this.

I stared out at the lights while Conklin told the Richardsons that we needed an uninterrupted hour with Avis. He said it would be easier on Avis if we talked to her here rather than down at the Hall. And he said that being with her alone might produce more truth-telling than talking with her while her parents were present.

Sonja Richardson said, "I don't think she has anything left to tell," but both parents agreed to let us talk to Avis alone.

Now the parents were having "light dining" upstairs at Top of the Mark, and Avis was in the kitchenette, looking at me over her shoulder with fierce antipathy.

"How many times do I have to tell you," she groused. She opened the refrigerator and took out a bowl of dip, then rummaged in the cupboard and put her hand on a bag of chips. "I told you everything I know."

"Come over here and sit down, Avis," Conklin said.

She looked surprised at the tone Conklin had taken with her, which was actually mild compared with the images I was having of grabbing her by the scruff of her neck and throwing her against a wall.

Avis took a defiant minute to gather her snack, along with a bottle of soda, and bring it into the sitting area, where she spread everything out on the coffee table.

"Tell us about your English teacher," I said.

"Mr. Ritter?"

"You've got more than one English teacher?"

"Mr. Ritter is okay. Not my favorite, but I get good grades in English. I have a talent for writing."

"Is Jordan Ritter the father of your child?"

"That's *insane!* I hardly know him."

I was sitting in a chair at her level, my hands clasped, my elbows resting on my knees. I leaned over the coffee table and said to the teenager, "Do you think I'm stupid?"

"What?"

"I said, Do you think I'm stupid?"

"What difference does it make who the father is anyway?"

I said, "That's it. Avis, stand up. Inspector Conklin, cuff her. Avis Richardson, you're under arrest for conspiracy, obstruction of justice, and child endangerment. If we find his body, we'll change that charge to murder."

"Oh my God, what are you doing?" she said as the cuffs closed around her wrists. "My baby's not dead. He's not *dead*."

"Tell us about it at the station. Let's go," I said.

"Here. I'll talk *here*," she said.

I nodded to Rich and he took off the cuffs. The girl threw herself back onto the couch, and then she started telling a version of the story that I hadn't heard before. I didn't know if she was telling the truth.

But truly, her story was taking a turn for the weird.

Chapter 60

"IF YOU TELL ME A FIB," I said to Avis Richardson, "or a half-truth or even an exaggeration—if you tell me any kind of lie at all—I will know it. And when that happens, you're going to jail."

"I'll tell you the truth," she said. "I'll tell you whatever you want to know. I can't stand it anymore."

"Start talking," I said.

"You're right about Jordan. He is the father of my baby. He has great genes."

Genes? Jeans? This kid was criminally deluded. I was afraid that if I opened my mouth, I'd lash out at her.

I put my hands through my hair and took a moment to get a grip on my anger. I couldn't remember when I'd felt so frustrated, but I didn't want to shut this kid down by letting her see the fury in my eyes. It was the time to let Conklin work his magic with women.

Conklin said, "Is the baby alive, Avis? Do you know where he is?"

"He's alive. I don't know where he is, though."

Conklin said, "Okay, Avis. Let's see if we can figure it out together."

"A lot of what I said before was true. I hid my pregnancy. I didn't even tell Jordan about it for five months. Then I told him, and he started to go asshole on me. 'How do I know it's even mine?' "

"Men can be jerks," Conklin said.

Avis nodded. "I went out to Prattslist and found an ad."

"There was no ad," I said.

"It wasn't the ad I told you about," Avis said. "It was a different ad and it was only three weeks ago. I contacted these two women. A couple. They were looking for a baby and they would pay twenty-five thousand dollars."

"Names?" I said.

"Toni and Sandy."

"That's it?" I said.

"You contacted two women," Conklin said to the teenage idiot on the couch. I looked at the door. With luck, the kid would tell us everything we needed to know before her parents came home.

Right now, Jordan Ritter was facing jail time. Avis Richardson was looking at juvie. And the last thing we needed was a thousand-dollar-an-hour lawyer sticking his fingers in the pie.

"They picked me up a block from the school, but — but they didn't drug me or anything. They said they had a place where I could give birth in peace. I fell asleep in the back of the car."

"When you woke up," Conklin said, "did you know where you were?"

"Not at all. It was dark. It was remote. I was in labor. I got into bed and for about six hours, I screamed my head off. I gave birth to the baby. I held him. He was absolutely the most beautiful thing I'd ever seen. And then I gave him to Toni and Sandy. They were nice and they really wanted him."

I'd reached my limit. Did this child care at all about her son? No.

I shouted, "That's the last you saw of that

baby? You have nothing else to tell us? Is any of what you told us true? If you gave birth with these nice women in attendance, explain to us why you were found bleeding out near the lake."

"That part was all my fault," said Avis Richardson.

Chapter 61

HALLELUJAH. Avis Richardson was finally about to take some responsibility. If she admitted something that led us to her baby, I thought I could possibly forgive her for driving us crazy for the past week.

How about it, Avis? Gonna give us a break?

I went to the fridge in the kitchenette, brought back a bottle of soda, and poured three glasses, no ice.

"Toni said she and Sandy would stay with me until I felt well," Avis told Conklin and me. "Then they were going to take the baby home."

"Did they say where home was?" Conklin asked.

"Nuh-uh," Avis said.

I was still comparing and contrasting Avis's new story with what she'd told us before, and the two versions hardly matched up.

The French-speaking man was on the cutting-room floor. The kidnapping was history. The father of her baby was her English teacher. Avis had answered an ad from two *women*, and now Avis said she had given up her baby voluntarily.

Was she capable of telling the truth? Toni and Sandy. I wondered if she'd made up those names on the spot.

"When I was in that house, right after I had the baby, Toni gave me her phone so I could call Jordan and tell him to come and get me," Avis said. "But when I handed the phone to Toni so she could give him directions, Jordan hung up."

Incoming phone calls would show up in Jordan Ritter's phone records. So maybe we would yield *something*.

"I just wanted to get out of there. I didn't want to be around the baby, so I waited for an opportunity and sneaked out the back door. I hitched a ride as far as Brotherhood Way, but the people who gave me the ride were going east, so I got out.

"What kind of car, Avis? Did you get the name of a person or a plate number? We're trying to connect the dots. Get me?" I said.

"I wasn't thinking of anything like that. I'd just run away, and I was still in the middle of nowhere. I didn't have my handbag, my phone, nothing, and I was starting to bleed again. And then I was bleeding really hard. I didn't expect that."

Finally the girl was starting to show signs of distress. She was sweating, wringing her hands. Thinking of her own pain.

Conklin said, "Can you go on, Avis? Or do you need to take a break?"

"I'm okay," she said. "There's not much more to tell. I found a rain poncho in the weeds near the lake, so I took off my clothes and put it on. I was feeling faint as I walked and I fell down a few times. A car stopped for me and took me to the hospital. I met *you*," she said, trying to give me an evil eye.

"Is Jordan in trouble because I'm underage?"

"Jordan will be fine," I lied. "The most important thing, Avis. More important even than Jordan Ritter, is to find out where your baby is and if he's okay."

That was the truth.

Where was that baby?

If these women were real and not more characters from Avis Richardson's creative-writing workshop, had they kept him?

Was he in a warm room somewhere covered with a little blue blanket? Did he have a full tummy? A teddy bear? Was he safe?

Or had he been smuggled out of the country with heroin in his colon, gutted as soon as he reached shore?

"How did they pay you?" I asked.

Please, God, let them have given this naive little girl a check.

"They didn't pay me. I didn't want the money. That would've been illegal, right? To sell my baby? I didn't sell him. So, what are you going to do now?" Avis asked Conklin.

"Everything is going to be all right," Conklin told her.

Really? For whom?

Chapter 62

WHEN WE LEFT the Mark Hopkins, Avis was being comforted by her parents. They barely looked up when Conklin said we'd call later, and we left their suite.

. My partner and I had a little confab outside my car—or rather, he listened to me rant about the stupidest, most morally challenged girl on the planet—and then we headed out to our respective homes for the night.

I called Quentin Tazio from my cell phone on the drive home.

Quentin is a police resource, a tech consultant who has been described as a "brain in a bottle." He lives in a dungeon of his own devising, a dark and drab two-floor flat tricked out with a million dollars in computer equipment.

It's how he spent his inheritance from his father, and it had made Quentin absolutely the happiest man I knew.

I told QT, as he liked to be called, about the ad on Prattslist, the call to Jordan Ritter's phone, and the two names, Sandy and Toni, which may have been real names, nicknames, or pseudonyms the women made up to use on Avis.

Maybe, for once, Avis had told us the truth to the extent that she knew it.

I cooked dinner for Joe and had a jumbo glass of merlot with my pasta. We went for a long walk with Martha and I told my husband the latest episode in the Avis Richardson story.

Joe said, "I have a hunch QT is going to find something for you, Linds."

Joe has first-class, FBI-trained hunches.

I had a great night's sleep wedged between Joe and Martha, and when I got to the Hall at 8:30 a.m., I discovered that QT had called.

I called him back, and while I waited for him to get my message and return my call, Brady asked me to come to his office and update him on Richardson. I gave him a detailed but concise report, and he asked good questions. I only wished I had something worthwhile to tell him.

"Get traction on this thing, or we'll send it down the line to Crimes Against Persons and move on," he said.

My phone was ringing when I got back to my desk. I was hoping it was QT, but I saw from my caller ID that it was Dean Hanover of the Brighton Academy.

"Boxer," I said, picturing the man with the polka-dot bow tie in his buttoned-up office.

"Sergeant, I'm glad I reached you."

"Is something wrong?"

"Avis Richardson is missing," the dean told me. "She came back to school yesterday, but she wasn't in her dorm room this morning. Now I just found out that one of our teachers is missing, too. Jordan Ritter didn't show up to class this morning. That's very unusual for him. Both of them are gone. No note, no nothing. They're just gone."

Chapter 63

LESS THAN TWENTY-FOUR hours earlier, Phil Hoffman had been in his office, rehearsing his defense strategy, when a phone call from the SFPD radically upped his client's chances for acquittal. It had sure felt to him like an act of God.

Now he stood behind the defense table in Judge LaVan's courtroom and said, "The defense calls Bernard St. John."

Bernard St. John entered the courtroom. He was wearing an expensive chalk-striped suit and a blue silk shirt. Not a spiked hair was out of place. After he had been sworn in and was seated, Hoffman approached the witness stand.

As expected, Yuki shot to her feet. "Your Honor," she said, "we only learned about this witness last night and haven't had a chance to do any investigation."

Hoffman said to the judge, "I only became aware of this witness myself yesterday evening, and we sent an e-mail to Ms. Castellano immediately."

LaVan peered through his glasses, looking down from the bench, and said, "Ms. Castellano, you'll have your chance to question the witness. Mr. Hoffman, you may proceed."

"Thank you, Your Honor. Mr. St. John, what kind of work do you do?"

"I play the piano for events, and I am also a piano teacher."

"Are you currently employed as the Martin children's piano teacher?"

"No. I was let go four months ago. The children were busy with a number of activities, and piano lessons were apparently not a priority."

"What was your job with the Martins before you were let go?"

"I mostly taught Caitlin," St. John said. "But Duncan was learning his scales and some beginners' songs."

"When did you first start working for the Martin family?"

"Two years ago last month."

"And do you have a friendship with other people who worked for the Martins?" Hoffman asked.

"Yes, I do," said St. John.

"Were you friends with Ellen Lafferty, the children's nanny?"

"Yes, sir."

"And did Ms. Lafferty confide in you about a connection she had with Mr. Martin?"

"Yes. A little over a year ago."

"What did she tell you at that time?"

"She said that she'd been having an affair with Mr. Martin. It had begun when Dr. Martin had surgery for breast cancer and was undergoing chemotherapy. Ellen said that at first she was just sleeping with Mr. Martin because he seemed so *sad*."

Hoffman waited out the titters that rippled across the gallery, then asked his witness to continue.

St. John said, "By the time Ellen told me about the affair, she said she had fallen in love with Dennis and didn't know what to do."

"Hearsay, Your Honor," Yuki said.

"I'm going to allow it, Ms. Castellano. Go ahead, Mr. Hoffman."

"Did Ms. Lafferty ever mention this romantic relationship with Mr. Martin again?"

"Yes. She showed me gifts he gave her. And before he...died, Ellen told me again that she was *painfully* in love with him—her word—and in love with the children, too."

"And why didn't you come forward with this earlier, Mr. St. John?"

"The police only asked me if I had witnessed any hostility between Dr. Martin and her husband. I said that I'd overheard fights. And they wanted to know if I was in the house the night of the murder. I wasn't. I hadn't been there in days."

"Did you tell the police that you thought Dr. Martin had killed her husband?"

St. John said, "No. I told them I *didn't* think she had killed her husband. The Martins were both under pressure, but I knew Candace wouldn't kill the children's father, and *that's* what I told the police."

"Do you think Ms. Lafferty was angry about being the other woman?"

Yuki stood up. "Speculation, Your Honor.

261

Speculation, leading the witness, as well as sneakiness and calculation."

"The jury will disregard," LaVan said. He pointed his gavel at Hoffman. "No more of that."

"Yes, Your Honor." Hoffman dipped his head, hid a smile from the judge, and said, "I'm finished with this witness."

Chapter 64

YUKI SCRIBBLED A NOTE to Nicky on her pad: "Do you know anything about this piano man?"

Gaines scribbled back, *"Not one thing."*

Christ. St. John hadn't supported the cops' theory of the case, so he'd been ignored. Now she'd been blindsided. Clearly, Hoffman had been trying to tell her about Ellen's affair with Dennis Martin when she'd blown him off.

Yuki fought the panic that was rising from her stomach and busied herself with her note cards as she thought through this surprise bombshell.

What St. John's testimony meant was that Ellen Lafferty had motive. And since Dennis Martin had a gun—evidence that Yuki herself had introduced—it followed that Ellen could have found the gun. If so, Lafferty had had the means to shoot Dennis Martin. Motive? Maybe. Opportunity? Every single day.

Dammit.

First rule any litigator learned was you don't ask questions if you don't know the answers. She was flying absolutely blind.

Yuki got to her feet and said, "Good morning, Mr. St. John."

"Good morning."

Yuki rounded the prosecution table, talking as she walked toward the witness.

"All I want from you are facts," Yuki said. "Not what someone told you. Not what you heard."

"Ms. Castellano," LaVan said wearily. "I'm wearing the robes, not you. I give the instructions, not you. If you have a question, I suggest you ask it."

"Yes, Your Honor. Mr. St. John, please answer my questions with what you know firsthand."

"Sure. Okay. I understand that," St. John said.

Yuki sent up a quick prayer to her dead mother, then said, "Mr. St. John, did you ever see Mr. Martin and Ms. Lafferty in what would be called a compromising position?"

"Having sex, you mean?"

"Yes. Or kissing. Overtly sexual behavior."

"No. I only know what Ellen told me."

"Thank you. That's all I have for this witness, Your Honor."

"You may stand down," said the judge.

Chapter 65

PHIL HOFFMAN STOOD UP from his chair beside Candace Martin. "Your Honor, we call Ellen Lafferty to the stand."

Ellen Lafferty entered the courtroom with her head up and confidently strode down the center aisle.

All eyes were on the pretty, young woman, impeccably and modestly dressed in a dark gray suit, a gold cross hanging at her throat. She looked to be just the kind of person you would entrust with your children.

Phil Hoffman did his best to hide his anticipation. Ellen Lafferty had been Yuki Castellano's star witness against his client. With the information he now had, he was going to destroy Lafferty on the stand and turn her into a witness for the defense. But he had to do it in such a way that the jury didn't see him as a monster.

After Lafferty had been sworn in and was seated, Phil approached the witness box. He greeted his new witness and then asked his first question.

"Ms. Lafferty, how would you describe your relationship with Dennis Martin?"

"In what regard, Mr. Hoffman?"

"I think that my question was pretty clear. Let me repeat it. What kind of relationship did you have with Dennis Martin?"

"He was the children's father. And I took care of the children. That was all that mattered to me."

"Your Honor, permission to treat the witness as hostile."

LaVan swiveled his chair ninety degrees and said, "Ms. Lafferty, for you as well as for the members of the jury to know, a hostile witness is one for the opposing side—in this case, a witness for the prosecution—who when examined by the other side—in this case, the defense—might not be forthcoming.

"In designating you a hostile witness, Ms.

Lafferty, I'm giving Mr. Hoffman permission to ask leading questions. You have sworn to tell the truth. Don't forget that."

"I won't, Your Honor."

Hoffman fixed his eyes on Lafferty and said, "Were you having an affair with Mr. Martin?"

"Oh my God."

"Yes or no? Were the two of you having an affair?"

"Yes."

"Could you speak loudly enough for the jury to hear you?"

"Yes. I was. We were."

"And when did this sexual relationship begin?"

Tears welled up in Ellen Lafferty's eyes and spilled down her cheeks. "Two years ago last April."

"So, more than a year before Mr. Martin was shot?"

"Uh-huh. Yes."

"And were you still seeing Mr. Martin at the time of his death?"

"Yes."

"You admit you were having a sexual

relationship with a married man in the home where he lived with his wife and children. Isn't that right?"

"Yes."

"And when Ms. Castellano had you on the stand, you didn't think it was important to tell us about this affair?"

"No, I didn't."

"And how did you feel about Dr. Candace Martin?"

"I think she's cruel."

"Were you jealous of Dr. Martin?"

There was a pause as Lafferty's eyes went everywhere. To Yuki. To the jury. To Candace Martin.

"Answer the question, Ms. Lafferty," Hoffman said. "Were you jealous of Dr. Martin's marriage to your lover?"

"Your Honor, do I really have to answer that?"

"Yes, you certainly do, Ms. Lafferty."

Lafferty sighed, clasped the cross at her neckline, and finally spoke, her words sounding loud in the hushed courtroom. "I wished that I had her life. But I would not have done anything to hurt her."

"How about Mr. Martin? He wasn't leaving his wife, was he? Would you have done something to hurt Mr. Martin?"

"No, no. Never. I loved him."

"And how did Mr. Martin feel about you? Had he promised to divorce his wife and marry you?"

"Why are you doing this to me? You see what he's trying to do, Judge?" Lafferty said. "He's trying to make it look like I'm the murderer, when it's her who did it."

"Ms. Lafferty, please answer the question."

Lafferty choked and began openly sobbing. It was as if she'd been saving up these tears for so long, the crack in the dam became a fissure and the lake just came barreling through.

Chapter 66

PHIL HOFFMAN jingled the keys and coins in his pants pockets. "Do you need a moment?" he asked Ellen Lafferty.

She nodded. Hoffman gave her a box of tissues and when his witness was more composed, he said, "Let me repeat my question. Did Mr. Martin tell you that he wanted to leave his wife and marry you?"

"Yes. He told me that a few times. Often, I would say."

"Did he firm up those plans, Ms. Lafferty?"

"What do you mean? I don't understand."

"It's pretty simple, really. Did Dennis Martin start a divorce action against his wife?"

"No."

"Did he take you out with his friends?"

"No. I wouldn't have expected that."

"Did you and he set a wedding date, for instance?"

"Dammit, no. He didn't give me a time or a place. I was taking care of his children. I saw him every day. He told me that he loved me and that he despised *her*. I thought he was going to leave her because he said he would. And I believed that until the day he died."

"Or—did he break off his relationship with you, Ms. Lafferty? Did he tell you to bug off? Did he treat you like just another one of his used-up girlfriends and tell you that he was staying with his wife? Is that why you were angry with him?"

"No. We were together and in love."

"The bastard lied to you, didn't he?"

"No."

"Were you mad enough at him to shoot him, Ms. Lafferty? Was this a crime of passion?"

Yuki said, "Your Honor, counsel is badgering the witness to death."

"Sustained. The jury will disregard the defense's last run-on question. Mr. Hoffman, that's twice. Do you have anything further for this witness? Or do you want to be sworn in so you can testify yourself?"

Ellen Lafferty gripped the edge of the witness box and said fervently, "I didn't kill him, I *didn't*. I am telling the truth. I would never have hurt Dennis. Never, never, *never*."

"Just like you would never, never, never lie? Right, Ms. Lafferty?"

"That's right. I would never lie."

"Did Candace Martin have a gun in her hand when you left the house on the night of the murder?"

"I think so. I thought so. I don't know anymore."

"Right. But you would never, never, never lie. Thank you. I have no further questions."

Chapter 67

A SHOCK OF ANGER blew all the dread and fear right out of Yuki. The defense had annihilated her damned witness, annihilated her and planted the seeds of reasonable doubt.

Yuki didn't know if she could rehabilitate a would-be home wrecker and probable liar, but she knew that her entire case might depend on it.

Yuki barely saw Nicky's note: "You go, girl."

She got to her feet and walked to the witness box that wrapped around the witness. She put her hand on the arm of the box as if to communicate to Ellen that she was placing a comforting hand on her arm.

"Ms. Lafferty, did you kill Mr. Martin?"

"*No*. I did *not*."

"Did the Martins fight?"

"All the time."

"Did you see a gun in Candace Martin's hand on the night of the murder?"

"I thought so. It was so long ago. And it happened so fast. I don't know for sure anymore."

"Okay. Were you telling the truth to this jury when you said you thought Candace Martin shot and killed her husband?"

"Yes, that is God's honest truth."

"The prosecution has no more questions for Ms. Lafferty."

Phil Hoffman watched the witness step down, wipe her eyes with a tissue, and head out to the rear of the courtroom. She was still crying as she went through the doors.

It was only eleven-fifteen.

Before the jury had a chance to even think of feeling sorry for Ellen Lafferty, Phil Hoffman would launch the next bomb.

Chapter 68

PHIL HOFFMAN SAID, "The defense calls Dr. Candace Martin."

For a moment, Yuki thought she'd heard him wrong. But when Candace Martin edged out from behind the defense table, wearing her game face, a two-thousand-dollar Anne Klein suit, and eight-hundred-dollar Ferragamos, Yuki knew that Hoffman was running the table.

Candace wasn't required to testify.

Judge LaVan had told the jury that the defendant was not obliged to take the stand and that the jury could not hold that against her.

So for Phil to call his client as a witness in her own defense was an act of either desperation or supreme confidence.

Hoffman didn't seem desperate at all.

Candace Martin put her hand on the Bible, and when asked if she swore to tell the whole truth, she said, "I do." Then she sat down in the chair facing the gallery and gave her attention to her attorney.

"Dr. Martin," Hoffman said, "some of this has been established, but for the benefit of continuity, were you at home when your husband was killed?"

"Yes."

"Where were Caitlin and Duncan?"

"They were each in their own rooms."

"And so that the jury can place everyone in the house, where was Cyndi Parrish, your cook?"

"She was upstairs in her room."

"And where was Ellen Lafferty?" Hoffman asked.

"I don't know where she was. She said good night to me about fifteen minutes before Dennis was shot."

"And where was Dennis just before the incident?"

"I don't know that either. I didn't see him. I went to the bedroom wing, passed the kids' rooms and said hello to each of them. Then I went down that hallway to my office. That's where I was when Ellen said that she was leaving."

"What were you doing in your office that evening?"

"I was returning calls."

"And were you still in your office when you heard shots?"

"Yes. I was about to call a patient's wife. It wasn't going to be good news. I had taken off my glasses and was massaging my temples, like this."

Dr. Martin took off her glasses and put them down on the armrest. She rubbed her temples with her thumb and third finger of her left hand.

"I had the phone in my other hand," she said, making a claw of her right hand as if she were clutching a receiver.

Yuki thought that this demo was a pretty ingenious way to visually put a cell phone in Candace Martin's hand instead of a gun, and she had to admire Hoffman for coming up with it.

"Please tell the jury what happened when you heard the shots," Hoffman said. He stepped aside so that he wouldn't obstruct the sight line between his client and the jurors.

Candace Martin listed the timeline just as

Hoffman had done in his opening statement. She said that she ran to the foyer, found her husband on the floor, blood pooling near his chest, and checked his pulse.

She went on to say that she wasn't wearing her glasses but heard the clatter of something metallic falling to the floor. She realized it was a gun at the same time that she saw someone in the shadows moving toward the front door.

Yuki watched Candace Martin's face for tells, facial tics or eye movements, and she listened for lies. She found Candace believable.

And she thought that the jury would believe her, too.

In a few minutes Yuki would have to discredit this heart surgeon, this good mother, and undo the work Phil Hoffman had done, polishing a halo and affixing it to the crown of Candace Martin's pretty blond head.

Yuki knew what she had to do.

She wondered if she could do it.

Chapter 69

PHIL HOFFMAN was winding up his direct examination of Candace Martin, trying to rein in any visible sign of the rush he was feeling. The gamble was paying off. Candace was the perfect witness for herself: Concise. Clear. Consistent.

And, of course, innocent.

"When you found Dennis on the floor and realized that he had expired, what did you do?" Hoffman asked.

"I remember grasping the gun. I had never held a gun before, but I saw someone leaving the house. The front door was open. Instinctively, I wanted to stop whoever had shot my husband. I ran after the intruder. I yelled, 'Stop!' a couple of times," Candace Martin told the jury. "And then I fired."

"Did you hit anyone, Dr. Martin?"

"No. I didn't see anyone outside. I just fired high to make sure he didn't come back. Then I came back into the house, locked the front door, and went back to Dennis. By that time, the kids had come out of their rooms and were crying. It was horrible. Horrible. I sent Caitlin to her room, and Duncan went upstairs to Cyndi's room."

"What happened after that?"

"I called nine one one. The police came in a few minutes."

"Please tell the jury how you were feeling."

"Me? I was almost paralyzed with shock and grief. And then, unbelievably, everything got worse. Shall I go on?"

"Please do."

The doctor nodded, swallowed hard, and resumed speaking.

"It was the routine end of a routine day. Suddenly—gunshots. Someone had come into my house and killed my husband. When the police arrived, they started questioning me. I had to leave my children at the most traumatic moment in their lives. I had to walk past my dead husband

and get into a patrol car so that I could be interviewed at the police station.

"I was questioned for eight hours, then held overnight. In the morning, I was charged with a murder I didn't commit.

"I was terrified then—and I'm terrified now. The fear never leaves me. Because I'm also afraid for my children and I'm not with them."

Yuki thought, Holy crap. Candace Martin had had the jury at *I do*. Under the best of circumstances, they would have a hard time seeing the killer in this woman. Yuki scribbled a note to Nicky that sent him to his laptop. He was opening files as Hoffman thanked his client.

"Your witness," Phil Hoffman said.

Chapter 70

YUKI RAN HER FINGER down the section of the transcript on Nicky's laptop, her deposition of Candace Martin from a year before. Then she stood and walked toward the witness.

"Dr. Martin, did you love your husband?"

"Yes."

"But you had been having an affair for more than a year before he was killed."

"Yes."

"How do you feel about Felix Ashton, your lover?"

"Objection. Relevance," Hoffman said from his seat.

"Overruled. Dr. Martin, please answer the question," said the judge.

"I have a lot of affection for Felix."

Yuki said, "Mr. Ashton testified that he loves you. But you don't return his feelings?"

"I don't know how to quantify my feelings for Felix."

"Did your husband tell you how he felt about you having an affair?"

"Not specifically."

"Did it upset him? Did it make him angry?"

"I don't think he cared if I had an affair," Candace Martin said. "If he did, it would only have made him a hypocrite."

"Well, your lover testified that your husband followed the two of you around. Is that true?"

"Yes. But, I don't think Dennis cared that I was seeing Felix. He was just trying to get me to agree to a divorce."

"And you wouldn't give it to him?"

"I wouldn't accept his terms."

"So you subscribe to the theory that it's better for the children if a couple stays together—even if they are both having affairs—than if they divorce?"

"Your Honor," Hoffman said from his seat, "counsel is badgering the witness."

"Sustained. Get to your point if you have one, Ms. Castellano."

"Yes, Your Honor." She walked to the center of the well, then turned back around to face the witness, the distance between them making it necessary for Candace Martin to speak loudly. Yuki said, "Ellen Lafferty testified that she was having an affair with your husband. Were you aware that they were involved?"

"Not until she testified."

"Were you jealous of the attention your husband lavished on other women?"

"No. I was used to it."

"So despite the fact that you loved him, his philandering in your own home didn't infuriate you? That's remarkable," Yuki said.

"Don't bother to object, Mr. Hoffman," LaVan said. "Ms. Castellano, your opinions are out of order. Don't do that again. Ask your questions, and let's move on."

"I'm sorry, Your Honor. Dr. Martin, let me make sure I understand your testimony.

"You were having an affair. You admit your husband was habitually unfaithful. And yet you maintain that you loved him. You were photographed with a known hit man. You found your husband's gun—"

Yuki made a gun with her thumb and forefinger, moved in toward the witness, and from five feet away pointed her "gun" at Candace Martin, saying, "And when you had an opportunity to kill him, you shot him dead."

Yuki squeezed the imaginary trigger and jerked the imaginary gun as if it were kicking back. And she ignored Hoffman, who was shouting his objections, and ignored the bang of the gavel—a sound as effective as if the bullets she'd fired with her hand were real.

She spoke over the commotion, saying, "And so, Dr. Martin, after your husband was dead, you fired a few rounds into the air to explain away the gunshot residue on your hands. Isn't that true?"

"*Your Honor,*" Hoffman shouted, "Ms. Castellano just gave her summation. Apart from her disingenuous 'Isn't that true?' there wasn't a question in that entire herd of bull," Hoffman said. "I move that this entire cross-examination be *stricken*—"

"For God's sake," Candace Martin said, gripping the arms of the witness box, leaning forward, the cords of her neck standing out as she shouted at Yuki over her lawyer's voice.

"If I were going to kill Dennis, why would I do it in my own home, where my children would see it? This travesty is the fault of bad police work and insane, rabid prosecution. Take a look at *yourself,* Ms. Castellano. I was angry at Dennis, but I didn't kill him. Just like I would never kill *you*."

Chapter 71

THE JUDGE SLAMMED down his gavel again and again, bellowing, "*Order!* Mr. Hoffman, get your *client* under *control*," he commanded, which only added fuel to the conflagration that was already consuming the courtroom.

Yuki stood in the well with her hands clasped in front of her, hoping the disturbance would rage on.

Even if her cross was stricken, even if she was fined, she had turned a blowtorch on Candace Martin's cool demeanor. The doctor's vehement protests that she wouldn't kill her husband had lost their punch.

The motive to kill was there.

Her going ballistic had demonstrated to the

jury that she could have lost her cool and gunned him down.

The judge banged his gavel once more, and at last the ruckus died down. He straightened his glasses, peered down at Yuki, and said, "Anything else, Ms. Castellano? Or have you done enough for one day?"

Yuki said, "I have nothing further for the witness."

Hoffman said, "Redirect, Your Honor."

But the judge wasn't listening anymore. His attention had gone to his cell phone. His face was pale.

A second time Hoffman told the judge that he wanted to reexamine the witness.

"It'll have to wait," said Judge LaVan. "I have to visit someone at the hospital, immediately.

"Dr. Martin, you may step down. Court is adjourned for the day. Ms. Castellano. Mr. Hoffman. Be in my chambers at eight a.m. tomorrow morning. Don't be late.

"We'll pick up the pieces then."

Chapter 72

I WALKED INTO Brady's office first thing in the morning, hoping to have the quickest meeting on record.

Brady put down his phone and said, "Boxer, I'm going to have to pull you off Richardson and send it down to Crimes Against Persons. Look at what's come in in the past week," he said, tilting his chin toward the whiteboard in the center of the squad room, legible through the glass walls of his office.

Six open cases were listed in black letters. Closed cases were always written in red. There were no closed cases.

"Lieutenant, we're getting some real movement on Richardson," I said, pulling out a chair, sitting down across from the big guy. His sunny hair was pulled back, but there was no wedding band on his ring finger. I thought about Yuki, no bigger than a bird, wrapped in the arms of this cop I barely knew, and I was afraid for her.

Yuki was a brilliant, gutsy prosecutor—and at the same time an absolute loser at picking men.

Brady was staring back at me, waiting for me to speak.

"Quentin Tazio found a connection that could crack this case," I said.

"QT's our computer consultant, right?"

"He's the best."

I told Brady that through the wizardry of telephony and electronic databases, QT had tracked a phone call to Jordan Ritter from the Lake Merced area during the time Avis Richardson was delivering her baby.

"According to Avis, she asked one of the two women who had assisted in the delivery to lend her a phone so she could call her boyfriend.

"The phone used to call Jordan Ritter belongs to Antoinette Burgess, age forty, used to be a schoolteacher. She lives in Taylor Creek, Oregon. Population three thousand forty-two."

Brady said, "You think Burgess may have the baby?"

"Avis says Burgess was there when the baby was born."

"I'm starting to feel a little hopeful. Seem okay to be hopeful, Boxer?"

I nodded and told Brady that Burgess didn't have a record and that I wanted to meet her. If she had the baby, I would get him out of Taylor Creek before sirens and helicopter and SWAT made an intervention dangerous.

"Conklin is going to stay here and work on locating Avis and her boyfriend," I told Brady. "Claire Washburn is coming with me. We're both working off the meter."

"Work *on* the meter," Brady said. "Let's wrap this up. I'll contact the local authorities in whatever the largest town is near Taylor Creek. I'll do it now."

"Lieutenant. With all due respect, I think we should get a feel for the situation first."

Brady and I went a few rounds about the logistics, but I could tell he was excited. After I assured him that I would call him as soon as I reached Taylor Creek and give him postings throughout the day, he gave me the green light.

I got out of Brady's office, relieved that I was still on the case. I knew that this one lead to a woman who lived in Oregon was probably my last chance to find Avis Richardson's missing child.

And it might be the baby's last chance, too.

WOMEN'S MURDER CLUB

Book Three

ROAD TRIP

Chapter 73

I MET CLAIRE in the parking lot outside the Medical Examiner's Office. She piled in next to me in the front seat of the Explorer with a diaper bag doing duty as a picnic carryall.

Like me, Claire hadn't gone on a road trip in more than a year. Unlike me, Claire was in a cheery mood.

I punched "Main Street, Taylor Creek, Oregon" into the Explorer's nav system and set out toward the Bay Bridge and I-80 East. It was a four-hundred-and-thirty-mile trip, and I planned to make it all in one day.

By this time tomorrow, I hoped to have Baby Boy Richardson in my care. I could almost see him all bundled up, lying in his car seat.

James Patterson

"I brought you a fried-egg sandwich," Claire told me as we passed the Berkeley exit and got a foggy-morning Bay view across the marina to the west. "I had the deli man put a slice of ham in there. And here's your coffee. Extra milky."

"You're a sweetie, ya know?"

"I *do* know," Claire said, chuckling. Man, she was glad to be getting out of town. By the time we hit the interstate, Claire was in full throat about her baby and my goddaughter, Ruby Rose Washburn.

She spared no detail in singing out stories about Ruby's adventures in the pots-and-pans cabinet, her first taste of hot dog with relish, and how Ruby's daddy was her favorite person.

"Edmund plays the cello for her," Claire told me as I got in the FasTrak lane. We crossed the Carquinez Bridge. I took in the view of San Pablo Bay and Mare Island, the site of the old Mare Island shipyard and the sugar refinery in the town of Crockett to the east.

"She lies in the puffy chair when he practices and coos along with the music. She loves Vivaldi, Edmund says. It's all so delicious, Lindsay."

"Uh-huh," I said. I couldn't say more. I love

298

Ruby Rose. I was looking for a missing baby. And I had babies on my mind.

I ached to have a baby with Joe. I wanted what Claire had—hot dogs and pots and pans and cooing babies. I wanted to hear Joe singing amazing arias to our child in Italian.

I didn't even know they were there, but salty tears leaked out of my eyes and rolled down my cheeks. I palmed them away, but Claire caught me in the act.

"What is it, Lindsay? What's wrong?"

"Just tired," I said.

"After all these years, you still think you can get away with lying to me?"

"No. No, I don't."

"So, what is it?"

I told my best bud, "Once a month I get body-slammed by the loss of another opportunity, you know? Getting married makes me want a baby more than ever. It's come over me like a freakin' baby-love tsunami," I said.

"You and Joe have been trying?"

I nodded.

"For how long?"

"A little while. Three or four months."

"That's nothing," Claire said.

By then we were on Interstate 5 about one hundred miles north of San Francisco. Knee-high thickets of scrub flanked both sides of the freeway, and wire fences separated the road from the plains of parched grass that stretched to the horizon.

The word "barren" came to mind.

"You having PMS right now?" Claire asked me.

"Yuh-huh," I said.

Claire reached over and gave my shoulder a shake. "You're getting a chocolate bar at the next gas station," she said.

I croaked, "What is that? Doctor's orders?"

Claire laughed. "Yes, it is, smarty-pants," she said. "It most definitely is."

Chapter 74

ANY COP WOULD SAY that emotional attachment messes with your objectivity. You just have to accept that innocent people get hurt, raped, scammed, kidnapped, and murdered every day.

But if you're a cop and you don't bring everything you've got to nailing the bad guys, what the hell is the point? For the same time and money, you might as well be punching tickets on a train.

We gassed up the Explorer outside Williams, then had lunch at Granzella's, a restaurant that looked like a feed store on the outside and a hunting lodge inside. Claire and I sat at a table under the mounted heads of deer and bear as well as zebras, water buffalo, and long-horned goats.

Along with the exotic taxidermy, Granzella's

specialized in a very nice linguine with a spicy red sauce. While we ate, I groused about Avis.

"She's wasted more than a week of our time, Claire. And she's such a liar, even *this* could be a flyin' goose chase."

Claire clucked sympathetically as I ranted, then raised the heat by reminding me about the last big case we'd worked together. Pete Gordon, a bona fide psycho killer, had murdered four young moms and five little kids a few months ago in a murder spree that had torn me and Claire to pieces.

I went to the bathroom, sat on the rust-stained throne, and got some major weeping out of my system. Then I washed my face, came out, and said to Claire, "I've got the check. Let's go, butterfly."

We were back on the road again by a quarter past two. About two hundred miles north of San Francisco, the freeway crossed a section of Shasta Lake.

For the first time in a week, I stopped thinking of babies. The sight of pink-and-yellow sandstone banks rising from the impossibly vivid bands of sea-green and peacock-blue water simply blew everything else out of my mind.

And then sightseeing was over. Surely we would find Avis's baby boy. Surely we would.

We pulled into Taylor Creek at 5 p.m.

It's a one-traffic-light town, a typical small town in the great northwest. Main Street was a row of western facades from the late 1800s. Brick buildings that were once banks or warehouses now housed boutiques and small storefront businesses.

Cars crawled along the main drag. Streetlights and headlights came on as the sunlight faded to a streak of pink.

"I want to drive by Antoinette Burgess's house," I said to Claire. "Get a fix on the place."

The disembodied voice of the GPS guided us to Clark Lane, a narrow, tree-lined street with a sign reading DEAD END. Green picket fences edged the front yards, and behind the fences was an assortment of homes from different decades— Victorians, ramblers, Craftsmans, and ranches.

The house belonging to Antoinette Burgess was a cedar-shingled A-frame with a wraparound deck and a satellite dish on the roof. I saw no lights on inside the house and no car in the driveway.

I parked the Explorer on a pile of fallen leaves at the curb, and Claire observed, "Looks like no one's home, Lindsay."

I thought, *Excellent opportunity to poke around.*

I turned off the headlights and said, "Be right back," and got out of the car.

Chapter 75

THE FRONT YARD was unkempt; the grass hadn't been mown, and the leaves hadn't been raked. To my right, a weedy gravel driveway flowed past the house to an open, freestanding two-car garage.

I flicked on my flashlight and proceeded down the driveway, the pea stone and dry leaves crunching loudly underfoot.

The garage smelled of motor oil, and there was grease on the floor. I flicked my light across a rowboat in the rafters, stacks of plastic tubs, and cartons of what looked like motorcycle parts: sprockets, valves, and brake shoes.

There was nothing of interest here.

I left the garage and headed toward the back

of the house. Flashing my beam through the multipane windows. I could make out worn furniture, a woodstove, and a baby's car seat on the kitchen table.

My eyes fixed on the car seat. It was blue and it was empty. My heart rate jacked up another twenty beats a minute as I put my hand on the doorknob and twisted.

The door was unlocked—but a half second before I pushed the door open, I saw a tiny red flashing light reflected in the microwave door across the room.

Burgess had an alarm system, and the house was armed.

I let go of the doorknob, and at that moment, I heard the distant sputtering and roar of motorcycles, a sound that got louder the closer it got to Antoinette Burgess's house.

The bikes were coming to this house, I was sure of it. I had to get out of here.

I turned off my flashlight and retraced my steps by the waning glow of twilight. Claire buzzed down the window and called out to me, "You hear that, Linds?"

"Couldn't miss it," I said.

I pulled myself up into the driver's seat and started the engine as a stream of seven or eight single headlights drew closer.

My wheels whinnied as I jammed on the gas, spun out, and left the curb in a sharp U-turn.

"That was smooth. You think anyone could possibly have noticed us?" Claire asked as she gripped the dash.

"Hey, that's me. Subtle as a jackhammer."

We passed the motorcycle cavalcade coming toward us and I continued up the street with my eyes on the rearview mirror. Bikes wheeled up to the Burgess house and turned down the driveway toward the garage.

Was Antoinette Burgess in that motorcade?

Where was the baby?

I glanced back at the mirror and saw the silhouette of a biker who had stopped at the entrance to the Burgess driveway. The bike was still there and the biker was still astride it as I took the next right turn and sped away.

Crap.

It looked like someone had taken down my plate number.

Chapter 76

THE HOTEL CLEARWATER was a faded blue two-story Victorian facing Main Street, with a second-floor exterior balcony supported by columns. It looked right out of the Wild West or maybe a movie featuring Sundance and Butch.

Claire and I entered the lobby, which hadn't seen any changes since the 1920s. I took in the Victorian flock wallpaper, satin-covered armchairs, and sepia photographs of long-dead people in ornate frames on the walls.

The man behind the desk was also a relic of earlier times. Not from another century, but definitely from another time. His thinning gray ponytail and frameless specs made me think the hotel had been named for Creedence Clearwater

Revival, a band I liked from the '70s.

I signed the register and credit-card receipt and collected the keys. As Claire called home, the desk clerk told me his name was Buck Keene and that he owned the place.

We chatted about the weather and the local restaurants, and then I said, "I'm trying to look someone up. Maybe you know her? Antoinette Burgess?"

"Everyone knows everyone here. Sure, I know Toni. She's the president of Devil Girlz — with a *z*. It's a motorcycle club, girls only. They mainly work as bouncers for one of the saloons in Winchester."

"She has a friend — Sandy someone?"

The man with the gray ponytail jerked back as if he'd said too much or I'd put ammonia under his nose.

"You're a cop," he said. "I should have figured as much." He opened a drawer to show me his sheriff's badge, and I showed him my shield.

"Is Toni in trouble?" Keene asked.

"Not at all. I just want to talk with her about an ongoing investigation."

"Then find another source," Keene told me.

"She's had a rough time, but she's clean. Getting her life straightened out. Being questioned by the cops…" Keene shook his head. "Checkout is at noon tomorrow."

The bathtub in my room had claw feet. The towel rack was brass, and there was a basket of toiletries on the pedestal sink. I ran the hot water, poured some bath salts into the tub, and called Conklin.

"Antoinette Burgess is in a motorcycle gang called Devil Girlz," I told him. "Outlaw type, I'm guessing."

Conklin said, "Hold on," and did a Web search while I tested the water temperature and pinned up my hair.

"I'm finding some stuff on these Girlz," Conklin told me. "Drugs. Weapon trade. They aren't Avon ladies, Linds. Watch your ass."

"I'm walking on tippy-toes," I said. "Rich. I saw evidence of a baby in the Burgess house. A baby car seat on the kitchen table. Blue one."

"*No kidding.* Yeah?"

"Yeah. Do me a favor and tell Brady."

Joe picked up my call on the first ring. I stepped into the tub, lowered myself slowly, and sighed as the hot water covered my shoulders.

"What's it like there?" Joe asked me.

"Sweet little town," I told him. "Imagine *Northern Exposure* crossed with *The Twilight Zone*."

"Be careful, Blondie."

Second guy in under ten minutes telling me to be careful. Jeez, I've been a cop for a decade.

"I've got a badge and a gun," I said to my husband.

"I don't like the way you sound."

"How do I sound?"

"Blasé. In a completely detached kind of way."

"I've been driving all day."

"Call for help if you need it. Promise me."

"I promise. Now, give me a kiss."

After I got out of the tub, I used the house phone and called the sheriff downstairs at the front desk.

"Sheriff Keene. Got a minute? I want to tell you about this case I'm working."

Chapter 77

AT JUST AFTER EIGHT in the morning, I turned the Explorer onto Clark Lane and headed south.

"Look at that," Claire said.

A thick knot of bikers filled the street—headlights on, engines revving—forming a wall between us and the Burgess house. As we closed in, the knot tightened, and the bikers showed no sign of parting to let us pass.

My plan had been to knock on Toni Burgess's door. Show her my badge. I imagined going inside that house and getting the baby out. I hadn't counted on a rumble. Freakin' Buck Keene must've given Toni Burgess a heads-up.

"What now, Kemo Sabe?" Claire said.

"We're winging it, Tonto," I said. "Going to rely on what I've been told is a lot of charm."

I braked fifteen yards from the bikers, close enough to clearly see their mannish haircuts and grungy clothes, their chains looped over their shoulders and around their waists, and their tattoos down to their fingernails.

I told Claire to lock the doors after I got out and to keep her cell phone in hand.

The moment I stepped out of the Explorer, there was no turning back. I was committed to gaining entrance to the cedar-shingled house. I made a path in my mind, saw myself sidestep the leader of the pack, walk through the gate, and approach the front door.

The biker in the lead position gunned her engine, then shut off the motor and dismounted. She closed the distance between us and stood her ground.

She looked to be in her late forties and about my height, five foot ten, but she had fifty pounds on me. Her blond-gray hair was greased back, she had gaps in her phony grin, and her nose was angled toward the right side of her face.

The patch over the breast pocket of her jacket

read "Toni." *This* was Antoinette Burgess? Not your typical suburban mom.

"What do you want?" she asked me.

My hands were sweating. There were a dozen ways this could go wrong. Devil Girlz trafficked in guns. I pulled the front panels of my jacket aside, showed her the Glock on my hip and the gold badge on my belt.

"Sergeant Lindsay Boxer, SFPD. I'm here about the baby."

"I don't know what you're talking about," the biker said.

That's when a baby's piercing wail came from inside the house. I looked up and saw the backlit form of a woman standing at the front window with a bundle in her arms.

I turned around, went back to the Explorer and, when the lock thunked open, got inside and asked Claire for the phone.

I had Buck Keene's number on my speed dial.

"Sheriff Keene, this is Sergeant Boxer. I need assistance on Clark Lane. If you're not here in five minutes, I'm calling the FBI. They'll take down anything or anybody who gets between them and that kidnapped baby."

Chapter 78

THREE GREEN-AND-WHITE PATROL CARS screamed up Clark Lane in the dim light of morning and braked on the verge. Sheriff Buck Keene got out of the first car, wearing a cowboy hat and a dun-colored jacket with fringe along the sleeve seams and a badge on the breast pocket. He had a rifle in his arms.

"Girls, break it up. Let's keep things simple, okay?"

There was some hooting and wisecracking. "What did you say? 'Keep it simple, stupid'? Who're you calling stupid?" someone called out.

But the Devil Girlz moved their bikes out of the way and made a narrow pathway through their ranks for Sheriff Keene.

Toni Burgess, Claire, and I drafted behind the sheriff, through the weed garden, along the fieldstone path, and up the creaking steps to the deck and the front door.

Keene knocked and called out, "Sandy, open up. It's Buck."

The door cracked open.

A woman's voice said, "Go away, Buck. We're not hurting anyone."

I said, "Sandy, I'm Sergeant Lindsay Boxer, and this is Dr. Claire Washburn, SFPD. We just want to talk to you."

"Call me on the phone if you just want to talk to me."

"We want to see the baby," Claire said. "Make sure he's okay."

Sheriff Keene shouted at the door. "What is this, Sandy? What have you girls done?"

"We haven't done anything wrong, Buck. Just back off. Unless someone has a warrant, get off our property."

"You can't send law enforcement away. You're making a mistake, Sandy," Keene said.

"Someone is. Go away. Don't make me say this again. You're trespassing."

I'd had enough of this. I took a half step back, then put my shoulder to the door and rammed it wide open. Claire and the sheriff barreled into the house after me.

"Subtle," Claire muttered.

"As a jackhammer," I reminded Claire, and that's when I saw the woman who had been standing behind the door. She was wearing coveralls and a long-sleeved pink T-shirt. Her face was pretty and her hair was long and brushed to a shine. She looked to be in her late twenties or early thirties.

She had a baby under a blue blanket over her left shoulder. It was a wriggling newborn.

Was this Avis Richardson's baby?

All I knew for sure was that he was *alive*.

And then I noticed that Sandy had a 9-millimeter handgun pointed right at my head. And from the look on her face, I knew she wouldn't hesitate to use it.

Chapter 79

"BUCK, GET THE HELL OUT of here!" Sandy shouted.

"I'm not leaving," he said, "until you put down that gun and tell me what the hell is going on. That *is* your baby, right, Sandy? You *were* pregnant. I saw you—"

"Aw, geez, Buck. Don't ask, don't tell. You ever heard of that?" said the girl with the baby over her shoulder.

"What are you saying? You were lying to everyone? You were faking your pregnancy? Toni? Jesus Christ. How could you two do that?"

Sandy put the barrel of the gun underneath her chin. "I don't want to talk about this anymore.

All of you. Get out. I'm not kidding," she said. "And I'm not lying either."

The blood left my face. Coffee climbed into my throat.

"Sandy," Keene said. "We'll help you. This isn't the way."

"It's *my* way. Now, get out, get out, *get out!*" she shouted.

The baby was crying now, real hearty wails.

My mouth went dry. So many ways for this to go wrong and I never even imagined it *this* way. I said, "You're not in trouble, Sandy. We just want to talk about the situation. Buck, let us have some privacy. Please."

"Toni, talk some sense into her, damn it," the sheriff said to the woman in the biker's leathers. "I'll be waiting outside."

As the sheriff left the house, I said to Sandy, "I'm putting my gun down." I reached under my jacket, extracted my Glock with two fingers, and put it on the floor.

Toni Burgess scooped up my weapon and walked across the open room, chains clanking. She put my gun in the garbage can under the sink and closed the cabinet doors.

Sandy dropped her gun into her coveralls pocket, then hugged the baby with both arms.

I let out a breath I'd been holding for far too long and looked around. I saw baby bottles on the counter, baby toys on a sheepskin rug on the floor. Pictures of the baby were stuck all over the fridge.

Sandy jounced the baby against her shoulder and patted his back, but he kept crying.

"My name is Sandra Wilson," she said. "And this is my son, Tyler Burgess Wilson. I'm his mother now. I answered Avis Richardson's ad in Prattslist, and I paid her twenty-five thousand dollars as reimbursement for her expenses in carrying and bearing the baby. And she signed the papers. It's all legal. You make sure to tell Avis that it's too late to change her mind."

"Avis ran the ad?"

"She sure did. I can show it to you. After Avis said she wanted us to have the baby, we wired the money into her bank account. Now, listen to me. We love Tyler and we're not giving him up. This little boy is ours."

Chapter 80

CLAIRE SAID, "I'm a doctor, honey. And I have a baby not much older than Tyler. Could I just take a quick look at him? Please?" She reached out her arms toward the baby in Sandy Wilson's arms.

"I can't get him to eat," Sandy said in a voice that suddenly cracked with emotion.

Claire hugged the girl and said, "It's okay. It's okay." Then she tugged the baby out of Sandy's arms and took him to the kitchen table. "Got some baby wipes and a clean diaper?" she asked, her voice as calm as if we weren't under the gun.

I was at Claire's side as she unwrapped the baby, and I could see that he was brown-eyed and pink all over and that he had all his parts, plus a little port-wine stain on the back of his hand.

I reached out and touched his little palm. He kicked his legs and let out a fresh new wail.

While Claire cleaned and inspected the baby, Toni Burgess disappeared. She returned a minute later with the ad from Prattslist and a sheet of paper in her shaking hands.

"Sergeant, I want you to see this so you can leave us in peace and tell Buck to go home."

"You go ahead and read it. I'm listening," I said.

"*I, Avis Richardson, being of lawful age and sound mind, do give my unnamed son to Sandra Wilson and Antoinette Burgess, who have paid me $25,000 for my expenses in bearing this child.*"

The ad was as Sandy described it. And the note was signed, dated, and witnessed by Antoinette Burgess and Sandra Wilson.

I sighed, and then I had to say it.

"Toni, the problem is, Avis Richardson is only fifteen years old."

"She's *eighteen*. She showed us her ID."

"She's a liar," I said. "And that's just the beginning."

"This is just *wrong*," Sandy said, collapsing into a kitchen chair and sobbing into her hands.

She was crying so hard, it was difficult to make out everything she said, but this much I got loud and clear: "We planned for him. We delivered him. We're giving him a loving home. Avis didn't want him. She had no love for him at all."

I went to Sandy and took her gun out of her coveralls pocket and ejected out the magazine.

She looked up at me, pleading. "Help us. What do we have to do to keep him?"

"You can't keep him, Sandy," I said, knowing that my words were like taking a hatchet to her heart. "This baby already has a family who wants him. I'm very sorry for your pain."

Chapter 81

OUR DEPARTURE from Clark Lane was excruciating; slow and tearful.

Cops, neighbors, and Devil Girlz crowded around the Explorer as Toni handed me a car seat and other things for the baby, and Sandy pushed papers into my hands.

"This letter is for Tyler to read when he's older," Sandy said. And she gave me her diary and a fat envelope of pictures documenting the baby's birth.

I put the photos in the door pocket, evidence that would do until Tyler's DNA was processed, and I set up the car seat in the backseat.

Claire fired up the ignition, and as soon as we cleared Taylor Creek, I reclined in the passenger seat and dozed, my eyes flashing open every few minutes over the next four hundred miles. I kept turning to look back at Tyler.

What was next for this baby?

Would he be okay?

As dusk blotted out sundown over Bryant Street, we pulled into the parking lot outside the Medical Examiner's Office. Conklin was standing next to his car, tossing his keys into the air, catching them, waiting for us to arrive.

He came over to the car, opened the back door, and stood speechless as he gazed down at the baby.

"This kid is adorable," he said. "So what's the plan?"

I unfolded my aching bones, got out of the Explorer, and said, "We're going to wait a few hours before calling Child Protective Services."

I hugged Claire good-bye, took Tyler and his car seat, and got into the squad car, Conklin behind the wheel. He said, "The last place Avis Richardson used her cell phone was Tijuana. She called her parents. That was twelve hours ago."

"Here's what I think," I said. "We introduce the baby to the Richardsons. Tell them to call

Avis's phone. Even if they just leave a message, that's fine. They just need to say, 'We got your baby back.'

"We put a trap on their phone line," I said. "And we take the baby to St. Francis. We have undercover work in neonatal until Avis comes to see the baby. We put another team at the hotel."

"And if she doesn't show?"

"I'll think of something else. You can bet I will."

"Works for me," said Conklin.

Chapter 82

SONJA AND PAUL RICHARDSON were waiting in the hallway outside their suite, shades of hope, expectation, and praise-the-Lord lighting their faces.

They ran toward us as we got off the elevator, and I braced for the imminent shock of separating from the baby.

I clutched the little boy as I told Sonja that by law we had to take him to the hospital, and the legal system would dictate what happened to him after that.

"But I knew you would want to see him first," I said and handed the child to his grandmother.

It was a beautiful moment.

Sonja's pretty face shone with tears as she

held him. Her husband curved a protective arm around her shoulders and put a hand on his grandson's chest. Sonja looked up at me and said, "Thank you so much for finding him."

"This is a great day," Paul said. "A great day."

Back in the suite, we all sat down for a serious conversation.

"Sonja, Paul," I said. "Avis has to come in. Avis was the one who placed the ad on Prattslist. We have a copy of the ad. She wasn't solicited. She put the baby up for sale and was paid twenty-five thousand dollars. That's child trafficking. We have a copy of the contract she signed."

Conklin said, "Avis is in Mexico, and that means that she'll be deported when she's caught. If Ritter is with her, he's guilty of transporting a minor across international lines. He's in enough trouble to keep a platoon of lawyers busy for years."

"But because Avis is a minor," I said, "if she comes in on her own, we can try to protect her. We'll work with the DA to get her into the juvenile offenders system. But if she's deported from Mexico...," I said with a shrug. "Trust me. You don't want her to be tried as an adult."

A look passed between husband and wife.

Paul Richardson sighed deeply.

"Avis is in the bedroom," he said. "Actually, Jordan is in there, too."

Chapter 83

I SAID to the Richardsons, "Please take the baby to the kitchen. Lie down with him on the floor. Go. Now."

The Richardsons looked startled, but they did as I said.

I pulled my gun, Rich pulled his, and we flanked the door to the bedroom.

I shouted, "Avis Richardson. Jordan Ritter, this is Sergeant Boxer. It's all over. Come out with your hands up."

There was silence, but before Rich could kick in the door, we heard Ritter's voice.

"Sergeant. We don't have any weapons."

The door opened and Ritter came out with his hands up. He hadn't shaved and his cheeks were sunburned. Even so, he still looked like an ad for an upscale men's clothing line.

Rich spun Ritter around and flattened him against the wall. He frisked him and was cuffing him as Avis darted out of the bedroom.

Avis had her hands up, too, but she was wiggling one of her fingers to draw my attention to a shiny gold band.

"We got married," she cried. "Jordan and I got married."

"Congratulations," I said as I threw her against the wall with great satisfaction.

Once again, in my heart I wanted to slap this girl. Instead I cuffed her and said, "Avis Richardson, you're under arrest for child trafficking, neglect of a child, and obstruction of justice. You have the right to remain silent..."

Suddenly a desperate kind of mayhem broke out around me.

Sonja and Paul Richardson swarmed around their daughter, and the baby wailed, then drew a breath and wailed some more.

To my left, Conklin arrested Jordan Ritter for kidnapping and statutory rape. Ritter was yelling, "I want to see my son," as Conklin read him his rights.

I stuck my face three inches from Ritter's nose. *"Shut the fuck up,"* I said.

Next I called for an ambulance for the baby.

"What's going to happen to Avis?" Paul Richardson asked me as I took the baby out of his wife's arms.

"She'll be booked and kept in holding until her arraignment," I said. "If you want my advice, hire the best attorney you can buy. Maybe he'll get her tried as a juvenile. I'd also make a few calls and get your daughter's marriage to this sleazebag annulled."

WOMEN'S MURDER CLUB

Book Four

THE HEARTBREAK KID

Chapter 84

MY EYELIDS FLEW OPEN. I stared up at the information that Joe's projection clock flashed onto the ceiling. It was October 11. Fifty-four degrees. 6:02 a.m.

I had been in midthought when I'd woken myself up, but what had I been thinking?

Joe stirred beside me and said, "Linds. You up?"

"Sorry to wake you, hon. I was dreaming. I think."

He turned toward me and enfolded me in his arms. "You remember the dream?"

I tried to backtrack, but the dream was gone. What was worrying me? Joe was safe. The Richardson baby was at St. Francis, perfectly well. Then I had it.

Candace Martin.

I was thinking about *her*.

I started to tell Joe why Candace Martin was surfing my nocturnal brain waves, but he was already snoring softly against my shoulder. I disengaged myself and put my feet on the floor.

Joe murmured, "What?"

"I've got to go to work," I said. "I'll call you later."

I kissed his cheek, ruffled his hair, and tucked the covers under his chin. I snapped my fingers and Martha jumped onto the bed. She circled a couple of times, then dropped into the hollow I'd left behind.

Less than an hour later, I blew into the Hall of Justice with two containers of coffee.

I took the back stairs two steps at a time, and elbowed open the stairwell door to the eighth floor. I negotiated the maze of corridors that led to the DA's department.

Yuki was at her desk in a windowless office. Her glossy black hair, parted in the middle, fell forward as she stared down at her laptop. My shadow crossed her desk.

"Hey," she said, looking up. "Lindsay. What's wrong?"

"Something is. Okay for me to see the picture of Candace Martin in the car with that hit man Gregor Guzman?"

"Why?"

She stretched her arm across her desk and took a coffee container from my hand. "You don't mind if I ask why you're still messing around with my case, do you?"

"Could I just see it again, Yuki? Please. That photo is bothering me."

Yuki glared at me, bent toward her laptop, and tapped a few keys. She swiveled the computer around so that I could see the screen.

"I could use a copy of that."

Yuki shook her head no. But at the same time, the printer made a grinding sound, and a black-and-white photo chugged into the tray. Yuki handed it to me.

"I'd give you a harder time," she said, "but the judge wants to see me in chambers. I'm in the bad-girl corner again. Don't make trouble for me, Lindsay. I mean it."

I wished her luck with LaVan and ran for the exit before Yuki could change her mind.

Chapter 85

MINUTES AFTER LEAVING Yuki's office, I signed the visitor's log at the entrance to the women's jail on the seventh floor. It was loud in this wing. The clanging of metal doors and the angry clamor of prisoners rose up around us as an officer escorted me to one of the small, bare conference rooms.

Candace Martin soon appeared in the doorway. She made eye contact with me as the guard removed her cuffs, then took the chair across from me at the scarred metal table.

"This is an unexpected surprise," she said.

Candace didn't have any makeup on, hadn't had her hair done professionally in a year, and was wearing a prison jumpsuit in a shade of orange that didn't flatter blondes.

Still, Candace Martin had her dignity and her professional demeanor.

I said, "I'm here unofficially."

"With good news, I hope."

I pulled the printout of the photo from my pocket and placed it faceup on the table. "Please look at this picture and tell me why you're inside this vehicle with this man."

She said, "I've seen that picture. That's not me."

The overhead light cast three hundred watts of bright white fluorescence, lighting every part of the small room. The red eye of a security camera watched from a corner of the ceiling as the woman in orange slid the photo closer and picked it up.

"I don't know *either* of these people," she said. Then, as though she had been struck with an afterthought, she studied the photo intently again and asked me, "What do you see in this woman's hand?"

She pushed the grainy black-and-white printout back across the table. The woman in the picture had her head tipped forward, her blond hair covering half her face, and she seemed to be clutching a chain that was fastened around her neck. I saw the glint of a pendant dangling from her clasped fingers.

"Maybe some kind of charm," I said.

"Could it be a cross?" Candace Martin asked me.

"I suppose."

"I don't wear thin gold chains with charms or crosses," Candace Martin said to me. "But you know Ellen Lafferty, don't you? Ellen always wears a cross. I've got to say, I wonder what it means to her."

Chapter 86

CANDACE MARTIN was due back in court in an hour, and if my belief in her innocence was warranted, I couldn't "mess around" with Yuki's case fast enough. Every day that Candace was on trial, she was a day closer to being convicted of murder in the first degree.

As hard as it would be to convince the court that the wrong person was on trial, it would be a snap compared with getting a murder conviction overturned.

I jogged down the Hall's back stairs to the lobby, thumbed a number into my cell phone, and waited for private investigator Joseph Podesta to pick up. His voice was thick with sleep, but he said, "Aw-right," to my request to see him in twenty minutes.

I crossed the Bay Bridge, drove to Lafayette, and found Podesta's yellow suburban ranch on Hamlin Road, a street lined with a mix of trees and similar ranch-style houses. I parked my car in his driveway, then walked up some stone steps through a rock garden and rang the bell.

Podesta came to the door barefoot, wearing a sweat suit with a sprinkling of bread crumbs on the front. I showed him my badge and he opened the door wide and led me to his home office at the back of the house.

I looked around at the warehouse of spy equipment Podesta had stored on his metal bookshelves. He wheeled his chair up to his computer, lifted an old tabby cat down from his desk, and put her on his lap.

"If my client wasn't dead," he said, palming the mouse, "I wouldn't show these to you without a warrant."

"I appreciate your help," I said.

Podesta clicked on the folder containing the digital photos he'd taken of Candace Martin in a car with someone who had been tentatively identified as Gregor Guzman, a contract killer who was wanted by cops in several states and a few foreign countries as well.

The first photo Podesta pulled up on his screen was the one Yuki had offered into evidence.

"I know these photos suck eggs," he said. "But I couldn't use the flash, you know? I can't swear that's Guzman, but that woman *is* Candace Martin. I followed her that night from her house on Monterey Boulevard right to the I-280 on-ramp north. She got off on Cesar Chavez, took a right on Third and then onto Davidson. I was on her tail the whole time.

"It's a very dodgy place. I'm sure you know it, Sergeant. I had to watch out for myself. It's a trash heap. A junkyard. I could have gotten mugged, and she could have, too.

"I watched her get out of her Lincoln and get into this guy's SUV. Ten minutes later, she got out."

"Can you burn those pictures onto a disc for me?"

"Why not, under the circumstances?" he said.

The computer whirred.

The cat purred.

And pretty soon I had a disc with a lot of grainy pictures taken a couple of weeks before Dennis Martin was killed.

Chapter 87

AT NINE-FIFTEEN I was back at the Hall of Justice, Southern Station, Homicide Division, my home away from home.

I hung my jacket on the back of my chair, then found Conklin in the break room. He was eating a doughnut over the sink, his yellow tie flipped over his shoulder.

"Yo," he said. "I saved you one."

"I'm not hungry. But I do have something to show you."

"You're being awfully mysterious."

"It's better to show than tell."

Chi was working at his desk, his computer humming, his coffee mug on a napkin, and about thirty pens lined up with the top edge of his mouse pad.

I handed Chi the disc Joe Podesta had given me and said, "You mind, Paul? I want you to see these, too."

The three of us focused on one frame at a time as the dozen digital shots PI Joseph Podesta had taken of a blond woman in profile, sitting with a possible hit man in his SUV, came up on the screen.

Conklin asked Chi to enlarge the best of them and to push in on the female subject's fist to see if she could be holding on tight to a gold cross. But the more Chi blew up the picture, the fuzzier it became.

"That's the best I can do," Chi said, staring at the abstract arrangement of gray dots. "What are your thoughts?"

"Run it through the face ID program," Conklin said to Chi.

"Face ID, coming up."

Chi opened the program, and two windows came up on his monitor, comparing Candace Martin's mug shot with the grainy shot of the blond woman in the car.

Chi turned to look at me and Conklin, a spark of excitement sailing briefly across his face like a shooting star. "It's not her," said Chi. "Whoever the woman is in this picture—it's not Candace Martin."

Chi then compared the grainy-pictured blonde against a database of tens of thousands of photos at blur speed.

And just as I was beginning to lose hope, we got a match.

Chapter 88

CONKLIN AND I got into an unmarked car and were soon speeding up the James Lick Freeway. As Conklin drove, I ticked off on my fingers the reasons I liked Ellen Lafferty for Dennis Martin's murder.

"One, she was in love with him. Two, she was frustrated by him. Three, she had access to his gun. She knew where he would be and where Candace would be at the end of the day.

"That's four and five. And six, if she didn't do it, she could have ordered the hit."

"All that," Conklin said, "and she's smart enough to frame Candace."

"She must be a frickin' evil genius," I said.

Fifteen minutes later, Conklin parked the car

in front of a pale yellow marina-style apartment building. Built in the '20s, it was a tidy-looking place with bowed windows facing Ulloa Street. It was about a mile from the Martins' house.

I pressed the buzzer and Lafferty called out, "Who is it?" And then she opened the door.

Conklin said "SFPD," flashed his shield, and introduced us to the twenty-something nanny, who hesitated a couple of beats before she let us in.

I had watched Lafferty's testimony from the back of the courtroom a few days ago. She'd looked quite mature in a suit and heels. Today, wearing jeans and a white turtleneck, her auburn hair pulled back in a ponytail, she looked like a teenager.

Conklin said yes to Lafferty's offer of coffee, but I lingered behind in the living room as the Martins' former nanny walked Conklin to the kitchen.

In one visual sweep, I counted five pictures of Dennis Martin in that small room, some of them with Lafferty. Martin was handsome from every angle.

I raised my eyes as Ellen Lafferty returned to

the living area with Conklin. She looked happier to see me than she could possibly be. She took a seat in an armchair and said, "I thought the investigation was closed."

I said, "There are a few stubborn loose ends. Well, one loose end."

I pulled the photo from my inside jacket pocket and put it down on the coffee table.

Ellen reached over to pick it up and said, "What is this?"

"That man may be a contract killer by the name of Gregor Guzman. The woman in this picture looks like Candace Martin," I said. "She's got the same blond hair, same cut as Candace—but it's not actually her, is it, Ellen?"

"It's hard to tell. I don't know," she said.

"You know how we know it isn't Candace?" Conklin said. "Because when we ran that photo through forensic software, it matched your picture from the DMV. The woman in this picture is you."

Conklin went to the mantel and picked up a gold-framed photo of Ellen and Dennis Martin on a sailboat out in the Bay.

"No," she said, getting up to snatch the picture

out of Conklin's hand. "You can't have that."

I said to her, "I think Judge LaVan will give us a search warrant to go through everything in your house. Meanwhile, we need to continue this talk at the police station."

I pulled out my phone and was calling for a patrol car, but Ellen said, "Wait. I'll tell you what you want to know."

I closed my phone and gave her my full attention.

Chapter 89

IF ELLEN LAFFERTY didn't try to hire a killer, why was she in that car with Gregor Guzman? I couldn't wait to hear her explanation.

"I didn't do anything wrong, certainly nothing *criminal*," Lafferty said. She reached into the neck of her sweater and pulled out a small gold cross on a thin chain. She kept yanking it from side to side, a nervous habit — and a telling one.

"Dennis sent me to meet this 'Mr. G.' in the parking lot of Vons," she said. "He gave me an envelope of money to give to this Mr. G., but when he opened it, he handed it back to me and said, 'Tell Mr. Martin thanks but no thanks.'"

"This Mr. G. gave back the money," Rich said.

Ellen nodded.

"So, you're saying you met with a man you didn't know because Dennis told you to do it. You gave him money—which he gave back to you, and you didn't know why you were there. Is that your story?"

"I didn't know he was an *assassin* until after the trial started and I read about him online. I was just a messenger. This is one hundred percent true."

"You're not in any trouble," Conklin said. "We're trying to piece some facts together."

"So, tell us about the blond hair," I said.

"It was a wig," Ellen blurted out. "It belonged to Candace when she was having chemo. She threw it out and I took it. Dennis liked me to wear it sometimes. Do you want to see it?"

Ellen Lafferty headed down a hallway toward the bedroom.

"You really think this girl hired a hit man?" Conklin asked me.

"I don't know. I know less now than I did when I woke up this morning."

I picked up the sunset-lit, highly romantic photo of Ellen and Dennis Martin and ran it all through my mind again.

Had Ellen hired Guzman to kill Dennis? Was Ellen the intruder, and had she killed Dennis herself? Did Dennis set up the meet between Ellen and Guzman so that his private eye could document a Candace look-alike meeting with a hit man?

If so, had Candace killed her husband before he could kill *her*?

As I was turning over the possibilities yet again, Ellen came back into the room holding a black satin bag. She opened the drawstrings and shook out a blond wig.

"Mostly I just wore this when we made love," she said.

I couldn't hold back.

"Help me to understand you, Ellen," I said. "Your lover liked you to wear his wife's wig in bed? Didn't you find that sick?"

Tears jumped to her eyes.

I muttered, "Crap," under my breath. Was I ever going to learn to be the good cop? Conklin took the bag and said to Lafferty, "We need you to come to the station, okay, Ellen?"

"But—you're not arresting me, right?"

Conklin said. "We want your signed statement to what you just told us."

I hung back as Conklin walked Ellen out to the street. I called Yuki but got her voice mail.

I waited out the beeps, then said, "Yuki, I need a search warrant for Ellen Lafferty's premises. Yes, we've got probable cause. Call me back ASAP. Uh—I think you're going to thank me for this."

I hoped I was right.

Chapter 90

YUKI SAT BESIDE PHIL, the two of them in matching leather chairs across from Judge LaVan's leather-topped desk. The room had been decorated in fox hunt–style: old prints of people in red coats on bay horses, and heavy wooden furniture against forest-green walls.

The judge's eyes were red behind his glasses, and he explained in the fewest possible words why he had been out for three days.

"My mother had lung cancer," he said. "She died. Badly."

He nodded his head as the two attorneys said that they were sorry for his loss. Then he cleared his throat and went on.

"I don't want any more of the crap that's been

going on in this trial. Ms. Castellano, you know how to ask a question without turning it into a summation. Mr. Hoffman, you know how to rein in your witnesses, so for God's sake, just do it."

Yuki wanted to object, but the judge was leaving no doubt about his intentions. He wanted the trial streamlined, and he wanted it over.

"Here are the new rules on objections," he said, as if he were reading her mind.

"If you have an objection, stand up. I'm a smart guy and I was a trial lawyer for twenty years. If I can't figure out why you are objecting, I will not acknowledge you. In that case—sit down.

"If I know why you are objecting, I will tell opposing counsel to knock it off. I don't expect to have to do that."

"Your Honor," Yuki and Hoffman said in unison.

"No theatrics. No drama. No stupid lawyer tricks. I will levy fines. I will find either or both of you in contempt. Do you understand me?"

Neither Phil nor Yuki answered.

"Good. I'll see you in court," said LaVan.

"This is a joke," Hoffman said to Yuki as they left Judge LaVan's chambers and walked down the hall toward the courtroom. "He can't tell us not to object."

"Apparently he can today," said Yuki.

Hoffman smiled at her and then said, "I've got a meeting. See you inside."

Chapter 91

PHIL HOFFMAN got to his well-shod feet, straightened his shoulders, and said, "The defense calls Caitlin Martin."

At that, Candace Martin leapt up and screamed in his face, "No! Don't you dare put my daughter on the stand! You have no right!"

LaVan slammed down his gavel and shouted, "Bailiff, please remove the defendant from the courtroom."

"Candace. Sit down," Hoffman said. "Your Honor, give me a word with my client, please."

"Mr. Hoffman, I'm fining you eight hundred dollars. If you'd prepared your client, this could have been avoided. *Bailiff!*"

After Candace Martin had been escorted

from the room, the judge called for order, and when the room had quieted into an expectant hush, he asked the jury to ignore the interruption.

He reminded the jurors that they were charged with weighing the evidence, not the commotion, and that they were to draw no conclusions based on his decision to remove the defendant.

Then he said, "Mr. Hoffman, present your witness."

Hoffman's expression was neutral as the eleven-year-old daughter of Candace and Dennis Martin stood by the stand, was sworn in by the clerk, and took the chair inside the witness box. She had to struggle to get into it, and her feet didn't quite touch the floor.

The judge turned toward the dark-haired girl in the flowered dress and blue cardigan, holding a matching handbag on her lap. He asked, "Ms. Martin, do you know the difference between a lie and the truth?"

"Yes, sir."

"If I said that I'm the president of the United States, would that be a lie or the truth?"

"It would be a lie, of course."

"Do you believe in God?"

Caitlin nodded.

"You have to say either yes or no. The clerk is typing what you say."

"Yes. I do. Believe in God."

"Okay. You understand that you have promised on God's word to tell the truth?"

"Yes, sir, I understand."

"Good. Thank you. Mr. Hoffman, please proceed."

"Thank you, Your Honor. Caitlin—okay if I call you Caitlin?"

"Sure, Mr. Hoffman."

Hoffman smiled. He had a nice smile. Nothing bad about it.

"Caitlin, I have to ask you some questions about the night your father was killed, okay?"

"Okay. Yes."

"Were you in the house when your father was shot?"

"Yes."

"Do you know who shot him?"

"Yes."

"Please tell the judge and the jury what you know."

"I did it," Caitlin Martin said. Her eyes darted to the judge and then back to her mother's attorney. "I killed my father. I had no choice."

Chapter 92

THE GALLERY EXPLODED in an uproar.

Jurors leaned forward, making remarks to one another, while reporters reached for their PDAs. Hoffman stood in the center of the well, his expression frozen, as if he'd just fired a gun himself.

Yuki wanted to rewind the last ten seconds and turn up the volume. Had Caitlin Martin just said that she killed her father?

It just couldn't be true.

Yuki shot to her feet, clutched her hands into fists, and kept her jaws so tightly clenched, they might as well have been wired shut. She'd been warned not to object, but she was screaming in her mind, *I object to this witness. I object to this — stagecraft. I object, I object, I object.*

"Counsel, approach. Both of you," LaVan snapped.

As the two attorneys came toward him, the judge swiveled his chair ninety degrees so that he would face the emergency exit rather than the witness and the jury.

Yuki and Hoffman stood at an angle to the bench and looked up at the judge.

LaVan said to Hoffman in a low voice that was thrumming with anger. "I take it that neither your client nor the prosecution knew that you were calling this child to the stand."

"I got a call from the young lady's maternal grandmother last night saying that Caitlin wanted to talk to me this morning. I met with Caitlin in the lobby of this building, Your Honor, right after our meeting with you. I knew nothing about her testimony until fifteen minutes ago."

"Your Honor," Yuki said, "this is an obvious ploy by the defense. Caitlin has either been coached, or she came up with this idea on her own. Either way, she is trying to save her mother's butt. And either way, she has created reasonable doubt in the minds of the jury."

LaVan said, "I'm calling a recess. I want to

see Caitlin in chambers. Don't either of you disappear. After I've talked to the child, I'll speak to the jurors.

"And after that, we can discuss the future of this trial."

Chapter 93

YUKI WAS in Len Parisi's office when her phone buzzed.

"Here we go," she said to her boss. She read the text out loud: "'Judge LaVan is ready for you in chambers.' What's your bottom-line advice, Len?"

Parisi hauled his bulk out of his chair, then opened the blinds on the Bryant Street side of the building. The light was translucent. Yuki couldn't see anything through the fog.

"You want to cross-examine the witness," Red Dog said. "It's the best and only thing you can do."

"What if she's telling the truth?"

"*Is* she telling the truth? What do you really think?"

"I think she's throwing herself under the bus. She's eleven. It's heroic, like in the movies. But it's a lie. I can shake her on the stand, but I don't know if I can do that and keep the jury on our side."

"It will be like walking a tightrope with diarrhea. But I have faith that you can do it."

Yuki walked out of Parisi's office and down the hall on autopilot. Phil Hoffman stood when she entered the judge's chambers, and after she took the seat she'd occupied only a couple of hours ago, he sat down.

LaVan had removed his robes and his tie and rolled up his shirtsleeves and was standing behind his desk. Yuki thought he was going to pace, but instead he reached down, picked up the metal trash can at his feet, two feet tall and eighteen inches in diameter. He raised it over his head and hurled it toward the far wall.

The trash can ricocheted against the edge of the liquor cabinet before taking out a framed picture of the judge with the governor.

After the explosion of glass and the echo of the racket died down, LaVan threw open the liquor cabinet doors and said, "Who wants a drink? I'm buying."

Hoffman said, "Scotch works for me."

"I'm fine," Yuki said, but she was not fine. Nothing in her experience had prepared her for a case that slid sideways every twenty minutes. Was she winning or losing? She had no idea.

The judge poured shots for himself and Hoffman, then retook his seat behind his desk.

"Phil, do you know the difference between a lie and the truth?"

"Yes, Your Honor. You are not the president of the United States."

"Did you have anything to do with shaping Caitlin Martin's testimony?"

"No. As I said, she talked to me at eight-forty-five this morning. She told me what happened. I bumped another witness I'd prepared who was suddenly irrelevant and decided I had to put Caitlin on the stand."

"I want to cross-examine her," Yuki said. "I have to discredit her testimony."

The judge said, "Hang on, Yuki. Let me tell you what Caitlin said in the half hour I just spent with her. This is for your benefit."

"Your Honor?"

"Caitlin told me that her father had been

molesting her. She was explicit. And I mean convincingly so. She knew where the gun was hidden. She saw an opportunity and she shot him."

"You believe her?" Yuki asked.

"I couldn't trip her up — and I tried. According to Caitlin, her mother heard the shots, found the girl holding the gun, and told her to wash up, go to her room, and never tell anyone what happened. Then, still according to Caitlin, her mother fired the gun outside the front door and called the police."

"Huh. Good story," said Yuki. "So, what made Caitlin decide to talk?"

"She said she wanted to tell the truth."

Hoffman leaned forward in his chair.

"Byron. Your Honor," he said. "We have an admission exonerating my client," he said. "I move to dismiss."

Chapter 94

YUKI STARED THROUGH the judge, her thoughts swirling in something that was pretty close to panic.

She didn't want a dismissal, not after all that she'd been through on this case, not when she believed she had the killer on trial. Dammit. If the judge dismissed the case, what then?

Was she going to go after the little girl? Would she really try to prosecute an eleven-year-old who was claiming incest and rape?

If so, based on what?

The only evidence against Caitlin was her testimony. No one had seen her shoot the gun. And even if Candace Martin did say that Caitlin was the shooter, the case was so fraught with reasonable doubt, the grand jury might not indict.

On the other hand, Yuki thought, if the judge didn't dismiss, Yuki would have to do that high-wire act Len had talked about. Turn that abused child into a liar. The jury would hate her for it, and if they believed Caitlin's story, Candace could walk free.

"Yuki. You want to say something?"

Yuki said, "Yes, I do, Your Honor. I certainly do. There is not a single shred of evidence to support Caitlin's testimony, and if her story *is* true, why is it coming out only now?"

Phil turned toward her and said, "Let's be logical, Yuki. There is more than enough reasonable doubt. We both know if the trial goes on, there's an excellent chance Candace will walk."

The judge said, "Let me make it easy for both of you. It comes down to this: Major new evidence has come in. I've decided to dismiss."

If LaVan dismissed, it was all over—forever. Candace couldn't even be tried again because it would be double jeopardy. Yuki suddenly saw an opening, a slim sliver of hope.

"I respectfully suggest that you not dismiss, Your Honor, but instead suspend the trial."

LaVan swiveled in his chair, pulling at his lower lip. The moment lasted for so long, Yuki thought she might scream.

"Okay," LaVan said. "I'll suspend the trial for sixty days. During that time, the defendant is free on bail. Yuki, go back to the DA and discuss this...mess. Really look at the downside of going forward. If you want to cross-examine Caitlin Martin, I'll go along with you.

"Otherwise, based on Caitlin's testimony, I'm going to call a mistrial. Okay? That should work for all parties. The ball's in your court until December tenth."

"Okay, Your Honor," Yuki said. "Thank you."

"You've got a lot to think about."

"I know."

LaVan pressed down the intercom button.

"Denise, bring my calendar. And call the clerk. I want to see the jurors again."

Chapter 95

I TRACKED YUKI DOWN and found her in her office, just where I'd seen her this morning, but she seemed smaller and paler now, like the air had been sucked out of her.

"Did you get my message?" I asked her.

"I just got out of the judge's chambers," she said. "I'm waiting for Red Dog to get back from lunch. How do I look?"

"You need some lipstick," I said.

She rummaged in her handbag.

"I went to see Ellen Lafferty," I said, and I waited for the explosion of anger that didn't come. Yuki found a tube of lip gloss and a mirror in her purse. I ventured on.

"Ellen Lafferty said she went to see Guzman.

That's her in the picture. She admitted it. And we also matched the picture to her photo at the DMV."

"She bleached her hair?" Yuki asked. Her hand was shaking as she applied the gloss.

"Candace Martin had a wig from when she was undergoing chemotherapy. Hey, Yuki, are you okay?"

"Go ahead," she said. She ran a brush through her hair. Sparks crackled.

"Dennis sent Ellen disguised as Candace to meet with the hit man and set it up so his private eye took pictures of her. He was probably going to use those pictures to force his wife's hand in the divorce—or maybe he was really going to set up a hit. We may never know. Look, I know you're mad at me, so just say it, okay? I can take it," I said.

Yuki said, "Caitlin Martin confessed to killing her father, and now either we take our chances with this jury or LaVan is calling a mistrial."

"Caitlin? Caitlin said she did it?"

Len Parisi came down the hallway and stuck his large head into Yuki's office.

"Hi, Lindsay. Yuki, I've got five minutes. Right now."

"Be right there," Yuki said.

She got to her feet and straightened her jacket. When she turned her eyes back on me, I saw that the fierce Yuki was back.

"Candace Martin killed her husband," she said to me. "Not Ellen Lafferty. Not Caitlin Martin. I know you don't think Candace did it, but I do, and I'm never going to have an opportunity to prove it. She's going to get away with it."

Was Yuki right?

Had I been chasing a flipping red herring?

I opened my mouth, but no words came out, and then Yuki was gone.

Chapter 96

AFTER WHAT WAS undeniably one of the worst days she had ever had as a prosecutor, Yuki left the Hall to go home. She had nearly reached the sidewalk when she heard Brady call out to her.

God. Not Brady. Not now.

Yuki turned and saw him coming down the steps toward her, his hair flying loose from that ponytail of his.

Very attractive man.

Yuki thought of what Lindsay had told her, that Brady was married, and dammit, she didn't want to go through another doomed relationship with another unavailable guy. She wanted stability, a home life...

"Yuki, I'm glad I caught you," Brady said, pulling up alongside her. "Have dinner with me?"

"Okay," she said.

Now they were at Town Hall in SoMa, the former Marine Electric Building, one of the best places around for casual dining with a sophisticated twist.

The interior was dark, with exposed brick, hardwood floors, and subdued lighting. Jackson Brady's hair seemed to draw light from the over-head starburst fixtures that had once hung in the ceiling of a theater in Spanish Harlem.

Yuki was having a margarita, a drink that she loved and that took her out of her misery—and, if she had more than one, out of her mind as well. If she'd ever earned a margarita, today was the day.

"A suspension of the case isn't the worst thing," Brady was saying. He was working on the Cajun shrimp appetizer along with his beer.

"No, it's not the worst thing," Yuki agreed, "but it's still a *disaster*. You know how many hours I put into that case?"

"Seven thousand?"

Yuki laughed. "Not seven thousand, but a

whole hell of a lot, and now it looks like that bitch is going to go free."

"Unless you find more evidence."

"Yeah. If we find more evidence, we can still try her with a new jury, but you know, the world turns, the files stack up, some other heinous piece of crap is caught, and we mount another case."

"I'll keep the Candace Martin file on my desk."

"Thanks, Jackson. Even if you don't mean it."

"I mean it."

"Now, tell me you don't lie, why don't you?"

"I lie sometimes."

Yuki laughed again. "Well, don't lie to me."

"Okay."

"I'm serious. I've been told that you're married. What's the story?"

"I'm still married."

"Fuck," Yuki said. "Waiter."

Brady took her arm out of the air. "I'm still married. But I hope not for long."

Yuki took a slug of her margarita, set the glass down, and as the waiter came by, said to him, "Could you take this drink away? Thanks." Then she said to Brady, "Tell me the whole story. I'm listening."

"You remember that shooting incident I told you about?" Brady asked her.

Yuki said, "You shot the guy who came up out of the crack between the bed and the wall holding a semiautomatic."

"Yeah. So Liz and I were already heading our separate ways, and that deal that went down—almost getting whacked, killing the guy, the IAB, the media on our lawn—all that tore it. Whatever thin connection we had left."

"Because you're a cop?"

"Yep. Because I'm a cop," he said. "She wouldn't be the first woman who said, 'I didn't sign up for this.' So after a year, we separated and I moved to San Fran. Alone. Divorce is pending. Pending on how much she can make me beg for it."

"You have kids?"

"Nope."

"Want any?"

"Maybe. I'm forty. But I'm not there yet. How about you?"

"I honestly don't know."

"We don't have to decide tonight," Brady said.

"Okay," Yuki said, laughing. This guy was funny. She liked him. A lot.

The waiter brought the buttermilk-fried chicken, a side of sautéed greens, and creamy-looking yams, and Yuki felt herself on the verge of coming back to life. She hadn't eaten all day.

Brady picked up his fork, paused with it in the air, and said, "I was going to tell you about Liz."

"I know."

"I was. And I want to ask you something."

Yuki had a forkful of chicken in her mouth. She was getting high from the chicken. She turned her eyes on Brady.

"Mmm-hmm?"

"Will you come home with me tonight?" Brady said.

Chapter 97

RAIN WAS IN THE FORECAST, but it came down only when Cindy was leaving her office for the day. She stood at the curb under her red umbrella, cold rain blowing up the skirt of her raincoat and soaking her new shoes.

She pulled a wad of tissues out of her pocket and caught the long, high-pitched, trumpeting *ahh-choooooooooo-ahh,* a sneeze that just about took off the top of her head.

It looked like every damn cab in the city was taken or off duty. Cindy phoned All-City, the cab company she used regularly, and after listening to background music and ads, she was told, "Sorry, please call back later."

Cindy sneezed again, damm it. Not only was

she fighting a cold, she was also half starving and now late for dinner at Susie's. She visualized the back room at Susie's, that haven of warmth — and the name Quick Express leapt into her mind.

She pictured the cab company she'd visited earlier in the week when she was working on the drug-and-rape story. Since then, there had been no reports of the serial rapist, and the story had taken a dive off the front page.

That was the good news and the bad.

Good that she'd scared off that psycho by turning the brights on him with her three-part, above-the-fold story.

Bad because he'd gone underground — and that meant he might never be caught.

Meanwhile, she had a connection in the taxi business. It was just before six. With luck, the dispatcher she'd met, Al Wysocki, would still be on duty. Maybe he'd do her a favor.

Cindy pulled the number up from her phone list and pressed *call*. The phone rang and a voice she recognized answered, "Quick Express Taxi and Limo."

"Al Wysocki?"

"This is Al."

"Al, it's Cindy Thomas from the *Chronicle*. I met you a few days ago while I was working on my story."

"Yep, I remember you. Blonde."

"That's me, Al, and I've got a problem. Could you send a cab to the *Chronicle*? I'm soaked to my skin and I'm late for dinner."

"No problem, Ms. Cindy. I'll have someone there in five."

Chapter 98

CINDY WAS DELIGHTED with herself. She described her raincoat and umbrella to Wysocki, folded her phone, put it in her pocket, and ducked back into the building, where she could see the traffic through the glass doors.

In five minutes, almost on the nose, a yellow Crown Vic pulled up and the window rolled down. She ran out to the street and immediately recognized the round face of the driver.

"Lady," he said with a grin. "You called a cab?"

"Al, I didn't mean *you* should come yourself, but thanks a ton. You're too nice."

Cindy closed her umbrella, reached for the door handle, and opened the back door.

"I was going off duty," Wysocki said as Cindy

settled into the backseat. "Happy to help you out. Hey. I gotta share this with someone who isn't going to get jealous. Where are we going?"

Cindy gave Al Susie's address, Jackson and Sansome, and leaned her umbrella against the door so the water would drip onto the mat.

"Share what?" Cindy asked, grabbing tissues from her pocket and blowing her nose.

"This is my lucky day," Al told her, stopping at the red light on 2nd. "I won the lottery."

"What?"

"Yeah, five hundred thousand dollars."

"Come onnnn. You're kidding me!"

"Seriously, I just kept playing my lucky numbers, and yahoo! — I won. I'm quitting tomorrow morning when I see the boss. This is Al Wysocki's last fare. I got a bottle of schnapps," he said. "Share a toast with me to my new life?"

"I don't know how that'll mix with Sudafed."

"Hey, just a sip. It'll do your cold good."

"Okay, then. Hit me," Cindy said. "You must be mind-boggled. Five hundred *grand!* So what are your plans?"

Wysocki opened the twist-off cap on the flask of high-octane spirits, poured Cindy a few ounces into a small plastic cup, and handed it to her through the partition.

"I'm going to buy a sailboat," he said. He clinked the bottle against her plastic cup.

"To your new life," she said.

"Thank you, Ms. Cindy. Yeah, I've been going to the boat shows for about eleven years. I know just the one I want."

Cindy smiled and said "What…kind of… boat?"

"I want to get a sailing yacht. Small one, hand-made, wooden hull," Al said, looking at Cindy in the rearview mirror as the light turned green. He said, "You okay, back there?"

"No…," she said slowly, casting her eyes toward Wysocki's mirrored reflection. What was wrong with her? She was having trouble focusing. "I…feel…"

Wysocki grinned.

"You should feel great," he said. "You were looking for me, missy. And now you've found me."

Chapter 99

CLAIRE AND I were at Susie's, all by ourselves, alone. First Yuki had blown us off, and now Cindy was a no-show; no show, no call, no nothing. Getting stood up by both of them had never happened before.

Claire said of Yuki, "Stop worrying yourself. That girl needs to get naked with a man every now and then. You know that, Lindsay. It's good for her."

"I don't have to like her getting naked with Jackson Brady, do I? I mean, come on. Of all the men in all the world, why him?"

Claire laughed. "A lot of girls would be clicking their heels to get naked with Brady."

"It messes with the chain of command."

"Anybody sleeps with anyone you know, it messes with the chain of command."

I wadded up a paper napkin and threw it at her. "Shut up," I said.

She batted it back. "You are so crazy," she said, still laughing.

I downed my Corona and said, "Let's order. Cindy can just catch up."

Claire agreed. Cindy had proven that she could start from behind, get down a half pitcher of beer and a steak, have dessert, and still be the first one across the finish line.

I signaled Lorraine to come over. She recited the specials, coconut shrimp and rum-sautéed chicken. We ordered the specials and more beer, and as soon as Lorraine left, Claire said, "You're not going to believe this one, Linds. It's right up there with my top ten most unbelievable cases. And it starts with a guy lying dead in the middle of the road."

"Hit and run?"

"It sure looked like a car accident," she said, "but there were no tire tracks, no bruising on the victim. A hat was lying a few yards from the body, a black baseball cap with an X on the back of it. And that's all we had. No witnesses. No surveillance tapes. Nothing except a dead body and a random baseball cap."

"Heart attack? Aneurysm?"

"Let me tell you, this guy was young, twenty-something. And he looked like he'd been laid out at a wake, only he was on the center line, stopping traffic," Claire said.

"So now I'm doing the post, looking over this young dude's perfect body. I do a full-body X-ray and find a twenty-two bullet behind his right eye. That gunshot wound was not visible, Lindsay."

"I'm not believing in invisible bullets, butterfly."

"It's like this. The round goes into the corner of the eye," Claire said, pointing to where one of her eyes met the bridge of her nose. "Eyeball moves away from the bullet, then closes up behind it so that you cannot see a sign of it."

"Huh. Interesting. So now you're saying it's a homicide."

"Yeah. Northern Station caught it, asked me to help."

"Did ballistics get a hit on the round?" I asked.

"Before we could get the bullet to the lab, we

got something better. At around the same time the roadkill dude took a slug to the eye, a liquor store owner was gunned down in an armed robbery.

"The liquor store surveillance tape shows the shooter is wearing tight black jeans and a black shirt and the exact same baseball cap as the one we found in the road. Black with an *X*," Claire said.

"So local cops know the liquor store shooter and ID him. His street name is Crank, and he's found at home, sleeping in his bed. Cops roust him and drag him into the station on the liquor store killing. Suddenly, Crank breaks down and then he starts to sing."

"Oh, yeah? And what was the name of the tune?"

"Called it, 'I shot the dude by accident, yo. I didn't mean to do it, yo.'"

"Come on," I said, laughing, digging into my chicken.

"I know, but this is *true*. Here's what happened in the missing middle of the story," Claire said. "There was a near-miss traffic accident.

"Crank is fleeing the liquor store homicide and cuts off this guy in a Honda Civic. Crank gets out to apologize to the Civic so the guy doesn't call the cops, and Civic says to Crank, 'You drive like a girl and you look like one, too.' I guess it was the worst thing he can think to say."

"Uh-oh."

"Yeah, how'd he know he was going to hit a nerve? So Crank whips his gun out of the back of his jeans and says, 'Well, this girl's packin',' and he shoots the guy."

"Oh, man."

"Yeah. Somewhere in that shooting, his hat falls off, the one that was caught on tape in the robbery. If Crank hadn't robbed that store, he would never have been caught for killing Civic."

"He didn't know his victim."

"Bingo. Total stranger calls him a girly man. Bang."

"And there you have an accidental shooting, yo."

"And he blames the victim..."

Claire's laugh cut off as she looked up at a spot right behind my shoulder. I turned, expecting to see Cindy. But it was Lorraine, coming to clear the table.

"You girls want coffee and dessert?" she asked.

"Hell, yes," I said. "We're eating for four."

Lorraine laughed and read off the dessert menu. I picked chocolate mud pie, and Claire went for a spiced-apple tart.

I called Cindy while we were drinking our coffee and left her a snarky message. I left another one when we paid the check, and then my cell phone battery died.

I don't know why, but I wasn't worried about Cindy.

I should have been. But I never saw it coming.

Chapter 100

I GOT HOME at eight-something that evening, left my wet shoes on the doormat, and went inside. Martha came wiggling up to me, her fur still damp, and I bent to hug her and got my face washed for me.

I called out to Joe, "Hey, sweetie, thanks for walking Martha."

I found him on the phone in the living room, teetering towers of papers stacked all around him. I heard him call the person on the phone "Bruno" and say something about containers, which meant he was talking to the director of Port of L.A. Security. This was Joe's freelance job that was supposed to last a month but had been his steady paycheck for the better part of a year.

Joe waved at me, and I waved back and headed to the shower: a six-head, low-flow, spa-type contraption that made me feel like royalty. I took some time in what I liked to call the car wash, lathered my hair with a lavender shampoo I love, and let my mind drift in the steam.

I toweled off with a man-size bath sheet and threw on my favorite pj's—blue flannel with clouds. Joe came in and hugged and kissed me and we got into it a little. Then Joe remembered and said, "Conklin called."

"When was that?"

"Just before you came in."

"Did he say what was up?"

"Nope. Just 'tell Lindsay to call' and 'can you believe the Niners, that dumb play in the last quarter?'"

I said, "I'd better call him."

Joe grabbed my ass and I smacked his. I wriggled out of his arms, saying, "Later, buddy."

I called Conklin from the bedside phone.

He picked up on the first ring. "Cin?"

"It's Lindsay," I said. "What's up?"

"I can't reach her," he said. "She's not picking up, not returning my calls."

I didn't like the sound of his voice. He was scared, and that scared me.

"She didn't show up to dinner, Rich. I called her a couple of times, left messages. Maybe her phone died. Did you try her at the office?"

"Yeah. I'll try her there again."

"Call me back."

I was hunting for my softy spa socks when Conklin called again.

"I got her voice mail, Linds. This isn't like Cindy. I called QT. I'm going over there."

"What are you thinking?" I asked him.

"I'm thinking this is probably unfounded panic on my part and she's going to be blistering mad. But what can I say? I love the girl."

"I'll see you at QT's," I said.

I took off my pj's and hung them on a hook on the back of the bathroom door.

Chapter 101

I'D BEEN TO Quentin Tazio's combination home and computer forensics lab many times, always when we were in a jam that required him to apply his skills in a strictly outside-the-box kind of a way.

His place is on Capp Street in the Mission, a former machine shop—squat, gray, two-story, and cement-faced with roll-up garage doors on the street level.

At nine-thirty at night, the streets were rockin' with people going in and out of taquerias, galleries, restaurants, and bars. Traffic was clogged and impatient. A drunk peed against one of the young trees dotting the sidewalk.

As I parked my car parallel to Conklin's, I told

myself that Cindy was fine, that she'd just gotten involved in a story and lost track of the time. That said, Cindy pushed herself into ugly situations and always worked against her fear, a trait we shared. But there was a difference between us.

I was a trained cop with a gun and a badge and a department behind me. Cindy had a press pass and a BlackBerry.

I put an SFPD card on the dash, then went to the doorway and pressed the button next to Tazio's name.

QT's digitized voice came through the speaker, and a second later I was buzzed in.

I hooked a left at the end of a narrow hallway and stepped into a vast, cold space lit by the glow of plasma screens. Monitors hung edge-to-edge on the walls, a built-in desktop went around three sides of the space, and there was a staircase in the middle of the concrete floor that went up to QT's living quarters.

Conklin called out to me and I crossed to the far side of the room, where he was standing behind QT.

"We're getting somewhere," Conklin said.

QT grinned up at me with his large, bright

choppers. His bald head gleamed. His long white fingers spanned the curving keyboard. He was good-looking in a naked-mole-rat kind of way.

"Cindy has a GPS in her phone," QT told me, "but it's not sending a signal. It's either turned off or underwater. I had to dump her phone logs to find her last ping."

Dump her phone logs without a warrant, I thought. Whatever it took to find Cindy, to know that she was okay.

Peering over QT's shoulder, I took in his computer screen, a map of San Francisco dotted with flags standing for cellular tower locations.

The best geek in the state of California clicked on an icon that stood for a tower in the Tenderloin. A circle appeared on the screen. He clicked on another tower, and then a third, and overlapping circles came up as he triangulated Cindy's last cell phone signal. I saw one small irregular patch that was common to all three towers.

QT said, "I can get accuracy up to two hundred and fifty meters. The location of that last ping isn't far from here. This is Turk," QT said, pointing with the cursor.

"Turk and what?" Conklin asked, completely

focused on the screen. "Turk and Jones?"

"Yeppers. You nailed it, Rich."

"That's where that cab company is."

"What cab company?" I asked. "What's this about?"

"Quick Express Taxi," Quentin said, zooming in on the intersection, rolling his cursor over it.

"Her phone isn't underwater," Conklin said. "It's underground."

I didn't understand any of this, but I read the urgency in my partner's face.

"Let's go," he said to me.

Chapter 102

I'D GOTTEN INTO the passenger seat of Conklin's unmarked car and barely closed the door when he jammed on the gas. The car leapt forward, slid sideways, then sent up a wake as we sped over the slick pavement.

Weaving around double-parked cars and inebriated pedestrians, Rich negotiated the six-minute drive through the traffic-choked streets toward an intersection in one of the roughest blocks in the Mission.

Conklin talked as he drove, telling me that Cindy had been poking around in taxi garages for a minivan cab with a movie ad on the side. So far, one vague sighting by one of the three rape victims was the slim and only clue to the identity of the rapist.

"She went to this hole-in-the-ground by herself on Monday," Conklin said. "She talked to the day dispatcher. A guy name of Wysocki. If she came back today, it had to be to see him. What do you think, Lindsay? Has Cindy taken this investigative reporter crap too far? Am I wrong?"

I saw the blinking neon signs up ahead on Jones, QUICK EXPRESS TAXI and CORPORATE ACCOUNTS WELCOME. Conklin parked at the curb in front of the grimy storefront before I could answer him.

The dispatcher was in a glass booth, her cage separated from the street by a grill in the plate glass.

I showed her my badge and told her my name, and she said her name was Marilyn Burns. She was forty, white, and petite and dressed in a blue-checked shirt hanging out over her jeans. She wore a wedding band and had a smoker's gravelly voice.

"I relieved Al right around six," Burns told us through the grill. "He was in a hurry. Want me to call him? It's not a problem."

"Have you seen this woman today?" Conklin asked, pulling out a photo of Cindy from his wallet.

"No, I've never seen her."

"Then, yes, call Al," I told Burns.

Conklin and I heard her say, "Call me when you get this, Al. Police are looking for someone who might've come in on your shift. Girl with curly blond hair."

The dispatcher put down the phone and said, "If you give me your number—"

"Okay if we take a look around?" Conklin said.

He didn't phrase it as a question, and Burns didn't take it as a request. She buzzed us into the grungy ground floor of Quick Express and said, "I'll take you on the tour."

Burns whistled up a cabbie to take over for her, and then the three of us walked between rows of parked cabs and past the ramp until we reached the stairs along the northern side of the building.

I asked Burns questions and answered a few of hers as Conklin flashed his light into cab interiors. She explained to me how the cab traffic worked inside the garage.

"Incoming cabs use their magnetic key card, enter the ramp on Turk," she said. "Drivers leave their vehicles on one of the three floors, then walk up the stairs, hand me their logs and keys, and cash out.

"When they start a shift," Burns went on, "it's the other way around. They pick up their log sheets on main, go down the stairs, take a cab down the ramp to Turk, and use their card to get out. We have a freight elevator goes down to Turk, but it's not working."

"Can cabs come in and leave without you seeing them?"

"We've got security cameras," she said. "They're not NASA-grade, but they work."

Taxis were parked on the perimeter and between the pillars on all three floors wrapping around the ramp in the center. We checked out minivan cabs and showed Cindy's picture to a half dozen cabbies we met as we walked.

No one admitted to having seen Cindy.

I turned over various possibilities in my mind.

Had Cindy met someone here who had a story for her? Was she interviewing that someone in a coffee shop with her phone turned off? Or was she drugged in the backseat of a taxi, one of the thousands cruising the streets of San Francisco?

I was accustomed to Cindy getting between rocks and hard places and equally used to the idea that she could chop her way out. But a bad feeling was coming over me.

Cindy had been missing for more than three hours.

We kept saying, "If Cindy's phone was turned off…"

But Cindy never turned off her phone. The last contact her phone GPS chip made was within two hundred and fifty meters of this building.

So where was she?

And if she wasn't here, and her phone wasn't turned off, where was she?

Where the hell had she gone?

Chapter 103

DISPATCHER MARILYN BURNS opened the stairwell door onto the lowest subterranean level, and Conklin and I were right behind her.

The windowless space was dark and dank and twenty-five feet underground. The fluorescent lighting was so dim, it didn't illuminate the corners of the room.

I thought about the crap-quality surveillance cameras high up on the walls and pillars — they would record nothing but snow. I stood at the foot of the ramp and tried to get my bearings.

Beyond the ramp was a motion-sensor and the magnetic key card–operated garage door that opened onto Turk Street. Beside that exit was the industrial-size freight elevator with its door rolled down and a hand-lettered sign duct-taped to it reading, "Out of Service."

To my right was the fire door to the stairwell we'd just come from. To my left was a door with another hand-lettered sign, this one marked "Storage." It was faced with metal, and I could see a shiny new dead bolt from thirty feet away.

"What's in that room?" I asked Burns.

"It's empty now. We used to store parts in there," she said, "but we moved the parts room to the main floor to cut down on thefts."

I moved my flashlight beam across the door and under the surrounding taxis—and then I saw something that just about stopped my heart.

Under a cab, about fifteen feet from the storage room, was a collapsible umbrella. It was red with a bamboo handle. Cindy had an umbrella just like that.

My hands shook as I put on gloves and picked up the umbrella and handed it to Rich. "This had to have fallen out of a cab," I said. "Doesn't it look familiar?"

Conklin blinked at the umbrella, then said to Marilyn Burns, "You have the key to that storeroom?"

"Al keeps the keys. All of them. He manages this place."

I opened my phone. The words "no signal" flashed. I told Rich and he said to Burns, "Go upstairs and call nine one one. Say officers need backup. Lots of it. Do it now."

I held my light on the storage room door, and Conklin pulled his gun, aimed, and fired three shots into the lock.

The sounds of the three shots multiplied as the echoes ricocheted throughout the underground cavern. But we didn't wait for the cracking booms to stop.

I took a stance behind Conklin. My gun was drawn as he pulled open the storage room door.

Chapter 104

IN THE SPLIT SECOND before my flashlight beam hit the room, pictures flashed through my mind of what I was afraid to find: Cindy lying dead on the floor, a man pointing a gun at my face.

I found the switch on the wall, and the lights went on.

The windowless room was a cube about twelve feet on all sides. Coils of ropes and tools hung from hooks on the walls. A dark-stained wooden worktable was in the center of the floor. Was this the rapist's party room?

Was that blood staining the table?

I turned toward Rich, and that's when I heard a muffled sneeze coming from outside the storage room.

"Did you hear that?" I asked.

There was a second, more drawn-out sneeze, definitely female, followed by an unforgettable grinding of large gears and winches. That cacophony of midtwentieth-century machinery could only be coming from the out-of-service elevator — and it was on the move.

I ran to the elevator, mashed the button, but the car didn't pause. Burns had told me that the only entrance to the freight elevator was right where we were standing and that the elevator emptied out onto Turk Street, three floors up.

Conklin beat on the elevator door with the butt of his gun, yelling, *SFPD! Stop the elevator!*

There was no answer.

I tried to make sense of what was happening.

No one could have gotten into that elevator since Conklin and I had come to Quick Express fifteen minutes before. Whoever was inside it had to have been inside it before we arrived.

Conklin and I stared at each other for a fraction of a second, then took off in tandem across the garage floor, heading toward the stairwell door.

I was right behind my partner as we raced up the stairs toward the light.

Chapter 105

THOSE SNEEZES had given me hope that Cindy was alive.

But Conklin and I had been unprepared for the elevator to start moving. If the car stopped between floors, if we got to the top floor and then the elevator descended, or if whoever was in the elevator beat us to the exit on Turk Street, we had very little chance of stopping him.

Conklin and I took the stairs two at a time, using the banisters to launch ourselves around corners. Conklin stiff-armed the NO EXIT fire door to Turk Street, and a piercing alarm went off.

I pounded behind him out onto the sidewalk, where I saw an assortment of law enforcement vehicles screaming onto Turk and Jones: fire trucks, cruisers, plainclothes detectives, and narcs pulling up in unmarked cars. Every law enforcement officer in the Mission had responded to the call.

I yelled out to two beat cops I knew.

"Noonan, Mackey, lock this garage down! No one comes in or goes out!"

Conklin was running up Turk toward the elevator exit, and I had to put on speed to catch up with him. He'd just reached the freight bay when the elevator door began to roll up.

A yellow cab was revealed by inches inside the mouth of the elevator. Conklin took a shooting stance square on the opening and was gripping his 9-millimeter with both hands when the cab rolled out of the elevator.

It was dark, but the driver and the backseat passenger were lit by headlights and streetlights. I could tell the passenger was Cindy from the light limning her curls.

The cab's headlights were full-on.

There was no way the driver didn't see Conklin.

Conklin yelled, *"Police!"* He shot out the left front tire, but the driver gunned the engine and the car leapt forward. Conklin was lit by the headlights, and yet the cab kept rolling, driving straight at him.

Conklin yelled, *"Stop!"* and then fired two shots high into the windshield. He jumped away in time to avoid being run down, but the cab kept moving, out of control now. It sideswiped a squad car on the far side of Turk, caromed off it, and plowed into a fire hydrant.

The cab rocked, then tipped, hanging on two wheels before settling down on all four. Water spewed. People screamed.

Conklin pulled at the passenger-side door, but he couldn't get it open.

"I need help here!" he shouted.

The fire crew came with the Jaws of Life and wrenched open the back door. Cindy lay crumpled on the slanted floor of the cab, wedged between the backseat and the divider. Conklin leaned all the way in, calling her name.

"Rich, is she okay?" I yelled to him.

"She's alive," Conklin said. "Thank God. She's alive."

He hooked Cindy's arms around his neck and pulled her out into the air. Cindy was fully dressed and I saw no blood. Conklin's voice cracked as he said to her, "Cindy, it's me. I'm right here."

She opened her eyes halfway and said, "Heyyyyy."

Conklin held her so tight, I thought he was going to crush the air right out of her.

And then her eyes closed and she started snoring softly, her cheek on his shoulder.

Chapter 106

MARILYN BURNS was screaming, "God, oh God, I can't believe this. What happened?"

She peered between her fingers and identified the dead man with one neat hole in his forehead, another in his neck, as Albert Wysocki.

I joined Conklin as he helped the paramedics strap Cindy in and load the gurney into the ambulance. He was panting and he was pale, and I knew he wanted to go to the hospital with Cindy. But he'd shot a man. He had to follow protocol for a shooting that was witnessed by thirty law enforcement officers. Conklin would have to wait for the ME, the Crime Scene Unit, and Brady to arrive.

I touched his shoulder, and his eyes met mine. His expression was flat, drained of emotion.

I've done what he had done. I've felt the same adrenaline overload covering rage and fear and the emotional numbness of shock.

"Is Wysocki dead?" my partner asked me. "Did I kill him?"

"It was him or you, Richie. You're lucky to be alive."

"I'm glad I nailed the bastard."

"Heeyyyy . . . Lindsayyyy," Cindy called out to me from inside the ambulance.

"I'm right here, girlfriend," I called back.

"You'll go with Cindy to the hospital?" Conklin asked me.

I nodded and climbed up into the ambulance. I gripped Cindy's hand and told her that I loved her and that everything was going to be okay.

"Did I get the story?" she asked me.

"You sure did."

Conklin stood at the rear doors. He said, "Lindsay?"

"I'll stay with her until you get to the hospital," I said to him. "She's going to be fine."

Chapter 107

LIGHT FROM THE SUNRISE was streaking through the windows when I greeted Martha inside the front door. I stripped off my jacket, my holster, and my shoes, and tiptoed down the hall to the master bathroom. I stepped into the "car wash," let it blast me pink, and then put on my cloudy blue pj's that were on the hook behind the door where I'd left them what seemed like a year ago.

Déjà vu all over again.

When I edged under the covers, Joe woke up and opened his arms to me, and that was good, because I wanted to tell him everything that had happened since I'd called him from the hospital.

"Hey," he said, kissing me. "How's Cindy?"

"Honestly? It's like it never even happened," I told him. "She was asleep a minute after she got into the cab and woke up in a hospital bed five hours later."

"Is she . . . all right?"

"He didn't get around to raping her," I said. "Thank God."

I made myself comfortable under Joe's arm, fitting my whole body tightly against him, my left leg over his, my left arm across his chest. "The doctor says she'll be fine when the drugs wear off."

"What did you find out about the bad guy?"

"He was some kind of lowlife freak, Joe. A friendless, unmarried, psychotic loner, fifty-five years old. He put in about eighteen hours a day in the Quick Express garage. Apparently he slept there in his car half the time."

I told Joe that Wysocki had managed the place for some guy who lived in Michigan, so he had run of the place. Had the keys. Kept the log sheets. Ran the scheduling.

"No one questioned anything he did. And so he hangs an 'Out of Service' sign on the freight elevator, and that box becomes his own private real estate."

"A big fish in a mud puddle," said Joe.

"Exactly," I said. "We found a date book in Wysocki's jacket pocket. Actually had the words 'Date Book' inked on the cover. Inside, he'd written a list of his victims, six of them, and times, dates, places, what they were wearing.

"He had Cindy's name in there," I said. "Just made me sick to see her name written in that lineup."

"He called it a date book?" Joe said. "So maybe he was acting like he was on a date."

"That makes some kind of psycho sense, I suppose. He picks up a girl, drugs her. Drives her back to his little out-of-service boudoir. I'm guessing he waits until his victims are semiconscious, then rapes them before the drugs wear off. Oh, yeah. Always the gentleman, he drives them home—or to a nearby alley. Perfect evening for Al Wysocki. Doesn't even have to send flowers the next day."

"How's Conklin doing?"

"Crazed. A wreck. He says to Cindy at the hospital, 'Don't you ever do that again.' She says, 'What? Catch a cab?'"

We both laughed.

My indomitable friend Cindy.

Joe turned onto his side and kissed me. I melted against him.

"I love you so much," I said. "I think I loved you even before I met you."

He laughed, but I saw that there were tears in his eyes.

Chapter 108

LOOKING INTO JOE'S EYES, I remembered the first time his baby blues locked on mine. We were working a case together. I was the lowest-ranking person there, and he was a top-of-the-heap Federal guy: Deputy Director of Homeland Security.

I liked his looks—his thick brown hair and solid build—and not only was he smart but he had an easy, confident manner, too.

He passed me his business card and touched my fingers, and we did a double take as electricity arced between us. It didn't take long for us to get involved, but our sizzling new connection had been disrupted repeatedly and for months by missed planes and crossed schedules.

Joe lived in Washington, DC and I lived in the

City by the Bay, and both of us had taken recent blows to the heart.

He'd been recovering from a savage divorce, and I was still suffering from the loss of someone close who had been shot and killed on the job.

Neither of us was prepared for the frustrating up-and-down year of long-distance dating that was later complicated even more by an insane—and unconsummated—crush between Conklin and me.

Through all of it, Joe had been a rock, and I'd hung in like I was clinging to a cliff by my fingernails. I knew what was good for me. And I loved Joe. But I couldn't give myself over to the permanence of the relationship.

Finally Joe got tired of it. He called me out on my ambivalence. Then he quit his job and moved to San Francisco. Somehow, while negotiating the zigs and zags, we'd found ourselves in each other.

"I just love you so much," I said to Joe. I kissed the corners of his eyes. He put his hand on my cheek, and I kissed his palm.

He said, "I love you almost too much, Linds. I can't stand it when you're not here and I'm lying in the dark, thinking about bullets coming at you. It's terrible to have thoughts like that."

"I'm very careful," I said. "So don't think about bullets."

I bent to kiss him, my hair making a curtain around our faces. That kiss went deep and it stirred me up. Stirred Joe up, too.

We smiled as we looked into each other's eyes. There were no walls between us anymore.

I said, "I sure would like to make a baby with you, Joe."

I'd said it before. In fact, I'd said it every month for a while now. But right this minute, it was more than a good idea. It was an overwhelming desire to express my love for my husband in a complete and permanent way.

"You think I can make a baby on demand, Blondie?" Joe said, unbuttoning my pajama top. "You think a guy in his late forties can 'just do it'? Hmmm?" He unknotted the tie on my drawstring pants and pulled the string as I unsnapped his drawers.

"Because, I think you could be taking me for granted. Maybe even taking advantage of me."

"Well," I said, "I guess I am."

10th Anniversary

Joe's hands on my breasts made my skin hot and my blood burn. I shrugged out of my flannels and lowered myself onto him.

"Go ahead," I sighed. "Try and stop me."

Chapter 109

IT WAS EARLY DECEMBER, about 10 p.m. on a damned cold night in Pacific Heights. Conklin and I were in an SFPD SUV, miked up, wearing our Kevlar and ready to go.

Six unmarked cars were parked here and there along the intersecting roadways of Broadway and Buchanan. Civilian vehicles provided cover for those of us on the ground.

Above and around us, snipers hid on the rooftops surrounding the eight-story Art Deco apartment building with its white-granite facade.

I'd been staring at that building for so long that I had memorized the brass-etched door, the ornate motifs and appointments, and the topiary boxwood and hedges between the side of the building and the street. I knew every line in the face of the liveried doorman, who was, in fact, Major Case lieutenant Michael Hampton.

There was a NO PARKING ANYTIME, NO LOADING zone in front of the building, and we could see every pedestrian walking past the door or going into the building.

If Major Case's confidential informant was telling the truth, all of our planning and man-power would culminate in the takedown of a legendary bad guy.

If the CI was wrong, if someone blew the whistle and called the game, there was no telling when, or if, we'd ever get this opportunity again.

I stretched out one leg, then the other, to get the kinks out. Conklin popped his knuckles. My breath fogged out in front of my face. I would have given up half my pension for a cup of coffee, the other half for a chocolate bar.

At half past eleven, just when I thought I'd never be able to walk again, a long Cadillac limo pulled up in front of the apartment building. Adrenaline fired through my bloodstream, chasing out the cramps and the lethargy.

The "doorman" left his post and opened the

door for the passengers. They had come from the opera and were dressed accordingly.

Nunzio Rinaldi, the third-generation capo of an infamous mob family, stepped out of the limo, wearing a smart black suit and a silver tie. He offered a hand to his wife, Rita, who had platinum-white hair you could have seen in a blackout. There was a high shine on the limo, and Rita Rinaldi's jewels sparkled in the night.

As the Rinaldis stepped away from the car and moved toward the lavish vestibule of their apartment building, a slight man in a dun-colored hooded raincoat, carrying a shopping bag and walking a small Jack Russell terrier, rounded the corner.

I saw him only out of the corner of my eye—he was one pedestrian out of many, and there were also cars speeding across my sight line to the doorman. But suddenly the little dog was running free and the man had dropped the shopping bag and pulled a gun from inside his coat.

It happened so fast, I doubted my eyes. Then I saw streetlight glint on the gun barrel.

The gun was pointed at the Rinaldis.

I inhaled and yelled, "GUN!" into my mic, blowing out eardrums all along Broadway.

Chapter 110

AS I YELLED, Lieutenant Hampton lunged for the gunman. Bringing down his arm, he yanked and twisted the would-be shooter around and fell on top of him.

Three bullets were discharged. Pedestrians screamed, but almost before the echoes died, it was all over. The shooter was disarmed and down.

Conklin and I charged across the street and were there before the bracelets snapped shut. I was panting, standing over the hooded gunman as Hampton leaned down and said, "Gotcha, you bastard. Thanks for making my day."

A few feet away, Rita Rinaldi pressed her bejeweled hands to her cheeks and wailed. She had to be thinking that the men in black had come for her husband.

Nunzio Rinaldi put his arms around his wife and said to Conklin, "What the hell is this? Who is that man?"

Conklin said, "Sorry for the commotion, Mr. Rinaldi, but we had to save your life. We had no choice."

But I had questions, and maybe I'd get some answers, too.

I ripped off the gunman's hood, grabbed a thin tuft of silver-brown hair, and lifted his head clear off the pavement.

He looked at me, his gray eyes glinting with amusement, a smile on his lips.

"What's your name?" I said, although I was sure I already knew. The face matched the fuzzy picture of the man sitting in an SUV with a Candace Martin look-alike.

He had to be Gregor Guzman. Had to be.

I'd read up on Guzman and learned that he was born in Cuba in 1950 to a Russian father and Cuban mother. He'd left home in a stolen fishing boat in the late '60s, and after landing in Miami, he'd made himself useful to organized guys in the drug trade. Later on, he carved out a career for himself as an independent assassin for hire on three continents.

That grainy picture of Guzman, or someone who looked a lot like him, had launched a fresh search for him. His picture was at airport security checkpoints, on BOLO alerts, in FBI agendas, and on my desktop.

Did we have him?

Was this the man who had met with Ellen Lafferty a few weeks before Dennis Martin was killed? Had Caitlin Martin really killed her father? Or had this hired killer had a hand in Dennis Martin's death?

"You tell me your name, and I'll tell you mine," Guzman said.

"Sergeant Boxer," I said. "SFPD."

"Nice to meet you, pretty lady," the killer said.

Sure. He was going to tell me everything, right here on the street. Hardly. I released my grip on his hair and his head dropped to the sidewalk.

I stood by as Lieutenant Hampton arrested Guzman and read him his rights.

Chapter 111

GREGOR GUZMAN had been charged with the attempted murder of Nunzio Rinaldi, but even if convicted, it wasn't enough to lock him up forever. That's why law enforcement agents from Bryant Street to Rio de Janeiro were digging up charges to throw at him, hoping they had enough Krazy Glue to make something stick.

By just after two in the morning, Guzman had a lawyer and had been interrogated by Lieutenant Hampton. When he spoke, it was only to say, "You've got nothing on me," even though he'd been caught with his loaded semiauto pointed at Nunzio Rinaldi.

Lieutenant Hampton wasn't bothered by Guzman at all.

Hampton had a lot to show for his work. He'd used the intel, set the trap, and had physically taken the hit man down. It looked like a guaran-damn-teed indictment. And now that we had him, we had his fingerprints, his DNA, and the possibility of linking him to unsolved crimes going back thirty years.

But I was more concerned about a crime that had happened just over a year ago.

I knocked on the glass window of the interview room.

Hampton came out to the hallway, ran his hand across the stubble on his head, and said, "Okay, Lindsay, I'm done. I'll stay with you if you like, and back you up."

It had been a long month and a longer night, and Hampton was ready to go home to his wife, but he held the door, followed me into the interview room, and said, "Sergeant Boxer, you've met Mr. Guzman?"

I said, "Yep, it was a pleasure."

"Pleasure was all mine," Guzman said in his oily voice.

"This is Mr. Ernesto Santana. Attorney-at-law," said Hampton.

I said hello to Guzman's lawyer, pulled out a chair, and dropped a file folder down on the table. I opened the cover to the short stack of 8 x 10 photos I had brought over from the squad room.

"Who do you have to screw around here to get coffee?" Guzman asked. No one answered.

I said, "Mr. Guzman, we're charging you with first-degree murder in the death of Dennis Martin."

"Who?" Guzman said. "Who the hell is that?"

"Dennis Martin," I said, showing him the ME's shot of the dead man lying in the foyer of his multimillion-dollar house, blood forming a dark lake around his body.

"I've never seen that guy in my life," Guzman said.

I took out another photo of Dennis Martin. In this shot, Martin was alive and well on a sailboat, his full head of hair blowing back from his handsome features. A pretty redhead by the name of Ellen Lafferty was under his arm.

"Maybe you recognize him alive," I said.

I thought I saw recognition flicker in Guzman's eyes. His irises contracted.

"I still don't know him," he said. "Look. Ernie.

Do I have to sit here, or can I go to my cell?"

I noted the slight Spanish accent, the well-tended hands, the aggression he didn't bother to hide.

Santana said, "Sergeant, this isn't evidence. It's nothing. So, what's this about? I don't get it."

"See if you get it now," I said. I took out one of Joseph Podesta's surveillance photos of Ellen Lafferty in a blond wig, sitting in an SUV with Guzman.

The Cuban peered at the picture. Smiled. Said, "Coffee first."

Hampton sighed. "How do you like it?"

"*Con leche,*" Guzman said. "No sugar. Served by a topless girl, preferably blond."

Chapter 112

TEN LONG MINUTES went by. I sat staring across the table at a piece-of-garbage contract killer while the killer looked at me and smiled. Just as I was ready to get him his damned coffee myself, the door opened and a cop came in, put a paper cup of milky coffee in front of Guzman, adjusted the camera over the door frame, and left.

Guzman took a sip, then turned the photo I'd brought so that he could see it better.

"Very bad quality," he said.

"Not so bad," I said. "Our software matched it to your spanking-new mug shot."

"Okay, I was sitting in a car with a lady. What the hell is that? You want to charge me with being heterosexual? I plead guilty as charged to liking girls. Ernie, do you believe this?"

"Let's hear them out," Santana said.

"The woman in this picture is Dr. Candace Martin," I said. "And she paid you, Mr. Guzman, to kill her husband. I think she'll be happy to identify you and cut a better deal for herself."

Sure, I was lying, but that was strictly within the law. Guzman called me on it—as I hoped he would.

"That's not Candace Martin," he said.

"This *is* Dr. Martin, Guzman. The widow Martin. We both know who she is."

Guzman drank down his coffee, crumpled the paper cup, and said to his lawyer, "I didn't kill Dennis Martin. They're screwing with me. I'll tell them what I know about it if they drop the charges in this attempted rubout."

"Drop the charges? Are you nuts?" I said. "We've got a witness to the shooting. We've got photographic evidence linking you to the woman who hired you to do the hit. And we've got a dead body. And since we've got you for the attempt on the life of Mr. Rinaldi, we've got time to fill in the blanks."

"You should be an actress, lady. You've got nothing."

I took back the pictures, closed the folder, and said, "Gregor Guzman, you're under arrest for the murder of Dennis Martin. You have the right to remain silent, as your attorney will tell you."

Anger crossed Guzman's face. He looked like he was going to spring across the table, all one hundred and forty pounds of him. I imagined the punch I'd throw if I had the chance.

"Don't say anything else, Gregor," said the attorney, putting a hand on his client's arm.

"Don't worry about it, Ernie. This is all crap."

"So straighten me out," I said. I clasped my hands on top of the folder.

"I can straighten you out, Sergeant Boxer, but I'm not doing it to hear the sound of my voice. I want this crappy murder charge dropped."

"We'll consider doing that if you point us to Dennis Martin's killer," I said, "and we can prove who did it."

"Look. I didn't kill Martin. You'll never connect me to that killing, and I'm not going to do your job for you, lady. I'm willing to trade information so that I don't get wrongfully convicted by an unsympathetic jury. That's it. That's what I'm willing to do."

"Okay. Done," I said to Guzman. "Tell me what you've got, and if I like your story, I won't charge you."

Santana said, "Sergeant, no offense. If you want Mr. Guzman to give you information leading to the arrest of this man's killer, we want an agreement in writing. From the DA."

"It's two-thirty in the morning," I said.

"Take your time," said the lawyer. "We can wait."

My dad used to say you have to "strike while the iron is hot." Well, my iron was sizzling.

"I'm here and you're here," I said. "I'll rouse someone from the DA's Office."

Chapter 113

YUKI ANSWERED HER PHONE on the first ring.

"He's primed and the grill is hot," I said. "You're going to want to hear this."

"Just marinate him a little. I'm bringing my appetite," she said.

An hour later, I brought ADA Yuki Castellano into the interview room on the third floor of the Hall.

Ernesto Santana stood and shook her hand, and Lieutenant Hampton did the same. Guzman groused to Yuki, "You seriously work for the DA? How old are you? Twelve?"

"Old enough to have been certified in spotting bull," she said. "Let's get started, shall we?"

I took the photos out of the folder again, and Guzman said, "This girl—I don't remember her name—she's the one who tried to hire me. She's connected back east. She contacted me through channels. I said I'd meet her.

"She was wearing a blond wig," he went on. "I know because I saw long red hair coming out the back of that thing. She brought an envelope of small bills, tens and twenties. About a thousand bucks. She wanted me to take out the doctor. Candace Martin."

"You're saying she ordered a hit?"

"Yeah. She brought money and a picture."

I found Guzman more believable than I'd found Ellen Lafferty, who'd insisted she'd been doing an errand for Dennis Martin. That she didn't know who Guzman was. That she didn't know what was in the envelope.

"Go on," I said.

"I said to this chick, 'Thanks, but you're crazy. I don't know where you got my name from, but this is not exactly my line of work.' "

"Okay, Mr. Guzman. We'll check out your story."

"Check it out?" he said. "Check out what? You

439

think that bitch is going to admit to wanting to have the doctor whacked? Candace Martin is alive, right? What more proof do you need?"

"Ms. Castellano," I said. "Have you got enough to charge Ellen Lafferty with solicitation of first-degree murder?"

"I do, indeed," she said. "And I'll be following up on that in the morning. Mr. Santana, I'll shelve the murder charge against your client for now. Sleep tight, Mr. Guzman."

Chapter 114

YUKI AND I left the Hall together in silence. We briefly clasped hands in the elevator, then walked out to Yuki's Acura parked outside the ME's office. We got into her car and sat staring out at the dim streetlight in the parking lot.

I was thinking that I'd gone way over the line. That Brady was going to nail my hide to the squad room door if this plan of mine didn't pay off, and maybe even if it did. I'd gone above, around, and behind my superior in investigating the Martin case, and saying "I was working on my own time" sounded lame, even to me.

Yuki was lost in her own thoughts.

I was about to break the silence and ask her to

talk to me, when a car door slammed on the far side of the lot. I looked over my shoulder.

"Okay, she's here," I said.

A minute later, the back door opened and Cindy slipped into the backseat.

"I can't believe Richie let you out at four in the morning," Yuki said.

"*Let* me? Very funny. What have we got?"

I filled Cindy in on the fake charge we'd dropped on Guzman for the murder of Dennis Martin, and I told her what he'd told us: that Ellen Lafferty tried to hire him to kill Candace Martin and that he'd kicked young Ms. Lafferty to the curb.

"He was credible?"

"He was motivated to be credible."

"Nice work, Linds," Cindy said. "But what do we have to show for it?"

"I think we can eliminate Guzman as a suspect in Dennis Martin's death."

"Agreed."

I said, "Ellen lies as easily as she breathes. If she knew that Caitlin was being molested, what did she do to stop it?"

"Do you seriously think Ellen killed Dennis?" Yuki asked.

"She had the means, the motive, and the opportunity," I said. "And she's smart in a vicious, clueless, stupid kind of way."

Cindy said, "She didn't have the opportunity to kill Dennis. Her alibi checks out for the time of the murder. Rich and I went to see her last night.

"Ellen told us that she left the Martin house at six p.m.—exactly what she's maintained since the murder. She texted her friend Veronica from six until she met up with her at six-fifteen. She showed us a record of text messages that fill her window of opportunity."

Cindy went on, "Ellen's friend Veronica verifies that they met for dinner at Dow's at six-fifteen, and the waiter remembers the time, because their table wasn't ready. And he remembers the two of them because they were hot and flirting with two guys who were sitting next to them at the bar.

"Ellen picked up the bar tab at six-thirty-two," Cindy said, "and he has her signature on the credit-card receipt."

"Okay, so moving past Ellen Lafferty, what about Caitlin?" I asked Yuki. "Did she take her father's gun and shoot him?"

"I'm talking to her court-appointed shrink in, uh, five hours. I'll let you know what he says."

I said to Cindy, "I don't need to say, 'Sit on this until we say go,' do I?"

"I haven't got a story yet anyhow."

"You sure don't." I grinned, slapping her a high five.

Yuki leaned forward and started the engine. Cindy and I reached for our door handles.

Yuki said, "Linds. I've been so sure Candace killed Dennis. If Caitlin hadn't confessed in open court to shooting her father, I think I would have gotten the doctor convicted. It scares me. What if I've been wrong?"

Chapter 115

OVERRIDING THE PROTEST from the director of security at Metropolitan Hospital, Conklin and I took the two empty seats at the back of an amphitheater above an operating room.

The room was packed with interns and specialists. Two monitors showed close-ups of the operating table fifteen feet below, and cameras exported streaming video to medical people all over the country who wanted to see Candace Martin perform heart surgery on Leon Antin, a legendary seventy-five-year-old violinist with the San Francisco Symphony.

The patient was draped in blue, his rib cage separated and his heart open to the bright lights. Candace Martin was accompanied by other doctors, nurses, and an anesthesiologist operating the cardiac-bypass machine.

A young intern sat to my right, Dr. Ryan Pitt, according to the ID tag pinned to his pocket, and he was currently bringing me up to speed.

According to Pitt, this was a complex operation under any circumstances, but even more so because of the patient's age.

Pitt said, "The surgery is not going to improve his longevity by much—he's an ASA class four. That's high-risk. But the patient wanted his chance now that Dr. Martin was available. He just wanted his friend to do the surgery. Only her."

Pitt explained that in the previous three hours, two of Antin's veins had been harvested from his thighs and three of four grafts had been implanted into the coronary arteries. Dr. Martin was stitching in the last implant now.

I was staring at the screen above my head when I saw the medical personnel suddenly become highly agitated. Green lines jumped on the monitors below, and Candace Martin began shouting at the anesthesiologist while massaging Antin's heart with her hands.

I said to the intern, "What is this? What's going on?"

Pitt spoke pure medicalese, but I got the drift. The patient's heart was beat-up and worn out, and it refused to work anymore. Dr. Martin was spraying curses all around the operating room, but she wasn't giving up.

Needles went into IVs. Paddles were applied to Antin's exposed heart, and then, once again, Candace Martin massaged the heart with her hands, begging her friend to stay with her. Demanding it.

After it was clear, even to me, that the patient wasn't coming back, a nurse pulled Candace away, and a doctor pronounced the time of the patient's death.

Candace ripped off her mask and made a rapid and direct line for the door. The video cameras blinked off.

I heard my name, turned toward the exit, and saw the security director beckoning to Conklin and me.

Security said, "Can I see that warrant again, please?"

Conklin took it out of his inside jacket pocket.

The security chief read it and said, "Dr. Martin is in the locker room. Please follow me."

We found Candace Martin still in her bloody scrubs, sitting on a bench, staring at a wall of lockers. I asked her to stand up, and she looked at me as though she didn't recognize me. Conklin showed her the warrant and told her we were taking her into custody for the murder of her husband.

All the fight seemed to have gone out of her.

Chapter 116

YUKI AND I sat across a small metal table from Candace Martin and Phil Hoffman. Hoffman looked as he always did: contained, dressed for a press conference at a moment's notice. Candace Martin looked like she'd been dragged by her hair through hell.

I was angry, feeling the calm before an emotional storm, pissed off at myself for the first time since Hoffman buffaloed me into getting involved in this case. But I'd done it, believed Candace Martin's lies, and if I didn't want to be patrolling the Mission in a squad car for the next year, I had to make this mess turn out right.

Yuki said, "Dr. Martin, it's over. We've spoken with Caitlin's shrink. She has recanted her testimony. She said she didn't kill her father. She said that her father forced himself on her, yes. But she said you did the shooting.

"The People are ready to proceed with your trial, or you can tell us what really happened."

Hoffman said, "I need to consult with my client. And she needs a little time to get her wits together. She's suffering a grave personal loss."

I was almost lit up with fury, the fighting-mad kind that you *can* control but just don't want to. I said, "Phil, you have lied to me, your client has lied to me, and she tried to get us to look at an innocent person for murder.

"Ask me how much I care about her personal loss. Not. At. All. This woman killed her husband. She's cooked, and this is her only chance to make a deal."

Candace was shaking her head, her face contorted in pain. "You don't understand."

I was unmoved.

Yuki said, "Phil. The judge gave us sixty days to determine whether or not the People wish to try your client. This is day fifty-seven. On Monday, we either tell Judge LaVan that the defendant pleads guilty or we go back to trial.

"The children will not be in court, but Caitlin's shrink will be standing by, and if you so much as hint that Caitlin killed her father, Dr. Rosenblatt will play the tape of Caitlin's recantation for the jury.

"So, Dr. Martin," Yuki said, "it's us or the jury. Take your pick. Honestly, I think your odds are better with us."

"Candace," Hoffman said, "it's your decision."

"I'm tired, Phil," she said. And then she was sobbing.

Phil nodded and handed her a tissue.

Candace dabbed at her eyes, blew her nose, and said, "Phil, I'm sorry I lied to you. I did it to protect my children. They don't have anyone but me."

"Let's hear it," Yuki said.

Chapter 117

CANDACE MARTIN SAID, "You want me to say I shot Dennis? I *did*. After years of torture, that bastard finally pushed me over the edge."

"What edge is that?" I asked her.

The doctor's eyes were flaming red. Her fingers shook and her voice wavered. The composed surgeon I'd met in this room back in October had been swapped out for a woman who still looked like her but was emotionally broken and ready to tell the truth.

"On the night in question, I was in my home office," she said. "Ellen had left for the evening and a little while later, I heard a muffled shout. It could only be Caitlin. I got up from my desk and ran down the hallway in time to see Dennis coming out of her bedroom.

"He didn't look right," Candace said. "He jumped when he noticed me. Then he screamed at me, 'Don't sneak up on me like that.'"

"I didn't even have a chance to answer before Caitlin ran out of her bedroom and into my arms. She was naked. She was flushed and crying and the insides of her thighs were *wet*. She cried, 'Mommy, Mommy, Mommy,' the most savagely sad cries I've ever heard.

"She'd been raped," Candace said, her face radiating horror. "My husband had done this to my little girl."

Neither Yuki nor I moved or said a word, and then Candace continued.

"I held her and told her that I loved her and always would. I told her to shower and get dressed, that I'd be right back. And then I ran back down the hallway to the bedroom I shared with Dennis— and he was there, stuffing cash into his wallet, and he said, 'Don't believe what she tells you. Caitlin lies.'

"Dennis picked up his car keys and left the bedroom," Candace said. "He had cheated on me for years, but whenever I tried to leave him, he said he would take the children and prove that I was an unfit mother. I knew that he would try. Even though he was never home, even though he was a horrible parent. I knew he would find a way to take them, just to make sure I didn't get them.

"He must not have heard me come home that evening. He was raping her while I was actually in the *house*. How could he have done that?

"I hated myself for missing the signs. But I hated Dennis more. I couldn't let him get away with what he'd done. I ran back to my office and grabbed my gun."

Candace's voice ran out and she just sat there, hands propping up her head, staring hard at the table, silent.

Phil went to the door of the interview room and opened it. I heard him ask someone to bring water.

As we waited, I went back over the pictures Candace had painted in my mind. I could see everything as if I'd been there myself and witnessed the horror.

It all rang true, but I still had questions.

Chapter 118

PHIL BROUGHT BOTTLES of water into the room and set them down on the table. Candace's hand shook violently as she drank down half of one of the bottles. After that, she told Phil that she was all right and wanted to go on. She continued her story of betrayal in the first degree.

"Dennis was heading toward the front door and I was right behind him, screaming at him to stop, calling him names, but he just lowered his head and kept going.

"I had no plan to kill him. You have to believe that. I only wanted to stop him. All I could think about was that he had raped my child, his own daughter. And I didn't want him to ever do it again."

"What happened next, Candace?" I asked.

Candace had fallen down a tunnel of memory. I repeated my question and she returned to her story.

"I was charging after Dennis, but as I passed Caitlin's room, she ran out to me and grabbed me by the waist again.

"I comforted her, but Dennis kept taunting me. He turned to me in the foyer and said that Caitlin was lying, that her hysteria was make-believe. I knew what he'd done. I knew full well what he had done to my little girl.

"He saw the gun in my hand, and I remembered that I was holding it. I said, 'Stay where you are. I'm calling the police.'

"He laughed at me. I lifted the muzzle and aimed the gun at him, and for the first time since I'd met Dennis, I saw fear in his face—but only for a second. I shot him twice, once while he was standing, once when he was down.

"Caitlin was holding on to me, screaming and crying, and then Duncan was there, too. He saw his father lying dead on the floor. I put Caitlin aside and swept Duncan up, carried him to the foot of the stairs, and told him to run up to Cyndi's room and stay there."

Candace came back to the present and she spoke directly to me.

"Sergeant, it had all become quite clear to me — I had to protect those children. If not me, then who?

"I went to the foyer and picked up the gun. After that, I called nine one one. When the police came, I said that an intruder had broken into the house and had killed my husband. They tested my hands for gunpowder. I told them I had opened the front door and fired after him. They brought me here. You know the rest.

"I'm sorry that it happened this way, but in that moment, I acted on pure instinct. I couldn't let Dennis live in the same world with Caitlin."

Chapter 119

YUKI AND I walked Candace back to the beginning of her story, and she filled in the sickening gaps. She said that Dennis Martin was a degenerate womanizer and a stalker with a well-honed gift for emotional abuse but that he had a good reputation in the community and was well spoken. Candace said she was convinced that in a divorce trial she wouldn't have gotten custody of the kids.

Dr. Martin said, "Had I known that he was abusing Caitlin before that moment, I would have taken her and Duncan and called the police. I would not have let my children see him die."

After Candace was locked up and Phil was on his way home to Oakland, Yuki and I gathered our notes and collected the videotapes. And then we were alone.

I said, "That was the worst."

"Awful. If the jury had heard it, even if they thought she was guilty, they might have let her off so she could be there for her kids."

"Caitlin told her shrink that Dennis had been raping her?"

"Yes. I didn't see any point in telling Candace that it had been going on for quite a while."

"What are you going to recommend?"

"Damned if I know," Yuki said.

She hurried upstairs to confer with Red Dog and I went down four flights to see Jacobi, my former partner, my longtime friend, and now the chief of police.

Jacobi cracked open a couple of Coke cans, and after I brought him up to the minute on Candace Martin, he said, "What's Yuki thinking?"

"She and Parisi are chewing it over right now. Brady is going to bust me back to the beat," I said. "I couldn't let this case go."

"You want me to talk to him?"

"Yeah. Would you?"

Jacobi nodded his head and began tapping on

the desk. He kept it up until under my prompting to just spit out whatever he was thinking, he said, "Lindsay, a message was forwarded to me this morning. It's not good news."

"What is it? What's wrong?" I asked.

"It's about your father."

"My father?"

"He died back in August. The pension people just got the word. I'm sorry, Linds."

I said, "No," and stood up, surprised that I felt light-headed, that my legs didn't want to hold me up. I grabbed the back of the chair for support. I thought about how Marty Boxer was hardly a father. In fact, I wasn't sure that he had even loved me. Had I loved him?

The next thing I knew, Jacobi had come around his desk and put his arms around me, and I was getting tears on his jacket.

"I wanted to be the one to tell you. He didn't ditch you at your wedding, my friend. He had a heart attack. He was already gone."

Chapter 120

CLAIRE'S HOME in Mill Valley is a dream of a house: wood-paneled inside with trusses and beams in the cathedral ceiling, stone floors throughout the open space, and a two-story fireplace. The bedrooms all have mountain vistas, and the patio has a multimillion-dollar view of a great, green, tree-studded lawn.

Edmund Washburn, a big teddy bear of a man, had fired up the barbecue, and Joe, Brady, and Conklin were horsing around with a football on the grass.

Yuki, Cindy, Claire, and I reclined on teak lounge chairs under woolly blankets, and baby Ruby slept in her rocking seat at Claire's elbow.

A Mozart symphony was pouring out of the

Bose, and Yuki was staring at the guys on the field, at Brady in particular, and she finally said, "I'm a goner. I just thought you ladies would like to know. I'm a very moony lady. Over my head for Jackson Brady."

We laughed out loud—couldn't help ourselves. Yuki wanted to be in a relationship and it looked like she was in one with my lieutenant.

Brady saw her watching him, tossed the football aside, and ran toward us. He grabbed Yuki out of the chair, hoisted her over his shoulder, and made a run for the space between the two saplings that marked the goal line.

Yuki shrieked and kicked melodramatically as Brady did the happy dance around the trees, then put Yuki on her feet and kissed her. With their arms around each other, they came back to the patio, laughing.

Man. They were disgustingly happy.

But I didn't begrudge Yuki a bit of it. Between Yuki and Jacobi, Brady had let my end run fade without so much as a wrist slap.

Damn. It was good to have friends.

Joe called my name. He had the ball, so I stood, ran out, and waved my hands in the air until he tossed it to me. Cindy threw off her blanket and went for a pass, doing some little moves with her hips that had never before been seen in football.

I threw the ball to her, a surprisingly tight spiral, if I do say so, and she whooped and yelled as she caught it. Conklin came off the sidelines and chased and tackled her, and then, even though I didn't have the ball, Joe tackled me. He tucked me under his body and rolled with me so that I landed on top of him, never even touching the ground.

We were all acting like a bunch of kids. And you know what? We needed to be kids. It was wonderful to just laugh our heads off. That's what I was thinking when a minute later Brady came over to me at the barbecue and pulled me aside. He leaned toward me, close enough to whisper in my ear.

He said, "For insubordination, Boxer, you're on night shift for the next six weeks."

It sucked, but I knew he was right. I had broken the rules.

What could I say? "Okay, Lieutenant, I understand."

Chapter 121

WE ATE like we never expected to eat again.

When Joe's secret-sauced ribs had been picked clean, the salad had been reduced to a film of olive oil in the bowl, and all that remained of the baked potatoes was a pile of foil in the recycle bin, we went inside the house.

Claire busted out the cake while Edmund popped the top on the Krug. It was one of the best champagnes, at least a hundred bucks a bottle.

"Introducing my original white-chocolate cheesecake with cream cheese and orange slices between the layers," Claire said, putting it down on the dining room table. "Baked sour cream frosting, and Grand Marnier in a graham cracker crust. Voilà! I hope you like it."

The applause was spontaneous and rousing, and I was pushed forward so that I could be next to my best friend. There were ten candles on the cake, standing for the tenth anniversary of the first time Claire and I met.

It had been a memorable occasion: It was my first week in Homicide, and Claire was the low woman on the totem pole in the ME's Office. We'd been called to the men's jail. A skinhead was down, three hundred pounds of swastika tattoos and muscle, wedged under his bunk and handcuffed. Not breathing.

The guard outside was in a high panic. He had cuffed the inmate and put him in his cell because the inmate was out of control, and now he was dead.

"He couldn't find the keys to the cuffs," Claire said. "And we couldn't turn the body over."

Claire was laughing as I told about her locking her kit outside the cell, then dropping her camera so hard she cracked the lens.

"And so Claire bends down for her camera, and I back into the guy's toilet, which sends me down," I said. "I reach out to grab on to something—anything—and end up grabbing his still under the sink. And the hooch sloshes all over me. I mean *all over*."

Edmund has this big laugh: "Hah-hah-hah."

He was pouring champagne into the good crystal glasses. I started to lift my flute of bubbly, but put the glass down.

Claire was snickering now, and Yuki's trilling laugh was sounding the high notes.

"We get back to the morgue," Claire continued, "stinking of hooch."

"Disgusting," I said. "But it was a no-brainer what killed him."

"No-brainer?" said Claire. "No-brainer for *you*. I'm the one stuck with doing the post while you go home and change your clothes."

"He OD'd?" Brady asked.

"Didn't take much," Claire said. "If you're distilling hooch in tin cans—and he was—it turns to methanol. Three ounces'll kill you dead."

"I can't hear that story too many times," Cindy said, laughing.

She plucked the candles out of the cake one at a time and licked the bottoms clean, making Conklin shake his head and laugh.

Yuki brought out the plates and forks, and

Edmund handed me my sleeping goddaughter, Ruby Rose Washburn, a child as cute as ten buttons.

Claire hugged me tight, the baby between us.

"Happy anniversary, Linds," said my best friend.

I had a lot of thoughts, and images came to me of a lot of murders and late nights working with Claire to solve them. It had been trial by fire every single time.

"And many more years together, girlfriend," I said.

We were still laughing an hour later, and then it was time to go. After I'd hugged and kissed all my buds good night—and yes, even my fine lieutenant—Joe and I headed back to town.

It was wonderfully peaceful inside that car.

I said to Joe, "It was hard not to tell anyone."

"I know. But let's keep it to ourselves for now, Blondie."

My handsome husband shot me a smile. Patted my thigh.

"Six weeks on night duty, huh?" he said.

"I dissed the lieutenant. I deserve it. Still, I did the right thing."

"I'm going to have the whole bed to myself for forty-two nights. And here I am, married at last."

"We can fool around when I get in at eight-thirty a.m.," I said.

I leaned over and kissed Joe's cheek as we took a turn onto Lake Street. Centrifugal force and a whole lot of love glued us together.

"Whoaaaaaa!" I squealed.

Damn, I was happy.

WOMEN'S MURDER CLUB

Epilogue

WIN/WIN

Chapter 122

YUKI AND RED DOG Parisi walked down the green terrazzo hallway toward Judge LaVan's chambers. Yuki was thinking, Anything could go wrong and as history had shown, it probably would. Red Dog said to her, "I've changed my mind."

"What did you say?"

"You don't need me. Just do what you do, Yuki. It's your party. Call me when you're done."

"I can't believe you're wimping out on me."

Parisi laughed. "Yeah, that's me. A big ol' wimp. Now, you go get 'em. I'll be in my office after lunch."

"Wus," she called after him.

Parisi laughed.

Yuki knocked on the judge's door and heard him shout, "Come in." She opened the door and entered Judge Byron LaVan's chambers. Phil Hoffman and Candace Martin were in place and the judge was behind his desk, wearing his robes to maintain formality.

The court reporter, Sharon Shine, was sitting at her own small table. She put down the phone, said hello to Yuki, and asked after the deputy DA.

"Len had an emergency meeting out of the building. I'll brief him later," Yuki said, attempting to convey with her body language that Parisi's absence was no big deal.

"Your Honor, everyone's present," said the court reporter.

"Fire up your transcription machine, Sharon. Everyone, this proceeding is now in session. Dr. Martin, do you know why you're here?"

"Yes, Your Honor."

"You've told the clerk that you've changed your plea to guilty. Is that correct?"

"Yes, sir."

"Mr. Hoffman, any objections you wish to put on the record at this time?"

"No, Judge."

"Ms. Castellano?"

"Your Honor, we're prepared to recommend sentencing based on the defendant's complete allocution."

"Okay, Dr. Martin. You're up. You're saying that you're guilty as charged, second-degree murder of your husband. Is that right?"

Candace Martin said, "Yes, Your Honor. I killed him without premeditation."

"Tell me about that," said LaVan. "Don't leave out a word."

Yuki thought Candace looked like she was sedated. When she spoke, her voice was soft but steady, even when she re-created the terrible scene that preceded the shooting. When she'd finished, she sat back in her chair and sighed deeply.

"Mr. Hoffman, have you spoken with the District Attorney's Office? You've worked something out?"

"Yes, sir, we have."

"Ms. Castellano?"

Yuki was unprepared for the rush of emotions she felt. Candace Martin had been part of her life for almost a year and a half. Even as she tried other cases, the Martin case had been on her mind, and new information had been added continually to a folder on her computer.

She'd rehearsed, lived, breathed, and dreamed this case, and when it blew up in court, when others would have given up, she'd stuck with it. And now it was almost over.

Yuki said to the judge, "Your Honor, due to the circumstances, namely that Dr. Martin's daughter had been violently abused and that the defendant acted to protect her daughter from further harm, we recommend a sentence of ten years.

"Because we believe that it is necessary for the good of the children to be able to see their mother, we are recommending that the first five years of that sentence be spent at San Mateo Women's Correctional. It's minimum-security and only eighteen miles from the children's home, and Dr. Martin will work in the infirmary.

"If Dr. Martin's behavior is good during that time, we agree that she be released from prison after five years and serve the rest of her sentence on probation."

LaVan swiveled his chair a couple of times before saying to Yuki, "Sounds good to me. So ordered."

Phil leaned toward Yuki and put out his hand.

She clasped his firm handshake and felt his respect and his sincerity when he said, "Thanks, Yuki. Congratulations."

That's when it really hit her.

She'd won.

Chapter 123

THE NOON RUSH was, frankly, horrible. Claire was driving because we were late and she was adamant that she didn't want to be a passenger with a "cowgirl" at the wheel. That cowgirl she was referring to was me.

I was fine with Claire dodging traffic for a change, so I just dialed around the radio as we headed toward Sansome Street.

"If you had answered my text," Claire groused, "we could have left ten minutes earlier. I hate to be late."

"We're only going to be a couple of minutes late."

A cab swerved in front of us, then jacked around to pick up a passenger at the curb. Claire leaned on the horn. Others joined in—and then we were driving cowboy-style. I laughed at Claire.

"Giddyup," I said.

"Am I okay on the right?"

"Go for it."

We cleared the worst of the jam at Folsom Street and found an open lane that took us from 3rd to Kearny, a straightaway to an office building in the heart of the financial district.

"Not bad," I said, looking at my watch. "I'd say we're actually on time. And you didn't even need a siren."

The wind blew through the canyon of office buildings, practically sweeping us past the entrance to the sixteen-story granite structure casting a long shadow over the corner of Sansome and Halleck.

The lawyer's office was on the eleventh floor, and while the elevator was swift, it took us time to find the right door and to clear reception. An attractive legal secretary in a pencil skirt and a ruffled mauve blouse walked us to a conference room and opened the door to let us in.

Avis Richardson was sitting in the seat closest to the door. She was scrubbed and dressed up, and although she looked grave, she resembled a fifteen-year-old girl more than she had at any other time since I'd met her.

I said hello to her and the Richardsons and introduced Claire, who was moving around the table to hug Toni Burgess and Sandy Wilson, the Devil Girlz we'd met in Taylor Creek, Oregon.

Correction: former Devil Girlz.

There was no sign of leather. Instead Toni was in a dress and had soccer-mom hair, and she said she was going back to teaching school. Sandy just looked sweet.

More people were introduced: lawyers for both sides, and His Honor Marlon Sykes, a judge from Portland who was in town for the ABA convention.

Baby Tyler Richardson's travel seat was in a chair pulled up to the blond-wood conference table. He was wearing a blue onesie with a duck appliqué on the front. His eyes were open. He was very little, but he was taking everything in.

I smiled at Tyler, thinking about what a very important day this was for this little boy.

Chapter 124

CLAIRE AND I sat down at the conference table and the process began.

Lawyers passed papers to Judge Sykes: the report from Child Protective Services giving a green light to the women from Taylor Creek; an annulment of Avis Richardson's marriage to Jordan Ritter; and the revocation of Ritter's parental rights in exchange for a couple of years off the twenty-year stretch he was facing for statutory rape and kidnapping.

There was also a revocation of Avis's parental rights, and adoption papers naming Toni and Sandy, who were beaming from across the table, Tyler's parents.

Avis signed the adoption papers without

hesitation. Toni and Sandy signed the same papers with barely contained glee, and together they got up and hugged Avis. She was stiff at first, but her nose pinked up and she started to cry.

Photos were taken and Claire and I were asked to be in the group shot. People came up to us and thanked us for our part in this wonderful outcome.

Avis was one of them.

She said to me, "I'm sorry for lying to you, Sergeant Boxer. I know you've done a good thing for Tyler. It's legal now."

The baby was in Sandy Wilson's arms and he laughed in the excitement. I reached out to him. He wrapped my finger in his little fist and gave me a good solid connection with his big brown eyes.

My heart swelled.

I was eager for this little boy to start his new life.

Back in the car, Claire texted Cindy and Yuki, saying the Women's Murder Club was on for dinner tonight at Susie's. She added, "Don't be late!"

I said, "By the way, I won't be drinking."

Claire put the phone in her lap and turned her eyes on me, pursed her lips, and said, "It's about time you told me, girlfriend." She reached over and gave my arm a shake. "I can read it all over your face."

We both cracked up.

Claire knew me that well. I didn't even have to tell her the news that had irrevocably and fantastically changed my world.

Joe and I were having a baby.

A History of the Women's Murder Club

2001   The first Women's Murder Club novel, *1st to Die*, is published. We are introduced to the series' main character, Detective Lindsay Boxer of the San Francisco Police Department, and her three friends – Claire Washburn, a medical examiner, Jill Bernhardt, an Assistant District Attorney, and reporter Cindy Thomas – who come together to form the Women's Murder Club.

2002   *2nd Chance* is published. Lindsay is left unsure whether to return to work after losing her partner in a shoot-out. But another horrifying case brings her back.

2003   *1st to Die* is made into a TV movie by US TV network NBC. The film stars Tracy Pollen as Lindsay Boxer, Pam Grier as Claire Washburn, Megan Gallagher as Jill Bernhardt and Carly Pope as Cindy Thomas.

2004   *3rd Degree* is published. The Women's Murder Club is devastated by the brutal murder of Jill Bernhardt. The three remaining friends continue to work together, however, determined to bring Jill's killers to justice.

2005   *4th of July* is published. Lindsay faces a court case brought against her for wrongful death. She befriends the young Japanese-American lawyer, Yuki Castellano, who helps represent her. Yuki joins the girls at their regular get-togethers at Susie's Café and becomes part of the Women's Murder Club.

2006 *The 5th Horseman* is published. The friends face one of their toughest battles as a string of unexplainable deaths occur in a San Francisco hospital and the hospital launches a court case that grips the entire nation.

2007 *The 6th Target* is published. A terrible gun attack leaves Claire Washburn fighting for her life. Lindsay has to cope with the possibility of losing another friend whilst keeping a promise to find the gunman.

   20th Century Fox Television adapts the novels into a television series titled *Women's Murder Club*. This series ran on US TV network ABC from October 2007 to May 2008. It starred Angie Harmon as Lindsay Boxer, Paula Newsome as Claire Washburn, Laura Harris as Jill Bernhardt and Aubrey Dollar as Cindy Thomas.

2008 *7th Heaven* is published. San Francisco is terrified by an arsonist wreaking havoc through the city. And it is up to Lindsay to stop him.

2009 *8th Confession* is published. Lindsay's relationship with her partner Rich Conklin is in danger of becoming far more than just professional. This creates a dilemma for Lindsay, and makes her question her relationship with Joe Molinari.

Spin-off computer game *Women's Murder Club: Games of Passion* is released on the Nintendo DS.

2010   *9th Judgement* is published. Lindsay is pushed to the limit with two impossible cases, putting her own life on the line. But a fatal accident helps to bring her to a decision about her relationship with Joe.

2011   *10th Anniversary* is published. Lindsay marries her long-term boyfriend Joe and begins to settle into married life. But trouble is never far away. As Lindsay investigates the case of a missing baby, Yuki's career hangs in the balance, and Cindy takes far too great a risk in the pursuit of a story.

JAMES
PATTERSON

**To find out more about James Patterson
and his bestselling books, go to
www.jamespatterson.co.uk**

Also by James Patterson

ALEX CROSS NOVELS

Along Came a Spider • Kiss the Girls • Jack and Jill •
Cat and Mouse • Pop Goes the Weasel • Roses are Red •
Violets are Blue • Four Blind Mice • The Big Bad Wolf •
London Bridges • Mary, Mary • Cross • Double Cross •
Cross Country • Alex Cross's Trial (*with Richard DiLallo*) •
I, Alex Cross • Cross Fire • Kill Alex Cross

DETECTIVE MICHAEL BENNETT SERIES

Step on a Crack (*with Michael Ledwidge*) • Run for Your Life
(*with Michael Ledwidge*) • Worst Case (*with Michael Ledwidge*) •
Tick Tock (*with Michael Ledwidge*)

PRIVATE NOVELS

Private (*with Maxine Paetro*) • Private London (*with Mark
Pearson*) • Private Games (*with Mark Sullivan*) •
Private: No. 1 Suspect (*with Maxine Paetro, to be published
April 2012*)

STAND-ALONE THRILLERS

Sail (*with Howard Roughan*) • Swimsuit (*with Maxine Paetro*) •
Don't Blink (*with Howard Roughan*) • Postcard Killers (*with Liza
Marklund*) • Toys (*with Neil McMahon*) • Now You See Her (*with
Michael Ledwidge*) • Kill Me If You Can (*with Marshall Karp*) •
Guilty Wives (*with David Ellis, to be published July 2012*)

NON-FICTION

Torn Apart (*with Hal and Cory Friedman*) • The Murder of King
Tut (*with Martin Dugard*)

ROMANCE

Sundays at Tiffany's (*with Gabrielle Charbonnet*) •
The Christmas Wedding (*with Richard DiLallo*)

11th Hour

James Patterson
& Maxine Paetro

**Detective Lindsay Boxer is pregnant – and investigating the
discovery of severed heads in a movie star's garden.**

Your best friend

Lindsay Boxer is pregnant at last! But her work doesn't slow for
a second. When millionaire Chaz Smith is mercilessly gunned
down, she discovers that the murder weapon is linked to the
deaths of four of San Francisco's most untouchable criminals.
And it was taken from her own department's evidence locker.
Anyone could be the killer – even her closest friends.

Or a vicious killer?

Lindsay is called next to the most bizarre crime scene she's
ever witnessed: two bodiless heads elaborately displayed in
the garden of a world-famous actor. Another head is unearthed
in the garden, and Lindsay realises that the ground could hide
hundreds of victims.

You won't know until the 11th hour

A reporter launches a series of malicious articles about the
cases and Lindsay's personal life is laid bare. But this time she
has no one to turn to – especially not Joe.

Century · London

Read on for an extract of

11th Hour

One

A GOOD-LOOKING MAN in his forties sat in the back row of the auditorium at the exclusive Morton Academy for Music. He was wearing a blue suit, white shirt and a snappy striped tie. His features were good, if not remarkable, but behind the blue tint of his glasses, he had very kind brown eyes.

He had come to the recital alone, and had a passing thought about his wife and children at home, but then, he refocused his attention on someone else's child.

Her name was Noelle Smith. She was eleven, a

cute little girl and a very talented young violinist who had just performed Bach's Gavotte with distinction.

Noelle knew she'd done well. She took a deep bow with a flourish, grinning as two hundred parents in the audience clapped and whistled.

As the applause died down, a gray-haired man in the third row popped up from his seat, buttoned his jacket, stepped out into the aisle and headed toward the lobby.

That man was Chaz Smith, Noelle's father.

The man in the blue suit waited a few seconds then followed Smith, staying back a few paces, walking along the tile-floored, cream-colored corridor, taking a right past the pint-sized water fountain, and from there into the short spur of a hallway that ended at the men's room.

Entering the men's room, he looked under the stall doors and saw Chaz Smith's Italian loafers under the door at the far right. Otherwise, the room was empty. In a minute or two, the room would fill.

The man in the blue suit moved quickly, picked up the large metal trash can next to the sink and moved it so that it blocked the exit.

Then, he called out, "Mr. Smith? I'm sorry to disturb you, but it's about your car."

"What? Who is that?"

"Your car, Mr. Smith. You left your lights on."

The man in the blue suit removed his semi-auto .22 caliber Ruger from his jacket pocket, screwed on the suppresser. Then he took out a tan-colored plastic bag, the kind you get at the supermarket, and pulled the bag over his gun.

Smith swore. Then, the toilet flushed and Smith opened the door. His gray hair was mussed, white powder rimmed his nostrils and his face showed fierce indignation.

"You're sure it's my car?" he said. "My wife will kill me if I'm not back in my seat for the finale."

"I'm really sorry to do this to your wife and child. Noelle played beautifully."

Smith looked puzzled, then, he knew. He dropped the vial of coke, and his hand dove under his jacket. Too late.

The man in the blue suit lifted his bag-covered gun, pulled the trigger, shooting Chaz Smith twice between the eyes.

Two

A LONG SECOND bloomed like a white flower in the blue-tiled room.

Smith stared at his killer, his two blue eyes wide open, two bullet-holes in his forehead weeping blood, a look of disbelief frozen on his face. He was still on his feet, his heart stopped.

Chaz Smith was dead and he knew it.

The shooter stared back at Smith, then reached out a hand and pushed him off his feet. The dead man fell back into the stall, collapsing onto the seat, his head knocking once against the wall.

It was a perfect setting for the late Chaz Smith. Dead on the toilet, a fitting a last pose for this crud.

"You deserved this. You deserved worse, you son-of-a-bitch."

It had been a good kill, and now, he had to get out.

He put the plastic bag containing the shell casings, the GSR, and the gun back into his jacket pocket and closed the stall door.

Then, he carried the trash can out of the men's room, put down so that it blocked the door from the outside. That would hold people off for a while, make them think that the men's room was temporarily closed.

The man in the blue suit heard a rush of sound. The auditorium doors had opened for the crowd. He headed back by way of the main hallway, turned left just as people poured into the lobby, chattering and laughing. None of them noticed him and if they did, they would never connect him to the dead man.

There was a fire alarm box on the wall next to the door marked "Teachers' Lounge."

Using his handkerchief to glove his hand, he opened the door to the box, lifted the hammer and broke the glass, pulled the lever and the alarm bell shrilled.

Then, he walked directly into the thick of the crowd.

Children were already starting to scream and run circles in the lobby. Parents called out to their kids, took their hands, lifted them into their arms and moved quickly toward the front doors.

The man went with the crowd, through the glass doors and out onto California Street. He kept going, turned onto the side street, past Chaz Smith's Ferrari and unlocked his scarred SUV parked right behind it.

A moment later, he cruised slowly past the school. All the good people, the kids and their parents were facing the building, staring up at the roof, watching for smoke and flames.

They didn't know it, but they were all safer now.

Chaz Smith was only one of his targets. The media had started tracking his kills, drug dealers, all of them. One of the papers had had given him a name and it had stuck.

Now, they all called him "Revenge."

Fire engines approached from 32nd Avenue and the man called Revenge stepped on the gas. Not a good time to get stuck in a traffic jam.

He had shopping to do before he went home to his family.

Guilty Wives

James Patterson
& David Ellis

Four best friends on a decadent vacation – thrown in prison for murder.

No husbands allowed

Only minutes after Abbie Elliot and her three best friends step off of a private helicopter, they enter the most luxurious, sumptuous, sensually pampering hotel they have ever been to. Their lavish presidential suite overlooks Monte Carlo, and they surrender: to the sun and pool, to the sashimi and sake, to the Bruno Paillard champagne. For four days they're free to live someone else's life. As the weekend moves into pulsating discos, high-stakes casinos, and beyond, Abbie is transported to the greatest pleasure and release she has ever known.

What happened last night?

In the morning's harsh light, Abbie awakens on a yacht, surrounded by police. Something awful has happened – something impossible, unthinkable. Abbie, Winnie, Serena, and Bryah are arrested and accused of the foulest crime imaginable. And now the vacation of a lifetime becomes the fight of a lifetime – for survival.

Guilty Wives is the ultimate indulgence, the kind of non-stop joy-ride of excess, friendship, betrayal, and danger that only James Patterson can create.

Century · London

Guilty Wives

One

THEY TELL ME I will die here. This place I do not know, this dark, dank, rancid dungeon, where nobody wishes me well and most speak languages I don't understand—this is the place I will call home for the rest of my life. That's what they tell me. It's getting harder to disbelieve them.

There are people in here who want me dead, some for retribution but most to establish their own notoriety. It would be a sure path to celebrity to kill me or one of my friends, known collectively as the Monte Carlo Mistresses. That was the moniker that stuck in the international media. More imaginative than the earlier ones—

the Gang of Four, the Bern Beauties, the Desperate Housewives. Less chilling, to me at least, than the one that ran on the front page of *Le Monde* the day after the verdict: *Mamans Coupables*.

Guilty Moms.

So I wait. For a miracle. For newly discovered evidence. A confession from the real killer. A sympathetic ear to my appeal. Or simply for the morning when I wake up and discover this was all a dream. The last three hundred and ninety-eight mornings, I've opened my eyes and prayed that I was back in Bern, or, better yet, back in Georgetown, preparing to teach American literature to hungover underclassmen.

And I watch. I turn every corner widely and slowly. I sleep sitting up. I try to avoid any routine that would make my movements predictable, that would make me vulnerable. If they're going to get to me in here, they're going to have to earn it.

It started out as a day like any other. I walked down the narrow corridor of G wing. When I approached the block letters on the door's glass window—INFIRMERIE—I stopped and made sure my toes lined up with the peeling red tape on the floor that served as a marker, a stop sign before entering.

"*Bonjour,*" I said to the guard at the station on the other side of the hydraulic door, a woman named Cecile. No last names. None of the prison staff was allowed to reveal anything more to the prisoners than their first names, and those were probably fake, too. The point was anonymity outside these walls: because of it, the inmates, once released, wouldn't be able to hunt down the prison guards who hadn't treated them so nicely.

"Hi, Abbie." Always responding to me in her best English, which wasn't bad. Better than my French. After a loud, echoing buzz, the door released with a hiss.

The prison infirmary was the length and width of an American gymnasium, but it had a lower ceiling, about eight feet high. It was mostly one open space filled with about two dozen beds. On one side was a long cage—the "reception" area—where inmates waited their turn to be treated. On another side, also closed off and secured, was a room containing medical supplies and pharmaceuticals. Beyond this room was a high-security area that could hold five patients, reserved for those who had communicable diseases, those in intensive care, and those who posed security risks.

I liked the infirmary because of the strong lighting, which lent some vibrancy to my otherwise dreary confinement. I liked helping people, too; it reminded me that I was still human, that I still had a purpose. And I liked it because I didn't have to watch my back in here.

I disliked everything else about it. The smell, for one—a putrid cocktail of body odor and urine and powerful disinfectant that always seized me when I first walked in. And let's face it, nobody who comes to the infirmary is having a good day.

I try to have good days. I try very hard.

It was busy when I walked in, the beds at full capacity, the one doctor, two nurses, and four inmates who served as nurse's assistants scurrying from one patient to the next, putting figurative Band-Aids on gaping wounds. There had been a flu going around, and at JRF, when one person got the flu, the whole cell block got it. They tried to segregate the sick ones but it was like rearranging chairs in a closet. There just wasn't room. JRF—L'Institution de Justice et Réforme pour les Femmes—operated at more than 150 percent capacity. Cells designed for four held seven, the extra three people sleeping on mattresses on the floor. A prison intended for twelve hundred was housing almost two thousand. They were packing us in shoulder to shoulder and telling us to cover our mouths when we coughed.

I saw Winnie at the far end, wrapping a bandage on an Arab woman's foot. Winnie, like me, was a nurse's assistant. The warden ordered that we not communicate, so we were assigned to different cell blocks and different shifts in the infirmary.

I felt a catch in my throat, as I did every time I saw her now. Winnie has been my closest friend since my husband and I moved to Bern, Switzerland, for his job at the American Embassy. We lived next door to each other for five years, mourning the late working hours of our diplomat husbands and sharing each other's secrets.

Well, not *all* our secrets, it turned out. But I've forgiven her.

"Hey." She whispered in her lovely British accent. Her fingers touched mine. "I heard what happened. You okay?"

"Living the dream," I said. "You?"

She wasn't in the mood for humor. Winnie was a stunning beauty—tall and shapely with large radiant eyes, chiseled cheekbones, and silky, ink-color hair—which made it all the harder to see the wear around those eyes, the stoop in her posture, the subtle deterioration of her spirit. It had been just over a year since the murders, and three months since the conviction. She was starting to break down, to give in. They talked in here about the moment when that happened, when you lost all hope. *La Reddition*, they called it. Surrender. I hadn't experienced it yet. I hoped I never would.

"Movie night," she whispered. "I'll save you a seat. Love you."

"Love you, too. Get some rest." Our fingertips released. Her shift was over.

About ninety minutes later, I heard the commotion as the hydraulic door buzzed open. I had my back turned to the entrance. I was helping a nurse dress a laceration on an inmate's rib cage when one of the nurses shouted, *"Urgence!"*

Emergency. We had a lot of those. We had a suicide a week in JRF. Violence and sanitation-related illnesses had been on the upswing with the worsening overcrowding. It was impossible to work a six-hour shift without hearing *urgence* called at least once.

Still, I turned, as guards and a nurse wheeled in an inmate on a gurney.

"Oh, God, no." I dropped the gauze pads I was holding. I started running before the realization had fully formed in my head. The shock of black hair hanging below the gurney. The look on the face of one of the nurses, who had turned back from the commotion to look at me, to see if it had registered with me who the new patient was. Everyone knew the four of us as a group, after all.

"Winnie," I whispered.

Two

"NO. PLEASE, NO."

I sharply parted the people around me, bouncing off them like a pinball, rushing to Winnie. Two guards saw me coming and moved forward to restrain me as the doctor and two nurses hovered over Winnie, working feverishly.

"Let me see her. Let me . . . *permettez-moi* . . . "

All I could see, between the two guards containing me, was the back of a nurse and the lifeless body of my best friend. The doctor was speaking quickly—too quickly for me to understand—and one of the nurses rushed to retrieve some medicine from the drug cabinet.

"What happened?" I called out to no avail, using the wrong language again in my panic.

I tried again to get around the guards. I just wanted to see her. I wanted *her* to see *me*. But one of the guards threw a forearm into my chest and my feet went out from under me. I fell hard to the floor. My head slammed on the tile. The guards dropped down, using gravity to their advantage, pinning me where I lay.

"Please. *S'il vous plaît*," I managed. "Winnie . . ."

Then, between the two guards restraining me, craning my neck as far off the floor as I could, I saw the doctor, a middle-aged man with long gray hair, straighten up, relax his posture, and shake his head at the nurse. He wrapped his stethoscope around his neck and turned toward the nurse who was retrieving the meds. "Marian," he called. "*Il n'est pas nécessaire.*"

"No!" I wailed.

He looked up at the clock on the wall. "*Le temps de mort . . . ah, il est quatorze heures quarante.*"

Time of death, 2:40 p.m.

"You . . . you . . . killed her," I said, the last words I heard anyone say before everything went black.

We support

National
Literacy
Trust

I'm proud to support the National Literacy Trust, an independent charity that changes lives through literacy.

Did you know that millions of people in the UK struggle to read and write? This means children are less likely to succeed at school and less likely to develop into confident and happy teenagers. Literacy difficulties will limit their opportunities throughout adult life.

The National Literacy Trust passionately believes that everyone has a right to the reading, writing, speaking and listening skills they need to fulfil their own and, ultimately, the nation's potential.

My own son didn't use to enjoy reading, which was why I started writing children's books – reading for pleasure is an essential way to encourage children to pick up a book. The National Literacy Trust is dedicated to delivering exciting initiatives to encourage people to read and to help raise literacy levels. To find out more about the great work that they do, visit their website at www.literacytrust.org.uk.

James Patterson